# SAM SUMAC

# Piss & Vinegar

Black Rose Writing | Texas

The author grants the final approval for this literary material.

First printing

This is a work of fiction. Names, characters, businesses, places, events, and incidents are either the products of the author's imagination or used in a fictitious manner. Any resemblance to actual persons, living or dead, or actual events is purely coincidental.

ISBN: 978-1-68433-480-3
PUBLISHED BY BLACK ROSE WRITING
www.blackrosewriting.com

Printed in the United States of America
Suggested Retail Price (SRP) $19.95

*Piss & Vinegar* is printed in Baskerville

*As a planet-friendly publisher, Black Rose Writing does its best to eliminate unnecessary waste to reduce paper usage and energy costs, while never compromising the reading experience. As a result, the final word count vs. page count may not meet common expectations.

**In Memory of Buster Brown,**
*a person who's made it so pleasurable*
*to walk a mile in his shoes.*

# Piss & Vinegar

"Friends of space, how are you all? Have you eaten yet? Come visit us if you have time."

English translation of the Amoy (Min dialect) greeting on the Voyager I spacecraft golden record.

# THE HIMALAYAN BLUNDER

Needless to say, the arrival of the Altoonians was the most momentous and catastrophic event to ever befall our planet.

Having a massive fleet of gigantic alien ships come here looking for asylum would've been impressive in and of itself, but the disastrously destructive events that followed can only be described as truly earth-shattering.

As White House Chief of Staff Morty Brahmson said so understatedly to me during those first days of our interspecies interactions, "Those Altoonians are certainly bringing a spark to our world these days, aren't they?"

It's funny to think about his wording now, since it turned out to be so backwards and wrong, yet spoke so directly to the inevitable combustion the aliens were going to cause. I mean, everything's certainly blown up in our faces, that's for sure!

Lately I've found myself wondering if we could've been spared any of this. After all, if the aliens had only found *some* other inhabitable planet in the galaxy, all of our lives would have remained intact and unchanged. Of course, we now know their coming to this planet was no accident –

they knew we had something to offer them before they all started heading our way – but we didn't learn this fact until it was too late. Because the collision between our two cultures was not in any way, shape or form a random occurrence, it could not have been circumnavigated by altering the conditions.

No, the only ingredient of happenstance in this entire story was the fact the Altoonians were so arrogantly myopic in their thinking that they believed they could take what they needed from us without having to pay a price for it. As advanced as they were, they could not see the devastating conflicts their attitude would ultimately unleash on all of us. I'd like to think if anyone involved had known our two peoples were destined to destroy one another, we would have waved each other off as frantically as a Navy Landing Signal Officer trying to dissuade a crippled bomber from landing on the deck of his aircraft carrier.

But that didn't happen. And while I've spent far too much time trying to affix some kind of blame onto a legitimately guilty party, this has been an act of futility. After all, if an experienced species of galactic space travelers like the Altoonians didn't have the foresight to see the explosive end to our mutual contact, how could we relatively innocent Earthlings ever have known what was really going to happen?

For most of us, the only preparation we had for any kind of alien contact came from those Hollywood monster movies we had watched as kids. So I guess it made some sense, once we knew an alien invasion was inevitable, for most of us to begin playing those roles we'd seen on the big screen. Instead of facing the trying situation calmly, we grabbed our heads with our hands and started screaming irrationally almost as soon as the Altoonian ships reached our corner of the universe. Talk about not being able to make a good first impression. Our species greeted the visitors with the embarrassing image of a gigantic flock of chickens running around aimlessly with their heads cut off.

That's not to say our initial, embarrassingly child-like response caused the turmoil which followed. When the initial shock that we were going to make contact with an alien species finally wore off, calmer minds did prevail. I'd like to think we did regain our composure enough to at least get things started off on the right foot. Once it seemed that the Altoonians were a peaceful species and not a conquering invader bent on our destruction, our two species did begin to establish a relationship together as we cautiously embraced one another like innocent teenagers at their first dance.

But this idyllic peacefulness did not last long. The appearance of an unanticipated mutual dependence instantly began to destroy the seemingly perfect alliance between our two species. It's been my personal experience that whenever something appears to be perfect, it's only a matter of time before it all topples down into an unrecognizable pile of shit.

As I look out the windows of my hotel suite now and I see the destruction and fulmination outside, I can state with a clear certainty that the seemingly perfect arrangement between us Earthlings and the Altoonians did just that!

Even though I am more than willing to accept full responsibility for my part in the destructive result, I think there were several other elements which combined with my own actions to make everything go up in flames as it did. I know it might seem like I'm splitting hairs here, but – let's face it — a brilliant chemist named Dr. Bernard Bishop, an impossibly enticing alien female we initially code-named Eve, and the free press all played their own role in what transpired. Unwittingly, each of us in our own way struck the fragile bonds between Earthlings and Altoonians from different angles until the whole battered mess was far past the point of no return.

Even though I may have doused the smoldering wreckage with gasoline, I truly believe these three entities would have been enough to do the job…all by themselves.

Dr. Bishop's initial discovery upset the whole unstable apple cart by creating a series of interconnected exchanges of needs and wants between the two species. Eve — God bless her — exposed the real and unholy cost to the new arrangement. And the free press finally was allowed to do its job and reveal to everyone what was really happening. Together they created a situation only one agent from a complete implosion.

Unfortunately, this agent turned out to be me. Sometimes you just can't win for trying.

Ah…I'm getting ahead of myself, aren't I?

Before I go any further with this account, I guess I need to introduce myself and explain how I ended up alone on the top floor of the abandoned Willard Hotel in the midst of the apocalypse. My name is James Fenimore Hunter, and I am the 43rd Vice President of the United States. Technically speaking, I am now currently the 38th President of the United States, since I assumed the position officially that moment when I stabbed President Ted Kennedy with a Pfaltzgraff Holiday Cake knife in the White House Kitchen three days ago.

The title of President no longer has any bearing, though, thanks to the fact that the country of the United States of America currently does not officially exist. However, since I have to live with the knowledge I simultaneously stabbed my dear friend in the neck and my country in the back on the very same day, I am forced to wear this official moniker and its inherent responsibilities like some kind of a god-awful tattoo of shame for the rest of my short life. Now that I can clearly see the horror resulting from my own actions, I can only fall back on the lamest of excuses.

I thought I was doing the right thing.

When the shit really hit the fan, my Secret Service security detail whisked me away from the White House. The two senior agents, Jim Richardson and Harvey Sanderborn, made a quick tactical assessment that the nearby old Willard Hotel provided a better defensible structure to stash me in while we waited out the oncoming strife we knew was going to momentarily hit the capital city. Before we hastily departed 1600 Pennsylvania Avenue, however, they instructed the other three agents of the team to grab whatever arms and mobile phones they could. With this task completed, we calmly walked down into the secret tunnel built back during the Truman Administration renovations of the White House. It led past the doorways of the bunkers under the Department of the Treasury building and out onto F Street.

When we emerged back into the sunlight after our subterranean flight, there was absolute chaos boiling over outside. Most people were justifiably panicking, so all of the city streets were a teeming scene of unchecked pandemonium. Due to this, no one noticed the passage of our ragtag group as we slipped into the courtyard of the Willard. There, hidden behind a fake garbage dumpster, we found the unmarked doorway. This opened to a secret staircase that led to the protective haven of the private suites on the top floor of the venerable hotel, and after the six of us entered that portal, we disappeared from the madness outside.

Looking back, I am greatly ashamed by the cowardice I showed during those hours. Not only did I not confess to the American people that it was I who had murdered the President or that it was I who had played a direct role in bringing this destruction to our beloved world, I also didn't act any better than the rest of those other bastards who knew the end was coming and still ran for the exits like the rats of a sinking ship. We all made sure to get our asses to safety, but we didn't let anyone else know they needed to do the same.

I'm pretty sure the small secretarial pool in my office in the Eisenhower Executive Building all came to the painful and blood-chilling realization that they were screwed at the same time. If they joined the mass exodus out of the building and ran into the streets, there's a fairly good chance they mixed in with the fleeing throngs and escaped. If so, they may still be alive today. But I can imagine my intensely loyal personal secretary, Mrs. Pretlowsky, and her two assistant secretaries, Nancy Bliss and Sarah Deminson, faithfully staying in the office to await my return until it was too late for them to escape.

If so, they probably became victims of The Army of Christ, and I can only hope and pray they were dead before the raping and the torture commenced.

The concealed entrance in the courtyard of the Willard Hotel, the unknown staircase to the top floor, and the ultra-secrets suites were not the only security features. The code of the punch key access pad on the external doorway not only allowed us to enter without detection, it automatically registered our group with the hotel staff as an unknown entity. The hotel's log for that day wouldn't reveal that the acting President of the United States was staying in the Presidential Suite. It would merely show that "*" was somewhere in the hotel.

This security feature was designed to allow high ranking government officials or visiting dignitaries to have more privacy than any of us probably deserved, but I'm now wholly convinced it saved my life. When the roving, killing teams of The Army of Christ were unleashed upon this city and they came to the hotel to find any potential targets inside, they didn't know to look for me there because the secret check-in system worked without a hitch.

Once we were in the safety of the suite, my security detail began busying themselves by fortifying our space to provide me with a refuge from the unthinkable violence building outside. Because I actually believed the country was going to be able to rebound quickly after a short-lived conflict, I went on behaving like I was still President. I sat down to prepare the speeches I was sure I'd soon be giving to outline the strategies for handling the defeated Altoonians and re-unifying what was left of America.

I actually believed I wasn't really in any danger. Even worse, I was convinced I would be in the perfect position to retake control of the country once this short and violent hiccup had passed.

To understand the extent of my delusion, you should know I thought the suite provided me a fabulous box seat to watch what I still believed was going to be a dramatic, yet brief flare-up down on the streets below. So, as I got myself settled in and comfortable enough to witness all of this, I even regretted I didn't have a big bucket of popcorn to munch on during the main feature. As it was, I just wanted to sit back and watch the show.

Ach, what an ass I was...and still am.

When the first thunderous concussion shook the entire building and torrents of lead began to hit the facade indiscriminately, I slowly came to understand I'd completely underestimated what was going to happen. The violent ruination of the Capitol building, the fiery destruction of the White House and the detonation of a bomb at the base of the Washington Monument were the irrefutable proof America was now in the tight grip of a major shit storm. And when the killing teams began to pursue the frenzied mobs of panicked people into the surrounding buildings and even into our very own hotel, I finally came to the undeniable conclusion that we humans, as a species, were completely done for.

But the decision to hole up in the suite of the Willard turned out to be a very good one, tactically speaking. For some reason, none of the gunfire being sprayed around like uncontrollable lawn sprinklers was aimed directly at our windows, and although we could hear the killing teams cleaning out the rooms below us, no one ventured up to our secure floor. Because of its secret access and the hotel's altered registers, the entire top floor of the hotel was overlooked. We did, however, have to listen to the grisly violence taking place beneath us and I knew the horrific sounds we were hearing were those of the systematic murder and torture of people less fortunate than us. This took its toll on all of us in the suite.

In the face of these desperate times, however, Jim Richardson and Harvey Sanderborn remained completely calm, cool and collected. When the nerves of the younger agents in their team began to fray, they kept them focused enough to discount the incomprehensible violence engulfing the world around us and make sure their president survived this conflict. Ah, those two men were such professionals! I was kept in the main room, far away from the windows, as they set about guarding the entrances and maintaining our perimeter. They quietly evaluated our situation, and then they confidently declared we were as safe as houses.

I knew better. As a student of history, I knew most fortifications under siege have capitulated because of the most non-violent of reasons. Sure, the destructive impacts of siege weaponry – be it battering rams, catapults, trebuchets, powerful long range guns like the Schwerer Gustav, the new strategic Wolverine bomber, or even the Minuteman ballistic missile – all have helped loosen the resolve of these fortified towns or cities, but the most common cause for surrender in these situations has resulted from two seemingly and wholly innocent factors, the presence of edible food and potable water.

While those Secret Service agents turned the suite into a kind of defensible bunker, they were beyond dismayed to discover we didn't have any food and had only two five gallon jugs of water. It'd been assumed the suite's small pantry was going to be as well-stocked as usual, but due to a recent renovation of the unit's kitchen during the prior week, there was no food anywhere to be had. With the dangerous darkness of the impending night beginning to engulf us and the swirling flames of violence beginning to consume the world all around us, we found ourselves safely ensconced in a formidably fortified shelter...but without one scrap of food.

As former military men, this fact was deeply troubling. Even though the great World War II general George S. Patton once said the gas for his tanks was more important than getting food for his troops — since the men could eat their belts — we all came to the conclusion that the six strips of leather around our waists would not be enough to keep us alive for too long. And, I can tell you, as the sun rose the next morning, we were so hungry we could've eaten a horse!

When Jim Richardson and Harvey Sanderborn called all of us together to discuss the situation and to make a plan for what to do next, we huddled together like a football team as those two laid it all out for us. As they saw it, the problem was quite simple. We were here, the food was there. We needed to get there to acquire the food and bring it back here. Their initial plan was for two agents to leave the suite and head down to the hotel's kitchen to forage for any food while the three remaining agents stayed up in the suite to protect me. All those men were so good, devoted and patriotic that the next few moments were filled with all of them talking at once as they each volunteered to go on what amounted to a suicide mission.

I don't know why I did it, but I raised my hand like a schoolchild. When the Secret Service agents all saw me acting like this, I think they were more than a little embarrassed for me. It obviously pained him to do so, but Jim Richardson eventually called on me. I told them that, although I didn't want to hurt their feelings in any way, I thought their plan, although a good and safe one, was somewhat heavily flawed. Even if the out-going agents were successful in finding some food, they could only bring back what the two of them could carry.

When you're in the midst of a survival situation, I reminded them, you usually had only one shot at getting things done the right way. If so, it made much more sense to have all of us scavenge for food, since we could bring three times more food back up to the suite than the original plan. Three teams of two would be much better for such a mission because it gave the group a solid force out in front to scout ahead, a middle worker bee pair, and a rear guard to provide cover.

While Jim Richardson and Harvey Sanderborn listened intently to me, the other agents waited for their response. After a brief moment of silence, they acknowledged the validity of my plan, but then they made it crystal clear there was no chance in hell I was going to leave the suite for any reason. They declared they hadn't risked life and limb to get me to safety, just to put me back in harm's way, but they did acknowledge I was correct about more men being able to carry more food.

So, they made up a new plan. Two teams of two agents would go on the mission to find the food while one agent remained with me in the suite for protection. The idea was to obtain twice the amount of food and not leave me completely vulnerable.

The agents then all resumed talking at once again as each volunteered to take the most dangerous parts of the mission.

I still was not happy, and — maybe due to the ravenous hunger I was starting to feel — I decided to pull rank. As the acting President of the United States of America, I *ordered* all five men in the security team to be directly involved in the mission. I pointed out, if I were given a firearm, I could protect myself sufficiently in the fortified suite while the two teams of two men and a fifth floater went out to scavenge for food. Since five men nearly made up a military squad, it was much more likely to succeed than two separate teams.

At first Jim Richardson and Harvey Sanderborn refused to accept that my plan made sense, but then its plausibility hit home. At the same time, they had to acknowledge the fact I had just issued a direct executive order. So, begrudgingly, they gave in and decided to enact my plan.

After I was given a loaded Colt M1911 semiautomatic pistol with two extra clips, I was told to situate myself under the bed to await their return. I took up my position as the five men headed to the front door. They were all stern as pallbearers as they double checked their armaments and listened to the two senior agents lecturing them about the rules of engagement and the modes of communication. With the violence outside our windows settling down from the maelstrom it had been during its nocturnal crescendo to a now scattered patt-patt of gunfire and an occasional explosion here and there, the five men walked out of the main door and disappeared without any fanfare or salutations.

I waited for their return under the bed for the rest of the first day, the next night, and half of the following day.

Every sound outside was like the ticking of a clock I could not ignore, and with each and every passing second, I found myself praying for the safe return of my security detail, even though the longer their absence became, the more sure I was about their mortality. However, up until to the very last moment, I held onto the faintest glimmer of hope in my heart that at least one of those brave and well-trained men would make it back safely with some food.

When the sun took its mid-day elevation during the second day, I knew the truth. I came out of my hiding spot and foolishly ventured over to one of the suite's windows to have a look outside. That's when I saw Jim Richardson's and Harvey Sanderborn's heads stuck atop the light poles across Pennsylvania Avenue. That grisly sight made it crystal clear to me that every one of those five men was now dead. The stark reality of my current situation took away my breath.

A sudden movement in a window in the National Press Building across 14th Street caught my attention. A man was looking down onto the destruction, and as our eyes locked onto one another, I thought about the moment of intimacy we were sharing as we both discovered just how truly bad things had become. Incredibly, the man had the gall to wave at me. Before I could return the gesture, I watched as his brain sneezed out the side of his skull and his lifeless body crumpled out of view. I instinctively dove to the floor and chastised myself for stupidly sauntering around exposed windows.

We'd given a hidden sniper an easy target and the chance to draw a bead on us. I knew if there were anyone else alive in these buildings, we were all like the moles in one of those "Whack-A-Mole" games kids play at the county fair midways. Seeing the stranger's unpleasant fate, I decided to crawl back into my den under the bed.

The fact there was a hidden marksman somewhere out there using a high powered rifle to pick off targets in the windows of the surrounding buildings put me on alert. I had proudly served in the United States Marine Corps during the Vietnam War as a spotter for one of history's most notorious snipers, so I'd seen, firsthand, the dangers a well-concealed shooter presented. Once, outside of Da Nang, I'd spotted our assigned target over a mile away. Concealed in the jungle foliage to the point of being invisible, my sniper had used his specially modified M2 Browning .50 caliber machine gun with a Unerti scope to take out the assigned Viet-Cong general.

Interestingly, that enemy general was about the same distance from us that day as the steps of the Capitol Building are from the base of the Washington Monument. In fact, the span was so great, there'd been a four second lag from the moment of the rifle's concussion to the hitting of the target by the bullet. If the Marine choir had been ready to begin singing the National Anthem at the moment the trigger was pulled, they'd have had enough time to get to *"Oh say can you see, by..."* before the bullet ripped through the general's chest and extinguished his life! Isn't that fascinating?

The shooting of the stranger in the National Press Building reminded me that any unessential movement in the suite could be an invitation for instant death. Underneath the bed I was safe, so I curled up there into a ball and thanked the fates the sniper hadn't spotted me first. As it was, I'd had enough of a glimpse of just how bad things had become outside – I didn't need to see any more! I could use my imagination for any future pictures, and perhaps that's really the safest way to view anything dangerous.

What was clear to me was that nothing made sense anymore. I mean, why would anyone behead such good and dedicated men like Jim Richardson and Harvey Sanderborn and then place their body-less heads on light posts? Why would anyone shoot strangers whose only sins were looking out windows at the carnage fuming on the streets below them? For no good reason I could see.

Once I understood that no member of my security detail was ever coming back, I had to accept the fact I was now on my own. If I was to have any chance of survival, I needed to get myself food and more water. And with my stomach making the mournful sounds of a Tibetan Death chant, I knew I needed to set off on this mission immediately.

However, since the only chronometers at my disposal were now disabled due the loss of electricity during the initial assault on the city, I wasn't sure exactly what time it was. The analogue clock beside the bed was as dead as the men of my security detail, yet its motionless arms continued to report the fact that this world had come to an unceremonious end at exactly 12:34, but the clock was no longer able to say whether the moment had happened in the day or at night. However, like the old saying states, it was right twice a day!

Even though I didn't know the exact time, I could tell from my hiding spot the shadows of the room were stretching and waning enough to signal another dusk was approaching. I was desperately hungry, so I decided to forego any caution and head right out to search for food. I crept over to the front door of the suite and slowly stood up to look out of the peephole. Because the hallway lights were off, it was too dark to see two inches in front of my face out there. The depth of the darkness coming through the tiny aperture was total, and all I could make out was the reflection of my cornea in the peephole lens. Foolishly, I began to unlock the front door to open it and get a better look.

As I peered out through this little crack, my view was completely blocked by the back of a Coke machine. At first, this perplexed me. But then I realized my security detail had moved the heavy vending machine from the end of the hallway to completely obscure the doorway to our suite. That's why it had been so dark through the peephole! Even though I hadn't heard any evidence the killing teams had made it onto our floor, even if they had, the Coke machine would have completely hidden our door from their view. My security team's attention to detail had ensured my room would continue to be safe from detection.

But the discovery of the protective barricade also made my current situation even more perilous. I was not only as hungry as a bear, I was now technically trapped inside a food-less and fortified hotel room with no way out. It seems strange now to recall this as being the very moment I first started panicking. After watching our entire world implode, I couldn't believe things could get any worse. But being ravenously hungry and, at the same time, cornered alone inside an empty and lifeless hotel room – well, these details all combined to create a devastatingly hopeless situation for me. I started to hyperventilate and I had to sit down on the floor and put my arms over my head to catch my breath.

When all hope seemed lost, my hand grazed a piece of paper sitting atop the narrow table next to the suite's front door. I pulled it down and took out my USMC butane lighter from my pants pocket to make a flame so I could read it. It was a handwritten note from Jim Richardson. In it, he described in great detail the strategy of the Secret Service agents and what my contingency plans should be in case they did not return from their mission. The note was brimming with optimism.

For a man who was destined to lose his head, he had been overly confident in his ability to return with ample food. He even had a positive spin on the possibility of not returning. He was certain I'd have the wherewithal to get the required food myself if left alone. I must say, reading his message left me both impressed and annoyed with the man. In the end, however, the faith he, and all of those poor sacrificed men, had in me turned out to be the motivation I needed to survive, if for no other reason than I couldn't let those dedicated and loyal agents down!

The note also contained the highly pertinent information about a secret door in the back of the suite's main closet. This was the entrance to a hidden tunnel which ran back to the stairway we'd originally used to get to the suite. Apparently, the camouflaged doorway in the courtyard, the automatic and anonymous check-in, and the unknown back staircase up to the top floor were not the only secret components of the hotel. The architect of the most recent renovation had also been charged with creating various other hidden devices to allow the high profile guests of the hotel a multitude of choices to escape whatever or whoever was pursuing them. He was definitely a believer in there being more than one way to skin a cat.

Harvey Sanderborn had opted to take his team out the front door and down the main hallway because he wanted to continue to keep the hidden passageway completely unknown. In other words, he had voluntarily taken his men down into the belly of the beast in an exposed manner to preserve the secret exit for me in case any last-ditched escape efforts were needed. Who knew anyone could show such selflessness and such foresight?

According to the note, once I traversed the tunnel to the flight of stairs and then used these to get down to the ground floor, I could possibly find the kitchen and, thereby, some food. I crept over to the closet and found the doorway behind the ironing board. I moved this aside, opened the door and slid inside the tiny and cramped space. It was completely dark, and I had to crouch down to fit.

As I made my way, I was too hopped up on adrenaline and ravenously hungry to be cautious and I blindly bumped into the perilously low-slung pipes criss-crossing the space. If there had been anyone with a stethoscope listening carefully through the walls, they'd have heard the repeated crack of my skull against these objects and my responding curses. But, fortunately for me, no one was there to listen, and I successfully made it to the end of the tunnel – bruised and battered, but alive.

Once I'd opened the concealed door there, I found myself back in the lightless secret staircase. I listened intently for any sounds. My heart was beating so loudly, it was hard for me to hear anything else. I tried to calm myself down, but was nearly apoplectic with fear.

Then, some of my repressed memories from the multitude of missions I'd participated in during the war came rushing back to me. During the countless operations undertaken, our little Marine sniper team had spent night after night traveling silently through the perilous jungles of Southeast Asia to get at our selected targets. These nightmarish experiences had gripped my stomach with tension at the time, but now the memory of them actually caused me to relax. I guess the fact I'd survived those murderous assignments in a faraway land now lent a new feeling of confidence to me, and I felt my body and my senses regaining their war-time preparedness.

I started descending slowly, one step at a time. Jim Richardson's note gave me specific directions to the hotel's restaurant, and it directed me to "head down" there to gather the necessary food. The macabre and unintentional pun between this direction and his current state out on the light post struck me as humorous, and I found myself tittering and giggling like a schoolgirl as I made my way as silently down those stairs as I could.

Looking back on what I've written down so far, it's clear I was certainly struggling with holding onto my sanity during those earliest moments of this crisis. Considering what had transpired and the current condition of the world all around me, I think it's completely understandable. I mean, even though I don't feel much pride in reading just how mentally unstable I was as I navigated my way through a world gone mad, I was more than a little justified in being a bit undone by the horrors of those times. I also feel compelled to add I'm doing much better now.

Anyway, going down this staircase in the pitch dark was akin to descending into the levels of Dante's Inferno. With each step into the abyss, the noxious aromas grew stronger. There was a mixture of sulphur, burning plastic, and grilled chicken in the air, and this last odor only amplified my hunger and made me impatient to quicken my pace. However, my military training continued to provide me with the restraint to slow down and let my alerted senses process my surroundings. I stopped for a moment and stood motionless in the pure dark void of the space. I could feel the slightest static upon my skin. My body hadn't felt like a dangerously honed weapon in quite some time, and the resultant rush made me giddy with excitement.

When I finally reached the ground floor, I found another hidden doorway. This one opened into the main hallway of the hotel. I listened for sounds coming from the other side, and when I didn't hear any, I slowly and silently opened the door and stepped out. This once lavish and ornamental corridor had been ravaged. Every piece of furniture, every piece of art on the wall, every chandelier, every light fixture, every mirror or piece of glass had all been smashed and shattered as completely as if they'd been put into a mortar and crushed down to particles by a massive pestle.

Undeterred by this, I made my way furtively among these ruins toward the kitchen. The space was so lifeless and barren it seemed as if a tidal wave of destruction had flowed in, smashed everything into tiny bits, ebbed after being sated, and then moved on to the next shoreline.

I was surprised to find the kitchen crudely illuminated. Apparently, the marauders had lit all of the hotel's cans of Sterno to create some kind of an all-hours chamber of horrors. The fading blue flames now lit up the space with an eerie marine habitat lighting effect, and I half-expected to find a mermaid with seaweed in her golden hair.

Instead, I came upon an old man in a fancy business suit seated upon a metal prep kitchen table like he was a member of a royal family. He was passively chomping on what appeared to be a turkey leg, and he didn't react at all when he saw me. His eyes were the color of watered-down Scope mouthwash, and he regaled me with such calmness I quickly became more unnerved by his quiet presence than I would have been if he'd made an aggressive movement towards me. The way he continued eating his meal while staring blankly back at me reminded me of one of those steers on the other side of the barbed wired fence who are chewing their cud while impassively watching the world with an air of disdainful oblivion.

My Colt was safely lodged in the back of my waistline, but I did not reach for it yet. There was no need to, since the man hadn't done anything to constitute himself as a threat. As the two of us continued to wordlessly stare at one another, our mutual silence became uncomfortable. I did not expect to meet another living soul, and certainly not one who would be so banal as they casually ate their meal in the epicenter of such devastation and death.

I looked more closely at the man. His white hair and beard were both scraggly and very dirty, but if they'd been clean, I had the feeling he'd have been a dead ringer for

Santa. As it was, he was so slight of frame the dark tailored suit hung loosely on his body and he looked like a child wearing his father's clothes. That's when I noticed the blood and the bullet holes in the fabric of his outfit. It took my mind a few moments to recognize the suit as belonging to one of the agents of my security detail! The anger from this discovery began to boil over inside of me, and I whispered hoarsely at the man, "Where the hell did you get that?"

The man seemed unsure of what I was asking about. He first looked at the piece of food in his hands and then down at the bloody front of his suit. His eyes rolled back into his head and he shrugged his shoulders.

"Aw, it beats the shit out of me," he said.

I asked him how he came to be there and what he had seen, but he gave the same response as his first one. It beat the shit out of him. I shook my head and clenched my jaw in frustration, but I couldn't get a straight answer from him.

From his appearance and his overall aroma, I think he was probably one of those street people who were so prevalent those days in the shadows of our city. Clearly he'd been a mentally demented individual even before the assault by The Army of Christ on Washington, D.C., and I'm sure the horrifying events he'd lived through as of late hadn't probably helped him in the least. Because he had neither any information nor any new advice to offer me, I didn't waste any more of my time on him and started my search for food.

I had not noticed the copious amount of blood on the floor when I first walked in, but now I saw how the off-white linoleum looked like it had been freshly painted with it. Since the warmth of the kitchen air was drying the blood and it was becoming more tacky, each step across the floor made the sound of some grotesque tearing and ripping noise. There was far too much blood on the floor to only be from the five members of my unfortunate security detail, and my brain struggled to comprehend the depths of the grisliness that must have taken place in the space.

I looked over at the fryolator and saw it contained fried amputated hands and feet. My brain refused to accept what it was seeing, and I kept staring at the sight, the gears slipping and skipping inside my head like a broken watch.

Then everything became clear at once, and I knew the homeless man wearing my beheaded security team's suit and sitting contentedly there on the table consuming his meal was not eating a turkey leg at all. He was devouring a human foot. I turned back to angrily confront him about this, but he was gone. Even though I frantically tried to find him, there was no trace. His silent departure made the hairs on the back of my neck stand straight up, and once again my fragile sanity was threatened.

I needed to gather up some food and get myself back up to the safety of my suite, so I stalked right over to the piles of canned goods inside the disheveled pantry to start picking them up into my arms. Right next to the piles I serendipitously found the two duffle bags my security detail had brought down with them, so I began filling them with whatever I could get my hands on. The growing darkness of the room made it impossible to know whether I was taking soup, SPAM, fruit, canned corn, or evaporated milk, but it didn't matter. I just needed to get as much food as I could before heading back upstairs and avoiding the killing teams.

By the time I'd crammed the two bags full, I could barely walk under their weight. I put them down softly on the floor and set out to find a can opener. It may seem ludicrous to risk getting captured by spending any time looking around for such a seemingly trivial detail, but I knew from personal experience having the proper tool would actually make all of the difference between my survival and a miserable death. My search ended when I found an old fashioned church key can opener in the piled contents of a drawer dumped onto the blood-covered floor.

I staggered back down the hallway. The duffle bags were not only heavy, the cans clinked and clunked so loudly with each step that I felt as stealthy as a medieval knight trying to sneak across a stone floor. The door to the staircase was designed to blend into the wall panels of the hallway, so I had to feel my way with my hand to find it. I was sure I was going to be pounced on at any moment by an attacker, so when I heard the noise of something stirring somewhere in the depths of the night, I froze with fear. I was convinced it was a member of a killing team, another cannibalistic street person, or even a stray dog. But, when nothing happened, I frantically pushed on the door and it reluctantly gave way.

After bringing the two duffel bags into the stairwell and starting to close the door, the golden lettering on the cover of a book lying in the detritus in front of me reflected enough light to catch my attention. Next to this book was a busted violin. For reasons that are still a mystery to me, I scrambled over and grabbed them both before bolting back into the secret staircase.

As if I could magically hold back any of the tumult, I leaned onto the backside of the door to catch my breath.

I started to ascend the stairs with my heavy booty. But with each labored step, I began to incant quietly to myself like a mantra the repeating answer the foot-eating homeless man had uttered to me in the kitchen when I'd confronted him. It seemed the most fitting thing to say in the middle of such an unimaginably bad reality, and by the time I reached the top of the staircase, I had repeated the saying 185 times. Like I said, my mental stability back then was as wobbly as the current ravaged remains of the Washington Monument. But I am much better now.

Back in the safety of my suite, I randomly opened two cans – one of fruit cocktail and another of tuna fish – and devoured them savagely. After not having had anything to eat for several days, neither my manners nor my palate were subtle at this point. After I had sated myself, I set about to store all of the cans of food.

My first plan was to put them in the suite's empty pantry, but then I realized it made the most sense to keep them close to me if I were going to continue to take refuge under the bed. I carefully constructed walls of cans around me under there, but because the room was now completely dark, the make-up of these tin barricades was totally helter-skelter. I looked forward to having enough light again in the morning to be able to assemble some sort of organization to my supplies, but I was becoming too tired and I decided to deal with them later. I lay my head down on a folded coat and shut my eyes.

Before I allowed myself to fall asleep, I turned over and grabbed the book I had risked my life to procure. I used my lighter to take a closer look at the front cover. In the faint illumination of the butane flame, I quickly identified the golden lettering on the red cover and saw it was, in fact, made up of Oriental calligraphy. There seemed to be something fitting in finding a book in a foreign language in the middle of a world that become so warped and alien. Actually, you could say it fit it to a tee.

I closed my lighter and let the darkness swallow everything whole again, closed my eyes, and, truthfully, slept like a baby.

When the sun rose the next morning, it wasn't just the dawn of a new day outside the Hotel Willard, it was also a new beginning for me inside it. Because the mission to get food had been a success, I was feeling a shred of hope. In spite of having my security detail meet such a most unfortunate end, I felt empowered by my own success, especially since others, much more qualified than I, had failed. Whereas I could have been bogged down with survivor's guilt, I let my small accomplishment give me the slimmest optimism. With an adequate amount of supplies and plenty of water, I knew I could hunker down and wait out this awful storm. Oh, how my spirits lifted.

My hips were sore from climbing the stairs with the heavy duffel bags and sleeping on the hard floor under the bed, so I tried to turn over in my cramped little sleeping space to get more comfortable. When I did, I brushed against the broken violin and it made a twangy protest about my movement. In the excitement of getting back safely to the suite, I had completely forgotten about the broken instrument. Now I picked it up and looked closely at it. I had no idea why I'd risked everything to stop and take such a useless and meaningless object with me, but there it was.

The violin was a wreck. It had only four strings remaining intact, and they stubbornly ran from the peg box, down the neck and to the tailpiece. As I gazed upon this ruined musical instrument, I wondered why it'd been in the Willard Hotel in the first place. Maybe there'd been a stringed concert in the luxurious lobby or there'd been a serenading quartet during a brunch in the lavish dining room before the murderous hordes invaded the capital. Either way, someone had smashed the beautiful and fragile instrument during the violence of the riots. If nothing else, it seemed rife with symbolism as to what was currently happening to our world.

When I strummed gently on the strings, it responded painfully, like some kind of castrated ukulele, and I stopped because I found the raspiness of the notes to be so unpleasant. There was, in fact, nothing pretty about this vestige of a more peaceful time, so I carefully removed one of the strings by unwinding its peg and taking its nub from the tailpiece. I coiled this piece of wire up and put it into the flaps of my wallet. I'm not a complete masochist, but ever since I had attended a performance of Dvorak's *Violin Concerto* by Itzhak Perlman, the sounds of violins continued to haunt my memories and I wanted a piece of the world I had helped destroy, no matter what happened.

The day's new light flooding into the suite allowed me to see the book I'd also recovered from the hallway. The golden calligraphy on the candy apple red cover stood out like they had electricity in them. I opened it, and, much to my surprise, I found the title page was written in English. It proudly declared:

> *THE DICTIONARY OF AMERICAN IDIOMS by Yan Bu Youzhong*

On the next page, Youzhong started his introduction by saying that, after the historic visit of President Richard Nixon to their country, the President of China had personally asked the author to compile a book of American idioms to help him when he was invited back to the United States. Youzhong then declares, in no uncertain terms, his book was written to help the reader understand the nuances of the colloquial dialects of the English language so as to avoid any embarrassing gaffes that could sabotage purposeful conversations.

The use of idioms, he goes on to explain, can be particularly difficult to master, as they involve using foreign words in such a different way that the implied meanings can be nearly impossible for many Chinese speakers to figure out on their own. He advises the reader to keep the book with him or her at all times to provide insights whenever needed.

I began to flip through the pages. The first idiom I came to was *a fish out of water.* The book translated this to mean *To flop breathlessly on the ground like a golden carp.* I turned a few more pages and came to *blow your mind.* The book's translation of this was *To cause the cerebral cortex of your brain to unexpectedly exit your head.*

The more definitions I looked up, the more errors I found. Somehow the author had gotten nearly every idiomatic explanation incorrect and he had given its literal translation instead of its meaning. On a lark, I looked up *it beats the shit out of me* to see what a visiting Chinese President would have made of an encounter with a cannibalistic street person in the kitchen of a devastated hotel. According to the book it meant *An event when a physical confrontation results in a sudden involuntary removal of feces.* I found this to be most amusing, and I cackled like one of the witches in *Hamlet*.

But then I had a Zen moment of enlightenment.

If the author of this silly book had gotten something relatively mundane like idioms so dead wrong, I needed to make damn sure people in the future knew the truth about me and my involvement in the apocalypse of our world. Even though I have great shame about my role in the destruction of life as we know it on Planet Earth, I still think — if my choices and decisions are taken in the context of the events we were all living with at the time — they do make a certain amount of sense. I can live with the thought of me being burned in effigy, but being labeled as some kind of a monstrous megalomaniac in the flawed history books of the future is too much for my pride to bear.

To ensure this doesn't happen, I've decided to become my own chronicler of these past events and to show what was occurring at the highest levels of the last American government from the very moment we first became aware that a fleet of alien ships was heading our way, to the current situation of the broken and burned world we now find ourselves having to endure.

As to who will be around to read my account when this is all over, well, it beats the shit out of me.

# OFF TO A FLYING START

~~On March 23rd, 1984, a fleet of twenty-three Altoonian interstellar transport ships came to Planet Earth.~~

This was how I started my first attempt to record the events leading up to this point, but I crossed it out because Congress had recently voted to stop using the Gregorian calendrical labeling. Instead, we were to adopt an entirely new system of time identification based on the arrival of the aliens. To many people around the planet, the appearance of Altoonians was so consequential it ushered in a natural beginning for a new era of our species. In their search to find a fitting and appropriate representation of this irrevocable moment, a small but powerful contingency proposed the replacement of A.D. (*Anno Dominum*) with the new P.A.A. (*Post Altoonian Adventum).*

This change was argued to be important because it put the aliens' humongous impact into the proper perspective. The modification only affected those peoples using the Christian-based calendar, so the Jewish calendar, the Hijri calendar of the Muslims, and the lunisolar calendars of the Hindu and Buddhists were not effected, as far as I know.

But before everything took its kamikaze nosedive, many of the nations around this world adopted this P.A.A. label. Therefore, the officially correct beginning of my story should now be:

On the first day of the first year of the *Post Altoonian Adventum*, a fleet of twenty-three Altoonian interstellar transport ships came to Planet Earth.

I personally think this system makes the date sound more like a noodle dish from a Bangkok food cart, but I figure if this new calendar system is still in place in the future, I need to use it to alleviate any confusion for the readers of my account. Please note, however, my usage of the P.A.A. moniker is not intended to show either my support of the change nor a flippant attitude about the impacts it represents. I merely want this document to be regarded as an official one. So I will use it throughout this text, but I do so with a heavy heart.

You see, it is my humble opinion this change of the calendric system was one of the first questionable choices in a long string of highly flawed decisions by Earth's leadership in response to the aliens' arrival. In fact, I think it could be easily argued all of us world leaders unknowingly did more harm than good every step of the way. By our failures to actually do what was right, we unwittingly threw ice cold water onto a piece of red hot glass.

To be blunt, our world was a bundle of nerves long before we even knew of the approaching space alien fleet. Our species had continued to taint this world with its racial, religious, cultural, political, and ethnic divides, and these had not only continued to fester, but had grown like a swollen boil, ready to erupt. By the time of the first hint of a possible contact with an alien race, the fractures and fissures of our species ran deep and extended everywhere across our little planet. One could even say it was so fragile, it might've imploded with just the slightest tap from a foam hammer.

That being said, I don't think it would have self-destructed on its own without the clear cut mistakes we all made in our handling of the Altoonians. I guess what I'm trying to say is the old proverb, *actions speak louder than words,* is, in this case, true. If the world's leadership had not given their populace pre-measured doses of mistruths – between their otherwise out-and-out silent treatments — from the moment we became aware of the aliens' arrival, and had instead led by example and gone down a pathway toward honesty and truth, I think the levels of devastation from this whole event could have been kept much lower. But, as a species, we're all captives to the myriad of our own foibles, so we tend to make mistake after mistake as we trudge down the coal chute to potential destruction.

After all, we're only human.

I feel compelled at this moment, by the way, to illuminate the difference between a proverb and an idiom. Although Youzhong got mostly everything wrong about idioms in his book, he shockingly was absolutely correct in his definition of proverbs. In his highly defective introduction, he instructed his readers, "A proverb gives straightforward advice or an accurate observation of life using the proper meanings of the words."

That's not bad, actually. I applaud him.

So, when I use a proverb, like "actions speak louder than words," to describe what a person does is more important than what they say, the idiomatic form of the same thought would be something like *when push came to shove.*

The truth is, when push did come to shove, the leadership of this planet should have acted more honestly and more honorably with their own people before attempting to interact with the Altoonians. If they had, we could have kept everything from going so badly. Instead, our world simply came apart at the seams.

But I digress. Let's go back to the beginning of this tale.

The exploratory drillings by several oil companies in the Yucatan Peninsula of Mexico in the late 1970's revealed the presence of a huge crater in the Earth's crust. This discovery gave the scientific community geological evidence for a theory it'd been debating for years about a massive asteroid striking the planet around sixty-six million years ago. It had been argued by several prominent geologists that such a cataclysmic event could have potentially caused the extinction of the dinosaurs and given rise to an age of mammals. The finding of the underwater and subterranean crater lent a whole new wave of credibility to the theory. Actually, the impact of this discovery, no pun intended, was far-reaching. Almost immediately there arose a deep-seated fear about our planet being at risk for having another calamitous space event. This time, however, we were more worried about it bringing about our own extinction.

The leaders of the most powerful countries of the globe came together under the guise of a scientific forum in Switzerland. After much debate and negotiation, they ultimately concluded we needed to develop an early detection satellite system before any more asteroids had a chance to strike our planet and kill us off. The theory was, even if we were faced with an un-winnable threat, just having some time to plan could give our species a fighting chance at survival. The result was the creation of IRIS or Interstellar Reconnaissance Infrared System, a network of ten high-powered satellites orbiting around Earth, each designed to act like a sentry looking for any uninvited approaching objects from the vastness of space.

You've probably never heard about any of this before. That's because the leaders of these countries chose to keep everyone else completely in the dark. The dangers from the general population getting their panties in a knot over being wiped out by a random piece of space rock were considered far more uncontrollable than the manageable fears arising from the Cold War or the Oil Crisis or the Middle East conflict. So this entire endeavor, from start to finish, was kept completely unknown to anyone who wasn't in the inner circles of the governments involved.

After the countries of the Western Bloc, the Eastern Bloc, OPEC, and even Communist China came together to create the necessary infrastructure, each of the ten richest and most technologically advanced nations were tasked with building one satellite apiece and launching it clandestinely into space.

One would think such a plan would've been impossible. But the usual red-tape and bureaucratic quagmires gave way to a shared and focused sense of purpose. Ahead of schedule, the planet had an early detection web of satellites orbiting around it. Ingeniously, as these technological marvels scanned deep space continually for threats, each of the reports from their vigilant observations was shared immediately and freely with the other leaders who were a part of the network. Even if something the size of a breadbox was detected approaching us, all the other satellites would take a look at it to assess the threat level, and then this information would be transmitted to the leadership of the planet simultaneously.

I need to take this moment to identify the IRIS project as an example of just how capable Earthlings were — and still are, I hope — to cooperate and work toward the common good. Because the satellites were located out and away from this planet to search space – extroverted group spying, not spying on each other — there was unanimous support amongst the collective of participating governments in spite of the fact many had been adversaries, enemies, and uneasy treaty members with one another before. It was truly the rarest of moments for humans to show such unity, and sadly — because it was kept so secret — no one in the general population ever knew anything about this amazing example of solidarity for our entire species.

This satellite network proved to be an overwhelmingly huge success. Any space object large enough to attract attention by venturing too close to our solar system was immediately picked up by IRIS and diligently tracked until the threat for a collision was over. Even though nothing came close enough to be considered a real danger, the detection system not only provided the human race with the ability to keep an eye on any approaching asteroids, it also created an instant line of communication between our governments.

Whereas we all had differing opinions about the matters of our world, providing safety from objects from outer space allowed us to transcend politics and philosophies and begin an earnest dialogue with one another. The fact that there hadn't been any real dangers detected did not create a sense of apathy or overconfidence, but the countries involved with IRIS clearly felt there was safety in numbers, and they were fairly relaxed in their belief an asteroid wasn't going to cause our extinction.

That was why it was so totally shocking to receive notification from IRIS of the sudden appearance of multiple space objects coming from out of the shadows of Venus. This information startled us all to the core! President Kennedy and I were at the Tidal Basin to meet with a group of survivors of the firebombing of Nagoya, Japan, on the anniversary of that calamitous event when the first warnings were sent around the network. In the middle of the serene ceremony among the blooming cherry blossoms of the Tidal Basin in West Potomac Park, White House Chief of Staff Morty Brahmson came sprinting down the sidewalk to inform us we needed to get right back to the Oval Office to address an immediate global situation of the highest importance. I worried at the time our premature departure would be misconstrued as an offensive act by our honored guests, but I was to find out an armada of approaching unidentified space objects always trumps a social *faux pax* every time!

By the time we were back in the Situation Room at the White House, the IRIS satellites were all in agreement something threatening was indeed coming our way. The most powerful telescopes on the planet were all trained on the approaching objects and the world's leading astrophysicists strained their eyes to identify what was headed towards Earth. The early conclusion was we were being approached by a group of twenty or so asteroids. However, as they came closer, the news went from bad to worse.

It became apparent they were not pieces of rock hurtling through space at all, but a fleet of alien crafts of immense size heading straight at us at speeds we couldn't even fathom. We were not only confronted with the realization we were no longer alone in the galaxy, we also had to handle an imminent invasion by a fleet of unknown spaceships from a possibly hostile and obviously technologically superior alien population!

The leaders of Earth's governments were unified in their belief that they should keep this information a secret. It was believed by all, if we told our citizens this shocking truth, the resulting panic would be uncontainable. So we kept this ground-breaking news about the approaching alien fleet from our peoples. While the scientific community was utterly stupefied by the shock from the discovery, as well as from our failure to disclose the news to the public, we governmental leaders put on a brave face and pretended nothing out of the ordinary was happening.

That is not to say we didn't prepare. The vast militaries of the world began to mobilize and arm themselves, but they did so in such a way that most of our populations didn't even notice. For example, to explain the nearly constant flights of armed fighter planes and bombers in our skies, not to mention the new presence of weapons and soldiers on the streets of all of our major cities, the U.S. government told its citizens the military was taking part in a massive celebration we code-named Pajama Bottoms. We hoped the overly innocent name would become a source of amusement, not fear.

Early on, everything seemed to be under control. The different leaders of the planet were unified in their preparation for the imminent alien invasion, and the people of the planet remained blissfully unaware of it.

Then some amateur astronomers spotted the objects, the news agencies somehow got a hold of the story, and the whole unpleasant truth was leaked to the world. As soon as the fact that our planet was about to be overrun by an unknown alien invasion fleet was put out on the airwaves, the entire human race, as predicted, hit the panic button.

Because we'd kept everyone in the dark, most people took our attempt at hiding the truth, and the militaristic preparation for the potential invasion, as evidence the world leaders were now only looking out for their own best interests.

Society reacted by breaking apart into its most individualistic, primal and potentially violent connections – clans, families, tribes, principalities, ethnicities, and even genders. The result of this was something to see, I can tell you! If the old adage of your life flashing in front of your eyes before you die is true, then the most selfish and self-serving sides of humanity were just as bared to us all during those uncertain days, as clearly as Marilyn Monroe's panties had been when she stood over the subway air duct in Sam Shaw's iconic "flying skirt" photo!

Meanwhile, in the White House, we feared all of this fractionalization was going to rip everything asunder even before the aliens landed, and this led us to wonder aloud if there was any reason to put up any resistance against the approaching alien fleet. After all, with our species doing a magnificent job of self-destructing on its own, we weren't sure there'd be anything left to greet our new alien house guests in the first place. The world, which now seemed on the brink of eradicating itself, was falling apart so quickly that we figured when the aliens did arrive, what remained would be an unassembled puzzle in a box.

But that turned out not to be the case. By the time the alien ships were just coming around our moon, the human species had bent, but not broken under the strain of its dissent. Because there hadn't been a total collapse, humanity seemed to step back from the brink of complete chaos and take in a huge inhalation to wait and see what would actually happen next. Although this had all the earmarks of an implausible miracle to be celebrated at the highest levels of government, we were soon to discover, as events continued to unfold after the Altoonians had landed, that the subsequent swelling from this worldwide breath-holding created the stretch marks that would become the seams from which our planet would finally burst, later on.

It was during this darkest time that President Kennedy shone his brightest. Just as the alien ships were about to breach our planet's atmosphere, he broadcast one of the greatest speeches I'd ever heard him give. In it he asked the world's inhabitants to remember two things: we were all in this same mess together *and* we needed to make sure there actually was a mess out there in the first place, before anyone did anything rash.

He argued that until we knew if the approaching aliens were hostile or not, it seemed silly to overreact. After all, if we started flinging nuclear weapons around like snowballs and the aliens just passed us by, or even turned out to be friendly, we'd be left with a bigger cleanup than any of us wanted. He urged restraint and cooperation from the entire international community, and to those leaders who were overly preoccupied with rattling sabers and doing war dances in preparation for the upcoming invasion, he begged everyone to take a wait-and-see attitude. And to those leaders who were feeling badly because they were frozen with fear, he admitted we were all scared to death at the moment.

The President's message proved to be insightful because the initially tight formation of the approaching armada suddenly broke apart and individual ships dispersed to various landing sites around the globe. This maneuver made the threat of an imminent invasion seem even more real, and it's my humble opinion that if President Kennedy hadn't reminded Earth's leadership to give the aliens the benefit of the doubt and let them speak first, the world would be an even bigger charcoal briquette than it is now.

Instead of hurling our weapons onto our visitors as they spread out, everyone around the globe stopped their agitation and looked up at the incoming Altoonian ships to see what would happen next.

Trying to act calm was beyond hard. Personally, I was a nervous wreck. The very first televised images of the gigantic alien ship hovering above the Pennsylvanian landscape sure didn't help. As the cameramen struggled to pan back far enough to fit the entire craft onto the television screen, the fact there were twenty two other gigantic alien ships doing the exact same thing around the globe only enhanced the feeling we humans were completely doomed. Believe me, there were times when I was prepared to strip naked and run through the streets screaming. But I didn't.

My military training had prepared me by demonstrating to all of us soldiers that the waiting for an upcoming action can be far worse than the actual event. You see, it's during those times of extreme apprehension when it's important to curb all thoughts since they are usually nothing but pessimistic prognostications about just how badly things are going to go. Because these dismal ideas are usually the manifestations of our phobias and deepest fears, they tend only to usurp clearer understanding and behavior.

So, as these massive crafts hovered and prepared to land, I knew most people around the planet were imagining nothing but swarms of little green men flooding out of these ships to zap us with their death rays. As I tried to squelch those very same images in my own head, I found the strength to continue to think about positive things and force myself to stay prepared for the worst, yet be hopeful for the best. Even so, the regrets of my own squandered chances and unrealized hopes during my life fluttered within me like butterflies. While discouraging, I didn't let these sentiments get out of control. I knew there was more to life than crying over spilt milk.

Earthlings had never seen anything like these Altoonian spacecraft. Even the seemingly realistic sci-fi movies of our youth did not get the scale of these vessels right. The alien ships were shining, smooth onyx discs, and they were not only floating magically in the air with no apparent means of propulsion, they were mind-numbingly immense. With a two mile diameter and a one mile height at its apex, each Altoonian ship looked like a gigantic flying *non la,* one of those conical Vietnamese bamboo hats. Except, in this case, they were each the size and shape of New Hampshire's Mount Washington.

As I watched the descent of these monstrously large ships from the virtual safety of the White House Situation Room, I could not help but feel we humans were as helpless as bugs on the sidewalk who are about to be stepped on by a gigantic shoe!

Each ship in the Altoonian fleet touched down on the Earth at precisely the same moment. While the synchronicity of this maneuver was more than impressive, it meant, in some places on the globe, the landings were happening in the middle of the night. For those of us inside the White House, we were very appreciative that the Altoonians had randomly chosen our landing time to correspond with early morning in the eastern United States since it gave us the benefit of daylight to ascertain and assess the situation with much more clarity. Those unfortunate places with nighttime landings had to deal with an exponentially larger dose of tension from not being able to see all the mind-blowing details of the arriving ships in the dark.

Our gathered group watched on the television screens as the Altoonian space ship arriving in Pennsylvania lowered itself down to the ground, and we all gasped as dozens of metallic legs, each the size and shape of sequoia trees, appeared magically out of the bottom of the featureless exterior and extended downward until the ship gently touched down onto the Earth like some kind of parachuting woodlouse. The surprisingly powerful final discharge of the ship's thrusters singed and scorched the land beneath them and created a charred circle under and around the ship. The sight of this was the most visually succinct sign of the aliens' arrival. It said the Altoonians had just landed on Earth – period.

The following moments were actually the most tense as we waited to see what was going to happen next. Either the aliens were going to start disgorging their armies or someone on our side was going to start launching a preemptive attack upon the intruders and begin the incineration of our planet. Either way, it didn't look like things would end well for us. The President and I watched the monitors to see which species would blink first – but, in this case, whichever one did would blink the other out of existence.

Suddenly, there was a broadcast in English coming across every radio and television frequency on the planet and a message being played across the alien ship's hull in an impressive visual display of lights. The message was simple.

WE COME IN PEACE. WE SEEK REFUSE.

This, of course, turned out to be a typo by the Altoonians and caused some initial confusion and — only later, much later — a little humor. The President, seeing what amounted to a goodwill gesture in their initial message, immediately had his staff get word out to the other leaders of the world what the Altoonians were broadcasting to us. In a matter of moments it became clear this same exact scenario was playing out in the other twenty two landing sites, except the message from the other ships was in the language of the host nation. (We hadn't experienced the power of the Universal Translator yet, so this fact amazed us nearly as much as the overwhelming size of the ships).

In this one moment of our human existence, we all found ourselves with our mouths open, a little shit in our underwear, and not a clue what to do next.

It was my suggestion we answer the aliens with an equally simple, yet similar reply.

WE SEEK PEACE. WE CAN PROVIDE REFUSE.

This, of course, caused the Altoonians some of their own confusion since they were still unaware of their typo at the moment. However, even with all the muddled aspects of the first communication aside, it was now clear neither species wanted to currently annihilate the other, and this allowed everyone involved to breathe a collective sigh of relief.

We immediately began receiving intelligence about the various landing sites around the planet. Three alien ships had landed in the United States. Because of its relative proximity to Washington, the one near Cherry Springs State Park in Potter County, Pennsylvania, garnered most of our attention in the White House. As for the two other ships – one north of the city of Shreveport, Louisiana, and the other outside of Reno, Nevada – we had to leave their reception in the capable hands of those states' governors. We hoped they'd handle their intergalactic visitors on their own. That might sound callous of us, but our hands were full with the ship nearest to us to worry about anything else.

The reports from the other twenty landing sites showed the Altoonian vessels had landed in seemingly random locations. One landed north of Mexico City, three on the continent of South America in the countries of Brazil, Uruguay and Peru, three in India, four in China, one in Thailand, one between Tokyo and Osaka, one in the Pyrenees Mountains between Spain and France, one in the Black Forest of Germany, one in the country of Belarus in the Soviet Union, one in the northern part of the Sinai Peninsula, one just north of Johannesburg, South Africa, one near Jakarta, Indonesia, and one north of Sydney, Australia.

Although we quickly understood our planet was now covered rather equally by their ships, none of the President's advisors, nor anyone on the Joint Chiefs of Staff, could see any rhyme or reason for why the aliens had chosen to land where they did. They were not all atop national capitals, nor were they near to any major centers of industry or agriculture. And, although some were nearby to active military installations, they didn't appear overly interested in those either. They also didn't seem to be threatening any specific worship, pilgrimage or historically important centers of any our world religions. There was no obvious climatic preference or avoidance to the sites as they included temperate to tropic regions.

We assumed they hadn't landed in the Arctic or Antarctic because of the complete lack of anyone to talk with in those places. But with no clear reason as to why they had chosen to go where they did, we all felt somewhat behind the eight ball when it came to initiating negotiation-like conversations with the visitors without revealing too much. After all, their motives were still completely unknown.

That is why the starkness of their next message caused us so much surprise. The Altoonian ships urgently requested to have a face to face meeting with two leaders from each region. Our ship specifically asked for the President and me to come to Pennsylvania. They added they sought some reassurance we wouldn't rush at them as they opened their doors to us. While I didn't read too much into this request, the leaders of the military immediately perceived this cautious approach as a vulnerability we could use to keep them from frying us with their death ray – if they had one.

After a short song and dance by both sides, involving the obviously fake *I'll have to check my schedule* – absurd, since there was nothing possibly more pressing for either species than dealing with one another – we agreed on the time and place for the first encounter.

All of these theatrics showed we might be immensely different from one another, but we certainly shared a similar way of doing business.

▪ ▪ ▪

On the date of our first meeting with the aliens, tensions were running ridiculously high. There'd been some strong resistance from Congress and the military over the demand that both the President and the Vice President be present at this summit. Although I appreciated the sense that everyone was looking out for our welfare, I also knew what they were really worried about. If the aliens did choose to barbecue us, the United States of America would be reduced to having Tip O'Neill, Speaker of the House, as the acting head of the country. Truthfully, no one in their right mind wanted him at the helm! I mean, we all knew what the puffy red nose of that Irishman meant.

But because the aliens had been so specific in their invitation, we decided we couldn't begin this new relationship on the wrong foot by disregarding their first request. It turned out to be the correct decision. We were to find out later that the Altoonians debated, negotiated, delegated and decided all issues in groups of two. Their requirement of a similar duo of leaders on the other side of the table from them was issued to assure a process that seemed harmonious to them.

When the President and I arrived on Army One to the Pennsylvania landing site, it was ringed completely by a very visible military presence. Tanks, artillery and missile launchers were all strategically positioned around the massive ship, and they all were clearly armed and ready. Bomb-laden fighter jets streaked across the sky while the throbbing rotors of helicopter gunships beat out a perfect cadence as they hovered just over the treetops. However, the Altoonians had been quite specific in their supplications for their own safety, so none of these weapons were brought closer than a previously prescribed distance from the ship. In spite of the size of the military arsenal assembled, there was so much tension right there at the landing site, you could have heard a pin drop as the convoy of jeeps brought us to the drop-off point.

As President Kennedy and I walked purposefully toward the meeting area, which was enshrouded in the growing shadows of the gigantic ship, this eerie silence quickly became utterly nerve-wracking. In front of us, the two Eames Lounge Chairs and Ottomans the aliens had requested had been setup for us across from the two immense backless settees in the small open place prepared for the meeting.

My heart beat out a conga tune as we made our way toward the designated site. The Altoonians had been downright stubborn in their specific demands for our encounter, and I remember thinking as we walked that I wanted the American people to see their President and Vice President acting completely unintimidated, even if we were to be publicly evaporated by the aliens. How ridiculous a thought to have, I know, but we all wanted to keep up appearances.

A shaft of black metal dropped down from the ship's underside and touched the ground. Instantly the outline of a door appeared in the metal and it slid open, revealing two large alien creatures inside. As they came toward us, their pace and size reminded me of two rhinoceroses walking erect on two legs. It was clear almost immediately the Altoonians were not being theatrical with their slow and deliberate gait – they could walk no faster. With each step they took toward us, the President and I both uttered nearly silent sounds of shock and awe under our breath, yet these utterances were drowned out by the click of camera shutters, the flashes of the photo bulbs, and the whirl of the movie cameras from the nearby press corps around the perimeter, the only other people the Altoonians had invited to the meeting.

When the two aliens had finally made their way to the edge of the meeting area and the President and I were standing facing them, an eerie hush lay over the area like an early morning mist. We took a moment to survey each other. The huge Altoonians towered over us. They were ten feet tall and they looked down at the President and me with large unblinking obsidian eyes. From their immense size, I quickly calculated they probably each weighed more than four grown adult humans!

Yet, despite their intimidating exterior, there seemed to be something benevolent in their expressions and their body language. They wore azure blue spacesuits, and the sky-like coloring of their clothing was neither too aggressive nor threatening. From the exposed skin we could see protruding from their suits, it was apparent they were the shade of a light green most painters refer to as *fern* in color. And, at first glance, they appeared to be completely hairless. Their heads were heavily muscled and powerful-looking, although much of their faces were obstructed by what looked like chrome tubes running from behind their necks and covering their mouths and ears. It was unclear whether these apparatuses were a breathing device, some type of muzzle or just decorative.

The awkward silence was finally broken by President Kennedy as he extended his hand forward with his introduction of us. I extended mine too, and we stood there for too long with our hands out like two sundials while the Altoonians looked down at us in discomfort. Finally, the bigger of the two seemed to smile — or grimace…it was hard to tell with its mouth obscured by the metal apparatus around its head — and then he spoke in the most robotic of voices.

"Ah, yes, your greeting ritual. If you do not mind, we will not engage in the shaking of hands yet. For, since we earnestly do not know how hard we can grasp your hands without injuring you, we are fearful any negative interactions from the first meeting between our two species would be disastrous to this whole process. But to make sure those members of your press personnel present don't misconstrue our hesitancy as some kind of rudeness or a fatal episode of distrust, we will place our hands out with the palms up. If you two would be so kind as to place your tiny hands atop ours, we feel this will create an image of a peaceful meeting. My name is Moog, and I am the Imperialtate of this ship. Next to me is Haag, the Second Imperialtate. We are from the planet Altoonia, and we are here to seek refuge on your planet."

The two aliens put their hands out in front of them, and they were the size of Truman service china chargers. As the President and I put our hands onto their palms, I could not help feel some trepidation that we were playing a dangerous game of "hot hands." The thought of those paddle-like appendages suddenly slapping my frail hands made me gulp, but we stood there, tenderly and awkwardly touching like that, for a moment without any incident. Their skin felt warm, but hard.

After we eventually pulled back, I dared to ask a question about their metallic headwear.

"I hope I'm not being rude by asking this at this juncture, Commander Moog, but I am wondering about the devices on your heads. Are they breathing devices? Is our air dangerous for you?"

The leader made a sound like the clicking of a roulette wheel — which was discomforting, to say the least – and I didn't know if I had insulted him or amused him. Either way, the creature turned its jet-black eyes on me and spoke.

"Not a rude question at all, Vice President Hunter. No, your atmosphere is nearly identical to the one on Altoonia. We were most lucky to discover our two planets share a lot of similarities. No, these devices are Universal Translators. The Altoonian language is one your species has never heard, and we are unable to speak the various human dialects, so we will use the Universal Translators to help us converse. The downside to it is the robotic quality of what we say and what we hear, but we feel it is better to be understood and to understand than to have proper inflection and intonation. Now, let's sit down and continue our conversation together. It is clear we all have many questions for one another. So, let us sit down and discuss them further."

We all moved to the meeting area and sat down. I was embarrassed to appear to be lounging in the chair with my feet up on the Ottoman, but the Altoonians were insistent they wanted us to be comfortable. They seemed quite at ease on their settees, so I attempted to give off a similar sense to them, but I must say I felt damn stupid to be reclining in my chair like I was watching the annual Army-Navy college football game!

Nonetheless, the meeting went well. The Altoonians relayed how their fleet of ships had been traveling through the universe searching for a suitable place to live after their own planet had been destroyed by war. They reiterated that they had come here with completely peaceful intentions and needed a haven from their exodus. And, as such, they were very aware they were now the guests of our planet, and they spoke at length about how they did not want to do anything to upset our hospitality.

Their goal was to design some kind of mutually beneficial living arrangement. Once settled, they promised they would give us Earthlings untold technological innovations. They went on to boastfully proclaim they would make the entire planet a better place for us all. In return, the Altoonians only sought a safe and war-free place to live. The specific details to the arrangement would, obviously, have to be ironed out by our two species as time went along, but they wanted the Earthlings to know they'd only come to find a new suitable home. They concluded by saying that if an overwhelming percentage of the inhabitants of this planet did not want them to stay, they'd leave immediately, no questions asked!

The President made no promises. He pointed out we were just the representatives of our people, and, as such, we'd head back after this meeting and discuss the details with the appropriate counsels to come to an acceptable and shared consensus in our country and around the globe. As we all stood and did the silly-looking hand-in-hand ceremony again, President Kennedy avowed that the Altoonians were accepted as current guests seeking asylum on our planet, but until further dialogues happened, he kindly requested the channel of communication be kept open so any new developments in our new and unfolding relationship did not cause surprises or create any kind of snowballing defensive reactions. Although relieved the visitors had come in peace, he reminded the Altoonians that the fragility of our situation required everyone to act with restraint and transparency.

As we were driven away from the site, President Kennedy turned to me and said, "Well, that certainly couldn't have gone much better!"

I nodded tentatively, for I was still a bit in shock from the experience. Suddenly, he spoke again.

"But they're definitely going to have to learn English if they want to communicate with us! I'm not sure how long I can stand to listen to them through the Universal Translators. It was like talking to Hal 9000 from *2001:A Space Odyssey*. Also, I sure hope we can teach them how to shake hands properly. That silly laying on of hands ritual isn't the image of strength I want to portray to our people."

I looked back and saw the door in the black metallic column close and the entire shaft rise up into the Altoonian ship and disappear like it had never been there in the first place. I felt a pang of uncertainty. As much as our entire understanding of our place in the universe had been put into a car crusher by the arrival of these aliens, I couldn't shake the feeling that the first meeting with them had been overly similar to so many other historical encounters, all of which had started out going well until they slid into the crapper because of unforeseen and unknown shortcomings. As our vehicle drove away past the military forces stationed there, I even dared to wonder when the other shoe was going to drop.

# THE CALM BEFORE THE STORM

Upon our return to the White House for our debriefing with the Joint Chiefs of Staff, it became immediately apparent from the unending stream of worldwide reports about the other twenty two meetings with the Altoonians that everything had gone similarly well elsewhere.

Those other encounters had been attended by state governors, lieutenant governors, envoys, dictators, presidents, emissaries, prime ministers, or even kings or queens, but the gist of the take-away from each one was overwhelmingly positive. The space travelers were here because they had nowhere else to go, and they thought our interspecies relationship would benefit both parties.

And, although we knew we couldn't dictate how any other government would approach the next rounds of negotiations, we were all fairly confident no one was crazy enough to start anything by committing a violent act against the Altoonians on their own. Because of this, the threat of global annihilation began to diminish as soon as it was clear the world's leaders were loosening up a little on the reins. The men of action, including our own generals and admirals, seemed more than content with just watching the Altoonians closely to devise a military plan to deal with them if things went south.

The next days were a time for gradual normalization – as much as a term like that can be used when referring to gigantic UFO ships parked on your land and asking for asylum. But with those successful first meetings going off without a hitch, most citizens of the planet felt they could go on with their lives again without the threat of instant death, enslavement or an imminent apocalypse. For those of us in the various branches of the government, we not only had the usual business of running the country to attend to, we also were now required to have countless additional meetings, briefings and planning sessions to determine our next steps for all future interactions with the alien visitors. That's not to say we were able to dictate any of the specific details about the next meetings, since the Altoonians seemed bound and determined to control all aspects of those. They were wed to the idea of following the exact same routine of the first meeting in all future sessions together. So, even though the President and I were busy with the usual daily duties of our positions, we had to put many of those on the back burner whenever the aliens beckoned us to have a meeting to work on developing another component of the living arrangement between us Earthlings and the Altoonians.

▪ ▪ ▪

About a week after our first meeting with the aliens, as we sat casually on the couches in the Oval Office to chat about some of our plans for what to do next, the President turned to me and asked bluntly, "You don't trust the Altoonians, do you, Jim?"

Even though I didn't, the bluntness of his question caught me off guard and I answered it too quickly.

"Of course I do, Ted!"

President Kennedy was petting his gray squirrel Jocko, and as he gently scratched the rodent under its chin, the animal gave him a stained-incisor filled grin. The animal was so content, I swear I could hear it purr with satisfaction. When the President saw me gazing at his beloved pet, he nodded down at it as if he were agreeing with something the animal had said.

"No. I can tell you don't. Honestly, I don't trust 'em as far as I could throw 'em – and with them being so *big*, we certainly couldn't toss 'em too far."

We chuckled at this comment, but the President became serious again. He continued to scratch his squirrel, but he turned his eyes back to me and sighed heavily.

"So, because I think it'd be prudent for us to stay cautious at this point, Jim, I want to do something somewhat silly right now. Although it might make me sound like some kind of love-sick teenage girl, I think we should make a list of what we know about the Altoonians and what we don't. It could help us weed through all the heavy-hitting topics. There's a pad of paper right there on the coffee table. You can use it to jot down everything we think up together."

I reached for the legal pad of paper, but couldn't find a pen. When the President noticed my looking around, he sat up and barked a command to the squirrel.

"Go get daddy his pen, Jocko! It's on my desk. Go get it!"

The rodent immediately set out on its appointed task. It hopped off the couch, scampered across the Presidential

Seal rug and clambered up onto the Resolute Desk. There, in the midst of a pile of loose papers, Jocko found the President's favorite fountain pen. He gently grasped it in his mouth and then took a running leap and landed at the foot of the couch. In another bound, the cute critter was back in its owner's lap.

The President carefully took his pen out of the squirrel's mouth and handed it over to me. As the man crooned his praise and scratched the animal's belly, I began to scrawl on the pad of paper. I know it might sound weird that the President of the United States had a pet squirrel roaming around the White House during those days, but the animal had been such a fixture of the man's life, none of us even took notice of it anymore.

"The Altoonians are huge in size, but they say they're peaceful," the President absently blurted out.

"Hm, uh-uh," I uttered as I wrote this down.

"They say they are from the planet of Altoonia, but we don't even know where that is."

I stated evenly, "You know, I asked Charlie Simmons, the head of NASA, about this. He told me that even though we first caught sight of them somewhere near Venus, we shouldn't assume their home planet is on a straight vector from where the IRIS detected them. He was insistent I remember that interstellar space travel across the various galaxies of the universe would be made up of constantly dodging celestial bodies and using other space features like worm holes and the occasional gravity assist to get to where you want to get to as quickly as you can. Because of this, there's just no way to plot which direction the Altoonians came from. All we know for sure is they came right at us like a bat out of hell!"

The President nodded and bunched a tiny blanket around his cherished pet, who was now dozing soundly with his feet straight up in the air.

"Yes, that's similar to the information passed on to me in my own inquiries. But what worries me more is how the Altoonians seem to be masters of deflection on the topic. Whenever we've asked them directly where their planet is, I've noticed Moog and Haag keep using the vaguest of terms and locations so often that they sound like they're describing a place in Willy Wonka's factory. I mean, it doesn't take a rocket scientist to figure out their ambiguous replies of, 'up there, next to a galaxy with a gigantic red sun and a smaller white dwarf' or 'far, far, far away' are nothing more than well-conceived non-answers. Not to say we'd be able to grasp the truth if they told it to us. We'd be just like a bunch of Yanomami in the Amazon rainforest trying to understand that an anthropologist visiting their village was from a place called Chicago!"

While we both had a good laugh over this comment, the way the Altoonians kept manipulating the truth with us obviously caused us great consternation, and we quickly became silent and glum again. Then President Kennedy pointed his finger at me.

"Here's a few more things for our list. Put these down, Jim. We know they require two people to negotiate with them. We know they are incredibly technologically advanced. We know they want to be here and appear to be peaceful, but they can be rigid in their thinking and can be down-right stubborn."

I wrote down what he'd said, but then I frowned because this short list was the extent of things we knew about the Altoonians. I cleared my throat.

"Maybe we need to put down all the things we *don't* know. I think that would be a much longer list."

"Good idea. Flip over a couple of pages. So, other than where the planet Altoonia really is, we don't know some crucial things about these creatures. We don't know how many of them there are in total. They've been very evasive answering questions about their population numbers. I'd like to know how many of them live on each of those ships, just for a census kind of data."

"Yes, that would be information we'd like to know about in any other immigrant or refugee situation, right?"

"Positively. I'd also like to know more about them as a species. What do they eat? Do they get married and are they monogamous? Do they commit crimes? Do they have a religion? What is their lifespan? How do the twenty three Imperialtates all interact with one another? I mean, is there a chief honcho or are their really twenty three ship captains all acting together in a confederacy? We don't even know what form of government they have! What will we do if they're communists? Or worse, social democrats. And what do they want from us other than letting them squat on our planet? I mean, they must have a vision for what their life on our planet will be like. What is it?"

I was furiously scribbling down these questions on the paper. When I had caught up, I looked up at him.

"It looks like we have some questions to ask when they demand our next meeting."

"Yes, Jim, we do. And I hope to get the answers to these. With the dangers of an apocalyptic event happening between our two species now fading, I find myself growing more worried the dangers we face as a species are not necessarily coming from the Altoonians, but from the gigantic egg of uncertainty we humans are currently sitting on and waiting to hatch. I'd like to know what the aliens really want. I don't want to say we need to know how to react to that, per se, but I'd like to be able to broadcast some good news to the citizens of this world to alleviate their building concerns. I cannot help the feeling the fears of the general population are just swelling and swelling from their growing anticipation of the unknown, and if we aren't careful, that could explode. If you and I are getting frustrated not knowing what these visitors are really like or really want, we can only guess as to what most people going about their normal lives are feeling or thinking these days. And two men such as ourselves are far less dangerous in the big picture than an entire population made up of distrustful, frustrated, or just curious individuals. This could all fall apart if the Altoonians don't start playing ball!"

▪ ▪ ▪

But the Altoonians didn't offer up any new answers to our questions the next time we met. They remained as defiantly stubborn as they'd been during the previous negotiations, and this caused some personal consternation for the President and myself. We'd begun to notice how some burgeoning issues were now stepping out from behind the curtain of the aliens' awe-inspiring arrival and taking their place at center stage. For example, we didn't know what to do with the gigantic ships presently sitting in the middle of our landscapes. The Altoonians seemed to want to stay on our planet, but right where they were.

Even though we argued it would work better for us if they'd move their ships to less populated areas – somewhere like the deserts of the Southwest – the aliens would not budge on this point. We even pointed out how such sites as these had been ideal locations for airplane boneyards and nuclear waste storage for years since they provided peace and quiet away from the hubbub of this planet. However, the aliens demanded to stay in their ships, on the sites on which they had landed.

Not to be deterred, we even tried to sweeten the offer by suggesting if they were so bound to their present landing sites, we would build them a new residential development for them there. We hoped the use of the term "Altoonian public housing" would strike some chord. We even showed them the artist's renderings of a complex of structures designed by none other than I.M. Pei. These modernistic structures were impressive in scale and scope, and the architect had made each living quarter resemble the shape of the Altoonian ship. The President and I were both impressed with the eye for details the plans incorporated and the cost evaluations of the massive project.

The aliens seemed unenthusiastic.

Things degraded even further when we pushed the Altoonians to tell us just how many of the housing units we'd need to build for them. They saw through this ploy to give us an estimate of their population and dug in their heels and declared that that information was superfluous since they weren't going to leave their ships. The meeting ended almost comically with the large aliens stamping their feet and repeating they wanted to be allowed to stay on their ships and keep them right where they were – like they were two massive toddlers having a public temper tantrum!

▪ ▪ ▪

Afterwards, back in D.C., we held an emergency meeting of the Joint Chiefs of Staff. Our military analysts informed us they'd surprisingly come to the conclusion it would be better to keep the aliens in their ships and in their present locations. From their calculations, any attempt to physically force the aliens out of their ships and into some kind of housing development was going to cause a war which would result in a terribly great loss of life and property. So, in their humble opinions, a forced movement was not the best course of action. Instead, they believed allowing the Altoonians to stay put made the most sense economically, logistically and militarily since, by doing so, we could keep our eyes on them in the three easily managed and centralized locations in our country.

From this it was clear to me these military men were really preparing for trouble. By insisting we keep the aliens isolated from the rest of the human population and in a separate and contained environment, then – if or when things went badly — it'd be far easier for their forces to get the jump on the Altoonians in their ships at the landing sites.

▪ ▪ ▪

When Moog and Haag called for another meeting, they were clearly relieved to hear we had given up the idea of removing them from their ships.

However, they did follow this conversation with new and strongly worded requests. They demanded we enlarge and more closely manage the security zone surrounding their ship to keep them safe from curious gawkers or even more serious threats. Because identical requests were going out from each of their ships at the different landing sites, compliance with the request would be not only be a show of solidarity, it would go a long way to sustaining the continued peaceful co-existence our two species sought.

Of course, we agreed with their request, and we continued to divert traffic around these areas and we established an even more secure area with limited access. This was challenging, though, since all the landing sites were now ensconced as major attractions and were usually filled with curious onlookers. But we'd all heard the thinly veiled threat — lying smack dab in the middle of the Altoonian request — about the fragility of our relationship, and we began to immediately make sure our guests' demands were taken care of first. Plus, we figured, we had bigger fish to fry.

With the stalemate over the living arrangements now side-stepped, the President and I decided it was time to broach the subject about getting an invitation to tour the inside of their ship and meet other Altoonian individuals. So, during our next meeting together, we proposed this to Moog and Haag. The two aliens instantly, but politely, shot down this idea with a typical dose of their vague non-answers. When we continued to push the issue, the two aliens gave each other a quick look and rebuffed our request by stating that a strict quarantine needed to be maintained between our two species to ensure no passage of potentially devastating diseases occurred.

Although the President and I tried to remain calm in the face of imagining such an unpleasant medical disaster scenario, their answer immediately caused our sphincters to clench. If anyone was going to get some form of an unknown dermatological condition or a fatal respiratory ailment from direct contact with the visiting aliens, it was going to be us. I can tell you, neither the President nor I was too thrilled to be the first victim of some kind of Altoonian Pox. We quickly withdrew our request, and said we were more than willing to wait until they deemed it was medically safe for our two species to meet together.

With this, the relationship between the two species began to cool. The aliens seemed content to stay in their ship and keep us at arm's length, and we Earthlings all took the hint and began to turn our attention back more onto our own lives. Even the press corps soon grew less interested in the landing site. After all, there's only a limited number of photographs and videos needed of an unchanging and featureless exterior of a gigantic alien ship. Many news agencies started to withdraw some of their anchormen and reporters back to the studios to give attention to more active local stories. Even the coverage of the aliens in the newspapers dwindled. As our meetings with the Altoonians went from daily to weekly to a more sporadic and random schedule, the few stories in print about the alien visitors were buried well onto the back pages of the publications.

Our life paradigms may have been shifted by the arrival of these space refugees, but the utter lack of murderous intentions and their own separatist inclinations caused most people to begin to think of the Altoonians as standoffish and aloof boarders who wanted to be left alone. In the same vein, even the President and I began to think about the aliens as nothing more than a distant and mostly content tenant.

Oh, my. What a horrible oversight that was!

# DIAMOND IN THE ROUGH

During our next requested meeting time, the Altoonians issued what seemed at first to be an utterly innocent proposition, but it certainly wasn't. In fact, it turned out to be a wolf in sheep's clothing!

As we sat out in the now familiar chairs in front of Moog and Haag, they asked such a mundane question that the President and I snickered at how similar it would be to hear their request coming from any human family traveling across the country in an RV. The two Altoonians reported their ship's sewage tanks had filled up almost to a critical level, and they asked if we had any objection to them dumping their waste products onto the ground outside their ships. We didn't have an immediate answer for this, but we informed them we'd check in with the experts of such things upon our return to Washington, D.C..

Of course, as soon as we posed this question to Rufus Witherspoon, the head of the Environmental Protection Agency, he immediately blanched at the request and then acted like he was going to pass out from fright. After all, if it's an unthinkable crime for a person to dump a Winnebago's untreated waste water onto the ground, the draining of the unknown contents of the septic system from an alien ship the size of a mountain was a completely unthinkable and unforgivable act to the EPA. Witherspoon immediately insisted samples needed to be taken and tested before any solution to their problem could be considered, and he even inferred litigation would immediately result if this request was, in any way, trifled with by either aliens or governmental officials.

Our next problem was to figure out who on our planet was qualified or crazy enough to test the aliens' waste. In the end, we decided the nation's preeminent expert in both organic and inorganic chemistry, a Dr. Bernard Bishop, was the man to contact.

He was absolutely brilliant, but he was not the most approachable person. After the death of his wife from pancreatic cancer, he'd become a virtual recluse on his research compound in North Carolina. He'd not only received a sizable death benefit from a very large life insurance policy, he had successfully sued the pharmaceutical giant Eli Lilly in a wrongful death case. On top of this second payout, he'd also patented several of his own groundbreaking chemical discoveries. So, at this point in his life, the man was so financially secure, he really didn't need to work.

This financial freedom gave him unprecedented opportunities to focus purely on those chemical projects he chose, but it also meant, for all intents and purposes, the man lived and worked entirely alone. He'd grown so accustomed to being without any other human beings around, he was considered to be somewhat of an anti-social hermit and a possible quack. But while many in the scientific community questioned his social skills and, potentially, his sanity, he was a man with unparalleled research skills and empirical ability who had often let his passions lead him to tackle problems alone in his laboratory that most in his field would have refused.

In other words, he was the perfect man for this job!

When it became clear to us that Dr. Bishop was the scientist to do the testing of the alien waste products, there was some serious hand-wringing during our planning sessions with trusted advisors in the White House as to the best way to make contact with the seemingly unapproachable genius in such a way as to not spook him. We came up with several approaches, including finances and fame, to help convince Dr. Bishop to head this project.

None of those were needed. He committed to the whole thing as soon as we asked him. I guess, to a man of science of the caliber of Dr. Bishop, being the first person on Earth to test substances that had origins in another part of the universe was the opportunity of a lifetime. His instant enthusiasm was so great, in fact, that the reclusive scientist surprised everyone by becoming more like the star pupil of an Emily Post Charm School whenever he returned our phone calls. Go figure!

But unlike getting a sample from the waste tank of an RV, this was not going to be as easy as just opening a valve under the Altoonian spacecraft and filling up a Mason jar. For starters, the aliens were incredibly reluctant to give us any access whatsoever to their ship for gathering a sample. We were forbidden from having a team of technicians go anywhere near the vessel, and the aliens remained defiantly skeptical as to why we would need any sample in the first place. When our first few polite requests were rebuffed, we finally played our host card and outright demanded the sample. After some tension-filled moments of indecision, Moog and Haag agreed to bring us one for the next meeting.

That was the first time the President and I had ever gone on the offensive during our negotiations with the Altoonians, and they were visibly perturbed by this. As we lined up for the now customary farewell ceremony of laying our hands inside theirs, they gave us the hairy eyeball, just like the parents of a teenager who'd asked for the keys to the family car without enough meekness or gratitude.

However, when we returned to the meeting site the next day, Moog and Haag carried with them a black onyx cube the size of a living room television set. As soon as they put it down in front of our chairs, we could tell it was made from the same seamless dark metal as the hull of their ship, and the way it gleamed and shimmered in the summer sunlight made it appear as if it were polished piece of jewelry.

As a matter of fact, as the Altoonians pushed the beautifully dark, glimmering cube toward us with their large feet, it was hard to imagine they were, in effect, shoving a bucket of shit in our direction.

The aliens, however, had apparently grown so unhappy with us that they stood up abruptly once the cube was handed over, gave a half-hearted excuse for needing to go back inside their ship, skipped the farewell ceremony, and walked back toward the waiting elevator without another word. The President and I exchanged glances as they entered the chamber and shot back up into the ship.

“Well, if they weren’t bald,” President Kennedy said under his breath, “I’d say we were just given the old ‘washing my hair’ excuse, huh?”

I nodded, but I had some grave concerns about the aliens’ visible displeasure with us over the waste sample. It certainly was not the best thing to have a new relationship like ours encounter such a rocky moment like this, and I could tell the President was anxious about it too. So I decided to use humor in my response. I spoke quietly out of the side of my mouth in an overly patronizing fashion.

“Maybe we should bring flowers to them next time we meet.”

The President snorted with contempt, and then we turned our attention to the cube. The Altoonians had made carrying it seem so easy, but when we bent down to lift it up, we found it weighed too much for just one of us to carry. We knew we were being watched — both by aliens and humans alike — so we tried to look like it wasn’t as heavy as a refrigerator.

As we both struggled to carry it back to the drop-off site and lower it gracefully to the ground without dropping it, the President and I muttered curses and grunted loudly. Men in their rubber hazmat suits and gas masks came down the walkway with a substantial dolly as soon as we’d gotten the cube close enough to still appear we were competent, and they worked quickly to put the cube onto the handcart to transport it to the specially modified tractor trailer truck waiting to take it directly to Dr. Bishop’s lab in North Carolina.

Due to their waste tanks being so close to overflowing, the Altoonians had made it abundantly clear time was of the essence, so we all knew we were on an extremely tight schedule. With a man as surly and academically aloof as Dr. Bishop, however, we were worried the usual assertive techniques of declaring a deadline, with threatened consequences for tardiness, would not work with him.

President Kennedy even volunteered to fly down immediately to discuss the urgency of the matter with the scientist. After all, time and tide wait for no man. Dr. Bishop accepted his offer for a quick visit.

When President Kennedy came back to D.C. after his very brief meeting with the scientist, he was brimming with confidence that the contents of the alien container were going to be analyzed as quickly as was humanly possible. From their time together, the two men discovered they had both attended Milton Academy, right outside of Boston, Massachusetts. This shared history gave the President a special "in" with the scientist, who was now even beyond eager to be working on such a tremendously important project for a fellow Mustang. He promised to get the answers we sought…or die trying!

The President and I were more than a little shocked when Dr. Bishop phoned less than twenty hours later. As instructed, the man called the direct line to the Oval Office, but he was so frantic with enthusiasm and exuberance that the White House operator thought he was a deranged madman calling and almost didn't patch him through. But since his name was about the only thing she heard in the midst of his titanic rambling and shouting, and since he was on the short list of important phone calls needing to be taken, she immediately notified the President of the call.

When he picked up the receiver, President Kennedy was also overwhelmed by the ravings of the man on the other end of the line. He tried to calm the scientist enough to understand what he was saying, and he was able to tell Dr. Bishop he was putting the call through the intercom so I could listen to his findings. There was a clear hesitation in the man's response, but then the President nodded and hit a button and we both could hear the man's excited breathing.

"Go on, Dr. Bishop. Vice President Hunter is here. Tell us. What did you find out?"

The man paused for a moment, then his words came out in a torrent.

"First off, you need to know the substance in the cube is unlike anything I've ever seen! It is made up of molecules not of this world. This shouldn't be a shock to anyone, but it is something so far outside the normal understandings of our sciences, it's almost enough to turn this agnostic into a religious fanatic. You see, these inhabitants of the Planet Altoonia are not – like us — based on carbon, and thusly there is no nitrogen or hydrogen involved with their makeup either. That is mind-blowing, to say the least! Mind-blowing!!"

The man's yelling made both the President and me flinch, but he quickly regained some calmness.

"But that's not the real source of my excitement. I ran the substance through the usual battery of tests to see if, even though it's not comprised of any known substance, it might respond similarly to earth-bound compounds. When I did a simple distillation process to the goo in the cube, something *earth-shaking* resulted! The liquid product of the test was as flammable as gasoline! As a matter of fact, I used a refining process similar to the one used by oil companies to isolate gasoline, and the liquid produced was one of the most efficient burning substances ever seen on this planet. I did a combustion test, and aside from a mild powdery residue, there were no pollutants lefts. Do you two realize what this *means*?"

The President leaned down to talk into the intercom.

"It would be safe to dump the Altoonian waste?"

There was no sound on the other end the line. Then we heard Dr. Bishop sigh with frustration.

"I'm not making myself clear here. If we were talking about a massive oil tanker brimming with high quality crude oil in our very midst, we wouldn't want to dump its contents onto the ground, would we? No, we'd want to pump it dry and use every drop of oil! The same with this Altoonian mixture. Their waste can be made into a super fuel, gentlemen. And, according to my calculations, if we were to send it through a slightly tweaked oil refinery, the result would be a completely pollution-free alternative to gasoline. If the aliens have enough of this stuff and can keep producing it, something like this could power everything on this planet for generations. We're talking, possibly, about making petroleum-based gasoline obsolete! We need to notify the other countries about this discovery at once. This could change everything for our entire planet!"

The President and I looked at one another. Even though we didn't have any idea at how much Dr. Bishop's prophecy would come true, we both understood some of the huge impact his discovery represented. But we also knew such a game-changing discovery needed either to be protected or at least managed carefully. The President leaned in closer to the intercom again and set about to make sure the chain of command was secure.

"But, Dr. Bishop, you won't contact the other countries on your own, right? I mean, it might be a better thing for us to do that at an official level. If information leaked into the wrong hands, this kind of thing could have disastrous results."

The doctor made a sound like he was digesting this news. Then he spoke low and in a near whisper.

"'Render therefore unto Caesar the things which are Caesar's and unto God the things that are God's,' I guess. No, I will keep my mouth closed so that the U.S. Government can do with this shocking information what it sees fit. But I'll tell you this, gentlemen, I'm washing my hands of any responsibility for a negative impact resulting from you keeping this information only on the official level."

"Agreed, Dr. Bishop. No blame will head your way."

"Okay. Instead, I only ask to keep the cube and its remaining contents for more testing, okay? As it's something truly unique to this planet, I'd like to run some more tests to find out more about its molecular makeup and its properties. Also, if I can turn the remainder of these wastes in this initial sample into fuel for my own personal use — even with this scant quantity — I can make enough fuel to power my lab for quite a while."

"Sounds good to me, Dr. Bishop," the President said with a nod toward me.

"Lastly, I'd like to write up my results and be allowed to submit my findings to the academic world whenever you deem it's ready for the information. Do we have a deal, gentlemen?"

The President pushed the button again and finished the conversation in private on the phone. I couldn't hear everything, but it was clear to me that while he gave in to many of the scientist's demands, he set down some strict rules to follow in the future for the research. He hung up and looked at me with a blanched face.

"Well, we certainly need to chew on this new news, don't we, Jim."

I nodded. It was almost too much to take in on so many different levels.

"I guess the first thing we need to do," I said, "is let the EPA have all of Dr. Bishop's results, right? And, after they give us permission to transfer and transport the wastes, we can go to the Altoonians and let them know we want all their sewage to make this new miracle fuel. It may take some time to design a proper way to transport it, but even if we have to mobilize every available tanker truck within five hundred miles of the sites to suck every drop out of their ship, it'd be worth it, right? With the announcement of this amazing discovery, the American people will have a new reason to continue to support the presence of the aliens!"

President Kennedy eyed me for a moment before speaking. He opened his mouth, but nothing came out, so he shut it again. He sighed and then spoke softly.

"Ah, Jim, I think we need to show much more restraint than that."

"I'm not sure I understand, Ted."

The President scratched his chin and looked off into space.

"Why did I just ask Dr. Bishop not to share his findings directly with the other countries?"

That was an easy answer.

"Because if we started throwing news of this magnitude without discrimination, someone less qualified might get wind of it, and there'd be a crush of people fighting to get their hands on the stuff to make the fuel. That kind of strife could potentially destabilize entire regions as the different factions wrestled with each other to take control of the waste supply."

President Kennedy arched his eyebrows and pursed his lips. I stared at his ridiculous expression for a moment and then I completely understood.

"Oh, I get it! You think the same thing could happen here."

"Yes, Jim. We can't destabilize our own country with the indiscriminate dispersal of this news either! We need to regulate the transmission of these facts…and stay in control of them."

"So we tell the EPA the waste material has tested as safe, but refrain from telling them about its potential as a new source of fuel?"

"Correct." President Kennedy nodded curtly.

"And we don't tell the American people anything about this amazing discovery at this point?"

"No, we can't. As much as I'd love to use this news to our advantage in terms of public support for the aliens' presence here, such explosive knowledge — no pun intended — is far too dangerous to put into the public's hands at this point. At some later date, once we've worked out all the details and there's a new infrastructure in place,

I'm sure we'll be able to tell the American people more…but not now.

"And you want to keep the truth of the matter from the Altoonians as well?"

The man nodded at me and then said loudly, "That's probably the most important thing we have to do, Jim. We can't put all our cards on the table with the Altoonians quite yet. I think, from what I've seen from them so far, they'd use our own excitement over the source of free fuel as a way to manipulate us, and I don't want to give them too much power."

President Kennedy stood up and went over to the windows to look out at the putting green on the South Lawn. He was silent for a moment or two and then he clucked his tongue several times before turning to face me. His facial expression was grave and tired looking, but his voice had a strength to it.

"The fact is, the Altoonians need us to empty their tanks just as much as we need the fuel. So I think this is one of those moments when, as the old saying goes, 'It is better to ask for forgiveness rather than to ask for permission.' We'll tell the EPA and the Altoonians we need to dump the waste far away from the landing sites to lessen the damage to the environment, and then we'll figure out how to secretly transport the stuff as quickly and quietly as we can away from the ship. Instead of taking it to some underground storage facility or a waste treatment plant, we'll need to get it to a refinery capable of producing this new form of gasoline as soon as we can. But we don't tell this to the Altoonians, the EPA, or the American public."

I shook my head and gave the man a worried look.

"That's mighty risky, Ted."

"Well, I don't see any other way, Jim. The EPA needs to know we're not hurting the environment. The aliens need to think we're just doing them a favor so we can keep the relationship at its present level. And, as for the American people, this knowledge would be way too much for them to handle. It might come in handy someday, of course, to give a positive spin to our whole relationship with the aliens. It could certainly appease all of those xenophobic and anti-government wackos who have begun to stir things up about these freeloading aliens on our planet being a part of a bigger conspiracy with the government. But, for the time being, I think it'd be best if we just sit on this info until the time to disclose it is right."

Even though I did not like withholding any information from the American people, I saw the value of this plan. The President watched me nod in agreement.

Then he added, "Okay, good. So you should make contact with the Altoonians to schedule a new meeting with them. During it, we will set into motion the idea we need to put their waste into transport vehicles. If they protest, we can use the guise that the substances could be very harmful to us and we do need to avoid a horrific polluting of our planet. Meanwhile, I will get together with my friend Sonny Ferguson, head of Texas Oil & Gas, and talk to him about the possibilities of refining the alien waste. Once I share what the good doctor told us about his simple refinement experiment, I'm sure Sonny's companies have the required infrastructure to take it to the next level. Plus, they already have the capability to transport, refine, store and distribute this new fuel. And, once we're sure we can do this ourselves, I will let Sonny make contact with each of the leaders of the other countries with the information about our plans to utilize the Altoonian waste products. Texas Oil & Gas has economic ties with these guys, so I'm sure he can figure out how to help them with what they're going to do at their own sites with the stuff. Whatever they decide to do, well, that's up to them."

"I really don't like not telling the American people the truth, Ted."

"Nor do I, Jim. But I don't want to get their hopes up about anything quite yet. I mean, if we cause a mass hysteria with the idea that this alien waste is going to be the answer to all our problems, and then it turns out there isn't enough of the stuff to make as much as we need, there'd be a severe fallout. We need to wait until we have all the facts. This means we need to continue to pressure the Altoonians for more information about their population and their waste generation rate. As soon as we know just how much of the stuff they have, and how much they produce, we can tell the people more. Maybe then — when we have pipelines and rail lines to transport the waste from the ships in a steady flow every day and to a nearby refinery — the relationship between our two species will be so cemented by this arrangement that we can disclose more aspects of it without rocking the boat. But, until we're absolutely sure this is even a possibility, we need to keep the news private."

"And what about Dr. Bishop?"

"We let him keep researching the cube and its contents. He'll be as happy as a pig in shit to be researching something so completely new and unknown. I've always found the best way to deal with someone like him is to keep them busy with their own endless projects. A curious scientist engrossed in an unsolvable puzzle has less time on their hands to cause any problems. So let's allow Dr. Bishop to dig as deeply into his own research as he can. When he comes up for air and wants to shout his findings from the rooftops, we'll have enough answers and solutions in place and the impact of his findings will be much easier to manage. That is, if he comes up with any more discoveries."

▪ ▪ ▪

During the next meeting with the Altoonians, the discussion about the transfer of the contents of their tanks went perfectly. Even though the aliens could not comprehend why in the hell we wanted to take their wastes, they were happy to hear we'd be providing a viable solution to their overwhelmed sewage tanks and disposing the material in such a way that the rest of the citizens would be more content with the alien presence. If it was in any way part of their lexicon, I'd gather the Altoonians would have said they were as pleased as punch to be killing two birds with one stone!

So, as the convoys of empty tanker trucks lined up for miles to get at the newly designed spigot the Altoonians had developed at the base of their ship to dispense the waste, we fed the fictional news story to the press that this endless line of trucks was due to the fact we were supplying the aliens with much needed and specially designed drinking water. We even had Rufus Witherspoon report this development. Although there were some people who were openly skeptical about this at first, most

Americans believed our story. It seemed as if the first insurmountable hurdle of the newfound relationship between the Altoonians and Earthlings had been just jumped over.

Ah, as if such lies could cover the truth for too long!

We should have known better. Lies are no better than those hand-crocheted comforters that aren't really big enough to keep all your extremities warm no matter how much your stretch them or reposition them. Sooner or later, something will get exposed.

Looking back, I think one of the greatest mistakes we kept making was forgetting we weren't the only ones dealing with the Altoonians. As ironic as it was, we repeatedly disregarded the brilliant message President Kennedy had originally issued as part of his calming speech to the world while the alien ships approached our planet. We're in this mess together!

We were so hyper-focused on dealing with the alien ship in Pennsylvania, we ignored the fact that there were twenty two other identical scenarios playing out simultaneously around the globe. So even though there was an open line of communication with the other governments dealing with the Altoonians to share all pertinent information about our negotiations and ensure these types of situations were being handled in a unified and almost identical way, we didn't see how the aliens were, in fact, taking note of the diverse human reactions from the different locales and coming to their own conclusions about us as a species.

Like viewers watching different channels on television, they assembled the information from all these different sources until they were able to clarify their understandings about us Earthlings. It didn't take them too much time changing the channels before they realized we humans weren't taking their waste products because of some kind of altruism or some basic benevolence on our part as hosts, but due to something a little more base.

As soon as the aliens figured out we were, in fact, feeding our own avarice, they knew the real score. Like most life forms in the universe, the Altoonians were well aware how greed always leads to need. So, once they saw our need for their "fuel," they instilled into our relationship one new value for our co-dependence.

They weren't dummies, after all.

▪ ▪ ▪

The next few weeks appeared to be a time filled with peacefulness, but, in fact, there was a three ring circus operating just under the surface of it all. As the worldwide energy consortiums got punch drunk on the profits from the free energy now coming from the aliens' waste, the leaders all around the world sat there with their shit-eating grins on their faces as they lined their own pockets and lied to their people to keep them distracted and disinterested. Meanwhile, the Altoonians pretended not to notice how we weren't just tolerating their presence on our planet, but beginning to become dependent on it.

I hate to admit it, but I, for one, bought this whole act completely. I was wholly convinced we'd achieved a happy harmony with the Altoonians through this situation.

Then the aliens flexed their muscle.

If you've ever been in the middle of a debate or a negotiation with someone who knows they have the upper hand on you — but doesn't let on — then you can appreciate our surprise when we noticed some obvious changes in Moog and Haag during the next meetings. The aliens suddenly began to ask for more and more freedoms, but with less respect...and certainly with less servility. We didn't know it at the time, but this new arrogance was betraying the fact that they now knew they held all the cards!

I don't know why, but we didn't realize what was happening until it was too late. I guess our own arrogance blinded us to the fact that the aliens were now playing us, and by the time they let us know this, we weren't able to do anything about it. Like the discovery of a small kitchen grease fire that seems so harmless — until you try to put it out with a glass of water — the President and I were smug with our ability to control things...because we didn't know that those 'things" were way outside of our limited capabilities. We were so enamored with the feeding frenzy resulting from the discovery of a free fuel that we didn't realize we were playing with fire until it was so out of hand, nothing was going to remain unburned by it.

# THE BEGINNING OF THE END

In one of his lesser known publications, Dr. Bishop had used the definition *"Combustion is a chemical reaction that occurs between a fuel and an oxidizing agent which produces energy, usually in the form of heat and light."*

No truer words were ever spoken, especially in regard to the events that occurred after the discovery that the Altoonians' waste products provided an almost unlimited and free fuel for us Earthlings. The only element missing was the oxidizing agent, and this was introduced to the mixture on July 4th, 1984. I'm dispensing with the silly nonsense of the post-Altoonian dating system, since the events on that well-known holiday caused the combustion leading to this charred mess we're now left to look at. Upon reflection, I don't really give a shit if this might cause some confusion with future readers of my chronicle.

Prior to the celebrations of Independence Day, the President and I met with the Altoonians to explain the importance of this holiday to our country and describe to them what events were going to happen. We didn't want the overt acts of patriotism or the fireworks to be misconstrued in any way by the aliens. They were greatly appreciative for the forewarnings and promised not to be too threatened by the explosions and the bared nationalistic passions of the celebrations, but then they made what seemed at first like an innocent comment about just how devastating any attack on them would be for everyone involved. They even warned us how we certainly did not want to allow our relationship to go to rack and ruin.

We concluded our meeting by assuring them we only wanted to strengthen the relationship between our two species, and to prove this we were nothing but smiles as we performed the ridiculous hands-on-hands farewell ceremony.

However, upon our return to the White House, the President and I digested the subtle threat in the middle of the aliens' seemingly innocent comment about the results of any attack upon them. We misinterpreted their comment as to mean they were worried about a splinter group of humans going on an offensive against them. The President and I had just been briefed about some of the usual fringe anti-government and anarchistic factions becoming more agitated and vocal in their displeasure about the alien presence these days, so we gave the various branches of the intelligence community a go-ahead to start immediate surveillance and even infiltration missions on those groups. We figured if we had an accurate pulse of their emotions and intentions regarding the Altoonians, we could keep them from disturbing the tenuous peace between our two species.

Clearly, we completely missed the bus in regards to the aliens' threat. They weren't expressing any feelings of their own vulnerability in their warning. No, they were exerting their own growing sense of importance in the relationship between our species. We just didn't see the writing on the wall.

The President and I were to be an active part of the bigger-than-usual festivities in Washington on Independence Day. Since there was a pervasive feeling in the leadership of the government that the American people needed a distraction from the Altoonian presence, it was thought an over-the-top national birthday party could refocus popular sentiment back onto the happiness of our entire country. As a result, most news outlets and agencies pulled their remaining photographers and reporters from the Altoonian landing site in Pennsylvania and brought them to report on these momentous celebrations in Washington and around the country.

That's why only one camera crew was present to film the tiny figure climbing down from the supportive leg of the Altoonian ship to the ground and then scurrying away as fast its little stubby legs would carry it. This little mystery creature ran directly into the arms of the U.S. Army commander at the site and was whisked away immediately, but these details only added to the intrigue later about the footage taken.

The President and I were attending the U.S. Marine Band's concert from the west front steps of the Capitol when Morty Brahmson strode over to whisper right into President Kennedy's ear. I saw the man's face wane as he closed his eyes and motioned for Morty to tell me the news. As he did, and I soaked in the momentous news about the sighting of the escaping alien, I detected a strange mixture of alcohol and sausage on his breath. He finished his report to me as I heard the culmination of John Philip Sousa's "The

Stars and Stripes Forever." This rousing musical moment initially distracted me from completely digesting the magnitude of the news, but one look at the President's stunned expression sobered me up enough to realize we needed to immediately leave this performance to deal with the fallout from this event.

This could not just happen matter-of-factly. If both the President and the Vice President of the United States of America got up and left in the middle of a televised and highly touted Independence Day celebration, there'd be too much unwanted curiosity and unchecked speculation about why. Since any answer involving the Altoonians would be interpreted as unpatriotically putting their needs ahead of our country's, we were obligated to proceed with extreme prudence. On the other hand, we were compelled to immediately address the pressing issue of a member of what seemed to be yet another unknown alien species running around our planet. And we needed to get some straight answers from the Altoonians about it too.

When the Marine Band began playing "Semper Fidelis," the President beckoned Morty to bend down while he bellowed something into his ear. Even though the music was loud, I saw the White House Chief of Staff stand up so quickly he looked like a soldier coming to attention. I could see the two men's eyes lock, and I looked quickly to see if the T.V. cameras were catching any of this, but they weren't. The ornately uniformed Marine musicians and their gallant performance were too captivating to snatch away any of their attention at the moment.

I turned back again to see Morty shrug his shoulders in such a way as to say he was dubious of the orders just issued, but he'd follow them completely. As Morty walked calmly away, the President turned to me and mouthed, "Wait for the signal."

I sat there not knowing what the signal was going to be, nor what was going to happen when it came, but I pretended to be wholly focused on the performance in front of me. With the eyes of the entire nation on us, the President and I both needed to appear captivated by the concert. Any deviation, and someone would know something big was happening – and we sure didn't want to alert anyone about that. So, even though I knew pulling that middle school maneuver of one person going to the bathroom and then not returning before the other person went off would not work in this situation, I couldn't think of a way to make the both of us disappear without arousing the suspicion of the American people. I sat there, sweating and fretting in my own personal discomfort, just waiting for what was going to happen next.

After the Marine Band had finished their performance of the venerable march, the huge audience in attendance was giving them a much deserved and sustained standing ovation while the orchestra leader came up to the microphone, leaned in, and spoke in a game show voice.

"Oh, hey, Americans! I've just been told we should all look skyward if we want to see our first glance at the United States Air Force's newest bomber, the B-1(TCH), also known as the flying Wolverine. One stationed out of Andrews Air Force Base will be doing a low-level pass-by for us all to get our first glimpse. So, hurry. Look up or you'll miss it!"

Just as I started to look heavenward to see the never-before-seen aircraft for myself, a large hand grasped me by the shoulder and pulled me to the ground. It was no one other than Secret Service agent Harvey Sanderborn, and he brought me and the President both down to the ground so quickly no one could see our body doubles take our places in the Presidential box. As I looked around at the feet of the other people nearby – each of them so transfixed by the approaching plane in the skies that they gave me far too clear a view up their nostrils – President Kennedy hissed to our bodyguards, "Get us the hell out of here!"

They scooted us out and away just as the distinctive shriek of the approaching plane grew louder and louder. The crowd was cheering and applauding wildly as we were given disguises to put on, and then we were escorted directly to a waiting military vehicle and driven away. As we made our undetected escape, I looked over at the President, now wearing a fake nose and glasses, a Schlitz beer baseball cap, and a military surplus poncho. He inflated his cheeks and then released the air inside as slowly as a leaky balloon.

"Sorry, Jim. I needed to enact the Gemini escape plan to get us out of there. I know the use of decoy actors is extreme, but we have to get ahead of this touchy situation before it all gets out of hand!"

"It's the perfect time to use the plan, actually," I said. "We got out of there without being detected. But I am bummed. I wanted to see one of those Wolverine Bombers fly overhead."

"Oh, don't worry, Jim. It's just an F-14 Tomcat with all its lights and afterburners on. No one will know the difference for a while. Plus, if we don't take care of this new situation with the Altoonians, we might need to deploy a squadron of Wolverines just to show them it'll be better to resume the peace. But God help us all if we have to use that force!"

We drove straight to the Andrews Air Force Base, and then an unmarked military Huey took us right to the Pennsylvania landing site. We were briefed along the way about what had happened, but there wasn't much new information for anyone to tell us. A diminutive, human-like creature had climbed down from the Altoonian ship and run directly at a surprised Army mechanized brigade guarding the perimeter of the site. One news crew had been there to film the flight of the creature, but they were all now being detained in the Command Center, and no footage or broadcast of the event had gone out to the public.

As for the Altoonians, they were more than a little agitated by the creature's escape and had urgently requested an immediate audience with the President and me. Even though we were hightailing it to the meeting site to attempt to assuage them, we needed to stop at the Command Center first to see this newly escaped alien for ourselves and to talk with the news crew beforehand. After all, we had to make sure we possessed all the facts necessary to go into such a potentially caustic confrontation with the Altoonians.

In a stroke of brilliance, President Kennedy radioed to talk to Admiral Paul Zumquist, the Commandant of the U.S. Coast Guard, who was manning the Situation Room during the national holiday. He was instructed to quietly pose a question to the other world leaders to see if there'd been any other unusual activities at the other landing sites around the globe. Because this simple question needed to be asked in such a way not to cause any suspicion whatsoever, the admiral scripted a truly benign and masterful message resembling an old town cryer call.

"It's nine o'clock," he broadcast, "and all is well here. Is everything fine there?"

After sending this innocuous transmission out to the other landing sites and only getting back positive responses of nothing out of the ordinary happening anywhere else, he quickly radioed us back with the good news. However, the President and I groaned quietly as soon as we'd heard his report. We were so used to entering into our negotiations with the Altoonians at the Pennsylvania landing site with the knowledge that similar meetings were taking place simultaneously at the twenty two other Altoonian ships, the news that we were now dealing with an utterly unique and potentially explosive situation all on our own shook us to the core.

We were greeted by Colonel Archibald Simmons at the Command Center. He was the commander in charge of the forces around the Altoonian landing site in Pennsylvania, and the man was a veteran soldier who wore his toughness like weathered leather. Without much prompting, he gave us a no-holds barred description of the events leading to this moment – the descent of the little female alien, her capture, the detaining of the news crew, and the sudden slew of forceful demands from the Altoonians to initiate immediate communication about the matter. He let us know he'd followed protocol and separated the two sets of his "visitors" into the opposite sides of the small complex and he had bluntly deflected all of the aliens' urgent requests for an immediate conversation.

The President and I decided to address the news team first, but no sooner had we walked into the room than it felt like we'd entered an agitated hornet's nest! These men and women were so steamed up and seething about the infringements upon their Constitutional rights that they could barely speak without issuing some kind of legal threat against us personally and against the government. I must admit I was intimidated by the fury of their vehemence. As a career politician, I knew the power the press possessed. Just how many governmental officials throughout history have had their careers ended by pissing off the wrong journalist? So, walking into a room full of absolutely furious news people was more than a little unnerving.

But President Kennedy commanded the room masterfully from the moment he entered. Speaking in a calming, but strong tone, he instantly smoothed over the reporters' ruffled feathers, yet made it clear that the event they had filmed was not to be shared since it could have truly devastating and destructive consequences if leaked prematurely to the world. He asked them to willingly sit on the story and let us do some fact-finding with the aliens before they released any news to the general public. After all, he argued, if they didn't have the details about what had happened, they weren't doing their job by reporting it. He gave them his word that once we had this information, the exclusive story was theirs to disseminate.

By the time we walked out of there, those reporters were not only anxiously awaiting the good meal being brought to them, they were so dizzy from the chance to be the source of this potentially historical and far-reaching news story — which would contain a promised exclusive interview with the captive, the President and quite possibly the Altoonians themselves — that they were as meek and mild as puppies.

As we made our way toward the hanger containing the mobile cell holding the escaped female alien the military had already code-named "Eve," the President and I remained silent, and this made the sounds we heard of hysterical ranting in some kind of gibberish coming from inside even stranger. The armed sentry outside the door turned to let us in, and I could not help but feel we were headed into a scene from the *Exorcist*!

As he moved aside to let us enter, the guard whispered, "Be prepared to be shocked, sirs. The Eve alien came out of the ship totally naked and, even though we've provided her with clothes and blankets, she refuses to cover herself up. Seeing her this way can be a bit...startling, especially because she appears to be some kind of combination of a troll with the Capitoline Wolf statue from the Romulus and Remus myth."

"That's a rather an obscure reference there, soldier," the President admonished.

"Sorry, sir, but I was a college professor before being drafted into the Army. Anyway, you'll see what I mean when you get in there."

There was a whole team of white coat-wearing doctors standing with clipboards in hand near the edge of what looked like a circular lion's cage from a circus. They tried to speak to the President and me as soon as we'd gotten abreast of them, but our eyes went straight to the creature within the enclosure. I'd love to report we acted professionally, but we both gawked at her as unchecked as teenage voyeurs. Even the soldier's seemingly odd description had not fully prepared us for what we were looking at, and our brains struggled to fully take in what we were seeing.

After all, we were still new to the idea we were not alone in the universe. But, this?

The creature was standing in the middle of her enclosure. She was about three and a half feet tall, and she had a head of purple-tinted hair that looked like it had never seen a comb. Her skin was light blue – like the softer shades of a robin's egg – but all of her features, her face, her hands, her shoulders and her legs, were heavy, like some kind of folktale troll or ogre. But she was far from ugly. There was something beautiful about her unabashed nakedness, and we couldn't take our eyes off of her.

The lead doctor came over and started addressing us.

"Mr. President and Mr. Vice President, we are not exactly sure what we have here because we're trying to show some restraint so we don't offend the Altoonians if it turns out the creature is important in some way to them. However, we're now assuming, from the three sets of apparent mammalian glands on the chest and belly, and what appears to be some kind of specially enclosed genitalia in the crotch, this specimen is a female — of a previously unknown species — living aboard the Altoonian ship. The specification of gender is only a preliminary observation using human knowledge to describe a new species. Of course, if nothing else, the Altoonians have proved none of our previous theories of basic universal physiology holds much water when it comes to aliens."

These medical observations sounded like gray noise, and I noticed the President and I were continuing to stare unabashedly at the alien within the enclosure with something deeper than curiosity.

Finally, the President said in a thick voice, "Good God! Her crotch looks just like a beak!"

"Um...er...the heavily muscled *labia majora* of her vulva does appear to be scaled," the doctor said with a nod, but then snorted, "But, hopefully, she does not have what's on the inside of a leatherback turtle's mouth. Such an unwelcoming environment might be contrary for reproduction, huh? Heh-heh."

His attempt of humor made us both turn toward the man and give him a strange look. He blanched under our scrutiny.

"Um, I was just making a reference to those keratinized prongs or papillae inside a leatherback's mouth. I don't know if you've ever seen them before, but those spikes look like a Hollywood version of an alien. If this creature has similar obstacles in her vagina, I wouldn't want to be the poor male supposed to mate with her."

When the President and I continued to stare at him wordlessly, he nervously cleared his throat.

"Well, I used to want to be a marine biologist, so I spent a summer at a sea turtle rescue facility in Marathon...."

The man's voice drifted off as the entire room came to the realization that Eve had stopped her outbursts and was now staring intently at the two of us. It was at this moment I noticed her eyes were the color of new copper pennies. President Kennedy absently took a few steps closer to the metal grates of the cage. The guards standing nearby tensed up and the doctor called out.

"Careful, Mr. President! We cannot assume the creature is completely harmless."

"Oh, Doctor, don't be ridiculous! How could something so beautiful, so pure, possibly be dangerous?"

The naked emotion in his statement must have caught the military personnel in the hangar off guard, but I understood exactly what he was feeling. Somewhere equidistant between the pit of my stomach and the bottom of my scrotum, I was feeling a sensation akin to the warm afterglow of a glass of good Hennessy cognac, and I knew this creature was something special. It was obvious she had some kind of bewitching quality to her which defied all explanation.

What I didn't fully comprehend at the moment was how much the President was already in love with Eve or how much she was going to be the agent of this world's destruction.

# THE NAKED TRUTH

When we met with Moog and Haag two hours later, our delegations were like two bighorn rams butting heads. We'd hadn't even fully sat down into our chairs before the Altoonians began demanding the immediate return of their lost possession. They were more forceful than we'd ever heard them be, and, in no uncertain terms, they implored us to do as they asked or face the consequences.

Meanwhile, the President and I were determined not to give in to their demands until we had been adequately given answers to all of our questions, and we eagerly declared we weren't going to do anything without getting a much clearer explanation about what exactly was going on.

After this initial, heated exchange was over, we all slowly shook off the effects from our powerful cultural collision, and attempted to formulate a new way for the conversation to continue.

The Altoonians were the first to recover, and as Moog issued another threat, we understood the relationship between our two species had now entered a new chapter.

He snarled fiercely, "If you do not return what we've lost, we will no longer give you our wastes."

President Kennedy chortled.

"That just means your waste tanks will fill back up to capacity. We're doing you a favor by emptying them!"

Now it was the turn for the aliens to snort contemptuously.

"If all of our ships were to dump their wastes on the ground rather than give it to the Earthlings, you'd not only be personally responsible for the largest and most destructive act of pollution this measly little planet has ever seen, there'd be an instant planet-wide revolt because of all the lost free fuel!"

The audacity of the comment caused both the President and me to recoil like we'd been punched in the gut. We exchanged only a quick glance because we now knew the aliens were aware of how much we needed their waste. The Altoonians had exposed the fact that they'd held the upper hand in our relationship for much longer than we'd known. If we'd been capable of seeing more of their faces underneath the Universal Translator, we might have seen them with smug expressions on them. As it was, we had no threat to top theirs, and they knew it.

The only thing we could counter with was a threat of an imminent military attack on them, which not only lacked any certainty of success, it made absolutely no sense. If we cooked the goose laying the golden eggs just to impress an alien girl we did not even know, we'd go down into the annals of history as the worst leaders the planet had ever seen.

The converse was almost as bad, however. For if we gave in to the Altoonians now, we were sure to be regarded as the morons who sold our species down the river. Oh, without a doubt, we were surely between a rock and a hard place!

I looked over at the President and saw his resolution was still unwavering, and I realized he was getting ready to unveil the threat of military escalation. To do so would be disastrous, so I attempted to intercede and let calmer minds prevail. I spoke up in a loud and clear voice.

"It would be such a failure on all our parts if we let this special relationship we've built up to this point fall apart over something as trivial as a little troll. Let us all take a step back and rethink the magnificent things we've accomplished together. Can't we please just all calm down a little."

The President's head snapped around and he stared at me with such an unpleasant expression on his face that I uncrossed my legs to free them up in case I needed to flee when he attacked me. But the Altoonians both nodded appreciatively.

"Well said, Vice President Hunter," Moog said. "We do not desire this conflict to escalate any further. Our two species are linked now, and it would be a pity if we let this new relationship dissolve over a matter of pride and egotism."

I waited for the President to take the opportunity to go through the small diplomatic opening the Altoonians had given us, but he just continued to glare at me. I tried to look strong.

"If we Earthlings are truly in a relationship with you Altoonians," I said bluntly, "we need to start sharing more than just your excrement. We need for you to start sharing more truths. More facts. More answers to our questions."

"So, if we were to give you some answers to your questions, we could have our possession back?" Haag asked too eagerly.

This seemed to bring the President out of his angry haze.

"Oh, no," he said. "The female creature has asked for asylum. And, since your species is currently enjoying the benefits of a similar offer from us right now, I'm sure you can appreciate why we cannot deny her request without a very good reason."

"It communicated with you?" Moog seemed astonished.

The President nodded once.

"She was able to convey what she wants. You know, it would be a lot easier to speak with her if we had one of those Universal Translators. Do you have any extra in your ship we could use with her?"

The sound the two aliens starting making was a familiar one. Over the course of our conversations, we'd heard it several times. It sounded exactly like a hand plane leveling a board, and we knew the aliens were now laughing at us. The President and I gave one another annoyed looks, but Moog put out his hands in a soothing gesture.

"Noosbits don't have a language! They only spew out gibberish. I apologize for our laughter, but it was such a silly idea to put a Universal Translator on one. I can tell you from experience, it would only register static and fart noises back to you!"

"Still," I interjected, "it would be a nice act of faith if you were to loan us one to try. Perhaps, when we found the futility in it, we'd concede the fact. What's the harm in trying?"

"Preposterous ideas are not the way to build new and stronger bonds between our peoples!" Moog stated firmly. "Unless you are prepared to give us back our possession, the Noosbit, we are back to the original impasse of this conversation. If so, we Altoonians offer up our same initial proposal. Give us the Noosbit or we will stop providing you with our wastes."

I was about to ask for some restraint to get the conversation back on track, when the President shrugged and said, "Have it your way."

When he stood up suddenly and turned away from the Altoonians to begin walking away from the meeting without as much as another word, my mouth dropped open in amazement. I watched him in disbelief until he called over his shoulder.

"You coming, Vice President Hunter?"

I looked at the Altoonians, who were watching the President's wordless retreat with what looked like concern in their black and beady little eyes, and I hurriedly spit out a silly sounding announcement to the aliens.

"Well, we'll be in touch."

I started walking as quickly as I could to catch up to the President, but he was so far ahead of me that he had to wait inside the Army transport vehicle for me to get up to it and get inside. I looked out as the black shaft retracted inside the Altoonian ship, and that image made me whistle.

"What are we going to do *now*, Ted?"

He looked at me with the most perturbed look. He opened his mouth to say something to me, but then he spoke directly to the driver.

"Take the Vice President and me directly back to the Command Center, soldier."

"Yes, sir!"

We hadn't gone very far before the President said quietly, "I think you're missing something very important now, Jim. You see, the exchange with the Altoonians — as unpleasant as it was — revealed a lot. Seeing their astonishment over my bluff about Eve communicating with us gave me an idea. You and I should make it our first priority to get her to talk with us. I think she has more to tell us than the Altoonians want us to know. The way she seems to get quiet with us could be a good starting point. Maybe we can get through to her and start the communication."

"But what about the Altoonians, Ted? What if they *do* stop the flow of waste? If they stop the production of the fuel, we could be headed toward an unavoidable conflict."

"The Altoonians can go to hell, Jim! I'm tired of them walking all over us. I'm telling you, Eve is the key to something big. We just don't know what."

As we sat in silence the rest of the way back to the Command Center, I stewed in my own thoughts about the matter. On the one hand, I totally agreed with the President that we couldn't give Eve back to the Altoonians without some kind of explanation. But the loss of their waste products meant more than just not getting free fuel – it was about terminating the chance to revolutionize the petroleum industry around the globe.

With our military's help, the Texas Oil & Gas Company had thrown its limitless resources into transporting the aliens' waste from the three U.S. landing sites to nearby mobile refineries to manufacture the alien gasoline. The copious amount of this now being secretly transported with the current inefficient tanker truck model only hinted at the unlimited potential of a new fuel supply with a better distribution system in place.

Sonny Ferguson himself was currently working on this. He was in the midst of top-secret negotiations with the municipalities surrounding the landing sites to lease the properties necessary for the construction of permanent pipelines from the space ships to the new refineries he proposed to build. He covered this up from the public by saying the necessary infrastructure to supply the aliens with their special drinking water was going to require such a pipeline. This was to be one of the biggest public works construction ever proposed, so the news that the Altoonians were stopping the availability of their waste would definitely not go over well. In fact, it truly gave me pause as I thought about it all.

Once back at the Command Center, President Kennedy bounded out of the vehicle and began barking orders. He wanted the hangar holding Eve to be cleared out so the two of us could have a private audience with the alien. Even though there were strong reservations expressed about his commands, the President would not back down. So, the space was vacated by all personnel and all the windows and doors were covered to give us more privacy.

Once again, Eve herself had stopped her agitated ramblings as soon as we'd walked into the room. We found ourselves standing inside the cavernous space of the hanger with the unnerving pall of silence hanging over us as we stared at Eve and she stared back at us.

"Okay, Jim, I've been thinking about this. Let's pretend the Altoonians didn't have their Universal Translators. How would we have communicated with each other without them?"

"I dunno. Maybe we would've played a charade-like game with gestures and whatnot."

"Exactly! My thoughts completely. Let's see if we can get some connection with her by using rudimentary signaling. What would be the most important thing to start with?"

"Our names. I think we gained a great deal of trust with the Altoonians because we could identify ourselves to one another. Let's start there."

He turned toward the cage and put his hand on his chest.

"I am Ted."

I took a step forward.

"I am Jim."

Eve tilted her head as she looked at us skeptically. We nodded and then repeated our names as we both hit our chests with our hands. We stopped to see if she was getting what we were trying to say. She just stood there, motionless. We did the same thing again, but then stopped and gestured at her hands. But she remained unchanged.

I exhaled loudly and whispered, "Maybe the Altoonians were right, Ted. Maybe the Noosbits are mindless creatures unable to communicate."

Suddenly the little alien seemed to have a moment of understanding and she lifted her chin. She hit her own chest.

"Grzzacka! Grzzacka!"

Even though we were amazed and delighted that our attempt had seemingly paid off, we needed to test it. We pointed at her and said the word back to her. Her face almost smiled and then she pointed at the President and said defiantly, "Ted!"

While he nodded enthusiastically and said her name back, she pointed at me.

"Jim!"

The President and I gave enthusiastic whoops at the success, but these outbursts scared her. We smiled and nodded to her to show our happiness, and then we repeated the circle of names once more. When it was clear we were all on a first name basis, the President turned to me and said nonchalantly, "Okay. I think it's time to strip, Jim."

"What?"

"She's still holding back. I think our clothes remind her of the Altoonian uniforms, so getting naked will make us as vulnerable as she is. It will help us build a sense of intimacy with her."

"You want us, the President and Vice President of the United States of America, to stand naked in front of this alien in this hangar in an attempt to find a better way of communicating with it?"

But the President was too busy untying his shoes to answer me. I stood there and watched to make sure the man was not playing some kind of cruel fraternity prank on me, but it was clear he planned on disrobing completely.

When I saw Eve looking intently at him and furrowing her substantial brow, I didn't want to be the one who appeared to be too much of a do-gooder to get naked, like the bookworm who is too prudish to play a Truth or Dare game. So I started to get undressed too.

I saw Eve's stare shift to me, and then I swear I saw a small grin show up on her face.

I cannot adequately describe the scene. As the two of us stood naked in front of Eve's cage, I averted my eyes from the President's body while taking in the way Eve was appraising each of us in an uncomfortable and unnerving way. Her face remained completely stoic, but her eyes thoroughly scanned our bodies from head to toe. And just when I thought the situation could not get any more bizarre, she pantomimed she wanted us to spin slowly around so she could see our backsides too.

As we both began to turn, like two ridiculous-looking hairless dancing bears, and started our slow motion pirouette, I suddenly was awash with the frantic hope there'd be no reason whatsoever for the soldiers to rush back into the hangar and find us in this embarrassing situation. There'd definitely be no coming back from such a moment. Our political careers would be instantaneously over.

When we finished our rotation and were looking back at her, Eve's face had a new expression of understanding on it. She quickly turned around in a circle to mimic ours, and we could see how her backside – her buttocks and back – were almost identical to ours. If President Kennedy wanted to make some kind of connection by getting naked in front of her, he had succeeded beyond all intentions for all three participants.

Even though there were some vast dissimilarities in our physiques, it was now clear the alien life form in front of us was not much different than us. The impact of this conclusion spread over the room like an invisible breeze of warm air, and it felt as if we were now clothed with the understanding that this little entity was not some unknown creature to fear, but a near cousin to welcome.

I found myself unable to refer to her by the name she'd given us. For some reason, my mind had locked onto calling her Eve, and to me she'd always be Eve, not Grzzacka. I tilted my head as I digested the impact of this realization, but then I looked over at the President.

His face was now frozen with a far-off look. He not only seemed to be completely entranced by her, but as I looked down at his body I saw, much to my dismay, he was – um, what's the best way to say this? — he was aroused by her.

This development did not go unnoticed by Eve. She was clearly seeing the change in the President's body, and she also seemed to understand its significance. I certainly did not want to see my friend, my boss, the leader of the free world, in such a compromised state, so I decided to plow ahead with an attempt to keep on communicating with her.

I pointed toward where the Altoonian ship was and barked, "Altoonians!"

After I repeated myself several times and got no reaction, it was obvious the word meant nothing to her. I growled and slumped my shoulders forward in defeat. The President continued to stare or, dare I say, swoon, so I decided to build upon the successes of our introduction. I began to do my very best imitation of Moog and Haag. I walked around slowly and puffed out my chest to attempt to look as big as the Altoonians. I had noticed how they let their hands rise and fall when they walked, and I started doing this, too.

I repeated the word, "Altoonians!"

Eve watched me for a moment before her face once again lit up with recognition. Instead of repeating my words, she contemptuously spat out a string of connected letters, "Ghzzippits!"

I said this back to her, and she hopped onto the cot within the cage and began to move just like an Altoonian.

It was clear to me we now knew what Altoonians were called in her language, so I began a ridiculous attempt to act out the arrival of the spaceship and the meetings with the Altoonians. The President now joined the performance by acting as if the Altoonians and we Earthlings were trying to be friends.

I can only thank my lucky stars there were no cameras present in the hangar as we made fools of ourselves in our naked condition, for we would never have lived it down. And, just as I was feeling that we had failed to actually explain anything to her, she started talking like some kind of alien auctioneer.

I heard the sneering use of "Ghzzippits" several times, but most of the rest of the diatribe was unintelligible. Both the President and I signaled nothing she was saying made any sense to us except her word for the Altoonians. She stopped and stood there, heaving from her outburst. We stared at one another for a moment or two, and then she went over to the tray of food and made the motion of putting some into her mouth with her hand.

"Aw, geez, Jim. The poor thing's hungry!" the President cried out sympathetically.

I saw the tray only had a small portion of food and drink left on it. I shook my head as I pointed at it for the President.

"No, Ted. I don't think she's hungry. She's got plenty to eat."

She continued to make the motion and then she began to repeat the words, "Grzzacka. Ghzzippits. Grzzacka. Ghzzippits."

For a second I just shook my head and shrugged my shoulders to indicate my lack of understanding. And then the truth hit me like someone had kneed me in my exposed crotch. I gasped loudly.

"Ted, I think she's trying to say the Altoonians eat her people."

He gave me such a horrified look that Eve stopped what she was doing and stared at us.

I ran over to where my socks lay and I grabbed one and came back to the edge of her cage. I repeated my impersonation of the Altoonians and then said with a snarl, "Ghzzippits." Then I took the sock and said, "Grzzacka!"

I melodramatically proceeded to put the sock into my mouth and pretend to chew it. Immediately, Eve unleashed another torrent of words as she repeated the action of putting something into her mouth. There was no doubt in my mind we were both indicating the Altoonians ate her kind, and as I pulled the sock out of my mouth, I turned to the President.

"Good God, Ted. Do you know what this means? This changes everything!"

But he was unable to answer because he was weeping uncontrollably. He walked up to the bars of the cage, squatted down to be at eye level with Eve, and he put his hand into the enclosure. And, just as I began to admonish him for his foolhardy action, the tiny female alien reached out and tenderly put her hand into his.

The intimacy of the moment was a soft jolt of electricity going through me, and just like the footage I had once seen of an F-89 Scorpion disintegrating in mid-air at an air show in the 1950's, I now realized the whole situation between the Earthlings and the Altoonians was about to come apart as we all flew toward the inevitable and the ineffable.

All I could hope for was that we'd find enough parachutes for everyone.

# THE HORNS OF A DILEMMA

The next few days became a horrifying kaleidoscope as the issues of the troubling times we were facing jumbled and magnified and interchanged in each twist of the frames and at a whirlwind pace.

As soon as we started to put our clothes back on in the hangar, Eve imitated us and put on the medical gown. When we brought the soldiers and doctors back in, they were more than a little surprised to see the clothed alien outside the enclosure crudely communicating and interacting with us. They were beyond surprised when the President announced he was taking Eve back to the White House as his own personal guest.

Even though there followed a howling of protests and warnings, President Kennedy was both unwilling to listen to reason and powerful enough to defy the authority of anyone else. So, with great secrecy and a crude disguise, Eve joined us on our helicopter ride back to Washington, D.C..

If the creature was overwhelmed by this experience, she certainly did not show it. She remained calmly seated next to the President as she glanced out the window at the terrain below the chopper with a curious, but controlled look upon her thick face. I watched in amazement, for if our two roles had been switched, I know I'd be beyond astonishment at all the sights and sounds of such a foreign world. But Eve seemed completely at peace.

She also appeared to be totally at ease with both the President and me. As she sat on the bench next to President Kennedy, she seemed as relaxed as any person traveling with good friends on a familiar trip. I did notice when Eve reached over and gently touched the President's upper thigh at the appearance of the capital's skyline approaching from off in the distance. I also took note he wasn't moving his leg away.

By the time we touched down on the South Lawn, it was quite late. We'd radioed ahead to enact the Romeo Protocol at the White House, so we were greeted by the solitary figure of Morty Brahmson with a folded black blanket over his right arm. Because President Kennedy had been the first divorced candidate who'd ever been elected to the Presidency, there'd been several different plans put into place to allow him to bring women to the White House without causing any scandals. Romeo Protocol was for those times when his trysts were not of a purely platonic nature, and it involved the use of darkness, concealing blankets, and the sworn confidentiality of a reduced staff.

As Morty now put the blanket over the diminutive Eve without as much as a glance at her, he did so because it was not his job to judge, but only to get the guest, whoever she was and whatever age she seemed to be, straight inside without being detected. If it was the choice of President Kennedy to now want to sneak in a blue-skinned circus midget into the White House, far be it from Morty to have any opinion on the matter!

I was to head off toward the waiting limo to go straight to my residence, but before we parted ways, President Kennedy gave me a command in a soft voice.

"Go home, Jim, and get some rest. Be back early tomorrow morning so we can go over what we've learned and discuss the options for what we're going to do next."

As he walked quickly to catch up to and put his arm around the tiny, shadow-like amorphous figure next to Morty, I watched their progress with a heavy heart. Knowing the Altoonians ate Eve's species, we now had to acknowledge we were in the middle of a troubling Mexican standoff with an alien race we were still hopelessly ignorant of. The burden of this made me feel completely overwhelmed.

Within a relatively short amount of time, we Earthlings had not only been forced to completely readjust the scope of our understandings of our place in the universe, but we were now also being challenged to find balance amongst all of the shortcomings of our own species while learning a whole new set of rules from creatures we couldn't even have imagined existing six months earlier. And, as we navigated this impossible course with a potentially imperfect moral compass, the future of the planet and all life on it hung in the balance.

▪ ▪ ▪

When I returned to the White House the next morning, I found Sonny Ferguson camped in the President's Outer Office awaiting a meeting with the President. The head of

Texas Oil & Gas was clearly angry enough to spit nails, and the redness of his face and unfriendly greeting let me know the man was on the warpath.

I walked past him, up to the President's door, knocked, and went right inside. I was grateful to get away from the oilman's unabated ire and find some sense of safety in the prestigious office. President Kennedy sat in his chair and was staring out the windows behind his desk. As I came up to him, he turned his chair slowly around to face me, and I was startled to see the man was still wearing his bathrobe and had an expression on his face of complete peacefulness.

After spending a tumultuous and sleepless night of tossing and turning as I tried to come up with solutions to the huge SNAFU sitting on our plates, I was somewhat peeved about the complete contentment I now saw on his face. With the complications now revealed by the appearance of Eve as well as the obviously irate head of the most powerful energy conglomerate in the world stewing just outside, I'd expected to see President Ted Kennedy upset or vexed, not enjoying what appeared to be a moment of....bliss!

Then my brain finally turned the corner and understood everything. It didn't take a rocket scientist from NASA to do this math problem. Eve had spent the night as a guest in the White House, which was still under the implementation of the Romeo Protocol, and the President looked like he was ready to smoke a cigarette and take a nap. The evidence was clear. The two of them had had sex during the night! I recoiled in horror as my understanding took on visual images in my head.

"Ted, how could you? For God's sake, don't we have enough of a crisis to deal with now? Here we are trying to save the day, and you had to get your pecker involved and stir up this mess even more."

President Kennedy looked at me and smiled guiltily. He sighed.

"You must understand, Jim. It was never my intention to become intimate with Eve when I brought her here. I just couldn't have her living in a cage anymore. After learning this creature and her kind are the food source of the Altoonians, I needed her to know that we are better than they are. So I set her up in the Lincoln Bedroom with the idea she'd be impressed by the comforts of her new surroundings. But, in the middle of the night she came into my room and got into bed with me. Then things just happened..."

"Good God, Ted!" I bellowed. "We've got way bigger problems than some kind of pubescent sexual tryst with a space alien! Sonny Ferguson, the head of Texas Oil & Gas, is out there, waiting on you, and he's more furious than I've ever seen him. It's my guess the Altoonians have followed through with their threat and shut off the supply of their wastes. And, if they did this here in the U.S., I'd bet they did the same at the other sites around the world. If so, there are probably a *lot* of pissed off people out there at the moment, Sonny Ferguson being the main one!"

"Sonny Ferguson can kiss my ass."

"Now, think about this for a moment, Ted. If we can't give anyone a good explanation for this stoppage, the situation's gonna get real ugly, real quick. And if these powerful people get angry enough at us, they could even give up the info about the waste for fuel trade just to get the public involved. Or, even worse, those more militant of the world leaders could decide they need to use force to make the wastes start flowing again. Either way, with an outraged and rebellious public flying out of control — a large-scale war underway – we need to get serious and address this situation before it gets out of hand!"

"Oh, Jim, Jim, Jim. When you experience something like I did last night, it changes you. It changes your whole perspective on things. I need to take a minute or two and soak it all in. Just give me another moment to relish my time together with Eve."

I had never seen him show such complacency before, and it enraged me to see it now. I grabbed the two arms of his chair and harshly pushed down on them until our faces were a mere inch apart.

"I don't think we've got a moment to lose here, Ted. So, wipe the stupid grin off your smug face and start acting like the President of the United States again! We need to do something!"

"You're jealous, Jim, and that's okay. If the shoe were on the other foot, and you'd just had a life-changing sexual encounter with an alien sex-kitty, I'd be jealous too."

"I'm not jealous, you prick!" I howled. "I'm doing my job! Oh, and trying to save the world at the same time! Stop thinking about sex with Eve, Ted! Snap out of it. I...we all...need you."

There was the strangest odor on his breath. It was a combination of soy sauce and moth balls, and I shuddered to stop the barrage of sexual images currently playing in my head. Even though our noses continued to be nearly touching, the President's breathing was even and calm. His eyes scanned my face, and then he spoke again, softly.

"Remember how that ridiculous Army doctor worried Grzzacka's vagina would be lined with spikes? Well, it's not. It's as soft as velvet. And it's a giant muscle, which tugs you inside it. You don't have to do anything. It does everything."

"Please, stop, Ted!" I said forcefully as I stood erect.

"No, you need to hear this, Jim. All I had to do was just lie there and let Grzzacka's body do what it does during sex. Whatever was clouding my vision before was removed as soon as I came…like the *Montrealer* into Union Station! Repeatedly!"

"No, I mean it, Ted! Please stop. This is becoming obscene."

"No, you need to hear this, Jim. I see it all now. I see what we've been missing up to this point. I was blind, but now I see. I see everything, and I see it clearly!"

His hand moved like a striking snake to the intercom.

"Sally? Send in Sonny Ferguson."

"Yes, sir."

I threw my hands up into the air because I now knew we were headed toward a complete disaster. The last thing Sonny Ferguson wanted to hear from the President at this current moment was any graphic details of his sexual exploits with a space alien concubine he had secretly stashed in the White House. But it was too late to stop it from happening, and as I spun to face the onslaught of anger that was going to come from the agitated oilman who was charging into the room like a member of a S.W.A.T. team assaulting a hostage situation, I put my hands out as if I would need to brace myself from the impact.

Ironically, Sonny Ferguson's furious outpouring of insults and accusations sounded remarkably similar to Eve's shouting of gibberish in the hangar the night before.

"Sit down, Sonny!" President Kennedy's voice boomed out, and it brimmed with so much strength, it caught the oil man off-guard immediately. Amazingly, he stopped his tirade and stared in astonishment at the President. It was as if he'd seen a Buddhist monk suddenly become Stephen A. Douglas.

"Don't you tell me to sit down, you son of a bitch!" the oilman finally hissed as he visibly seethed with rage again. "I've been out there for over an hour waiting for you two nitwits to get off your asses and tell me why the hell the aliens turned off the taps to their waste. I know you know why they stopped, and I'm here today to get some reassurances you've got this situation all handled. And I might add it weren't only our taps turned off, neither. It was all of them around the planet. Did you know that?"

"If you don't sit down, Sonny, I'm going to call my Secret Service detail to come in here and baton the backs of your knees. You *will* sit down and you *will* begin to address the Vice President and me with the respect we deserve."

The President's surprisingly calm threats seemed to pull the rug out from underneath our visitor's anger, but he still had enough fury to make himself stand taller with pride.

"You wouldn't dare! Do you have any idea what kind of blow back you'd get from having me assaulted?"

The President put up his finger.

"Hang on, Sonny. I will answer your question after I make this quick phone call."

If the man was bluffing, I couldn't tell. Neither could Sonny Ferguson. He began to eye the couch he was supposed to sit in, but then he stiffened again.

"I don't know what the hell's going on here today, but you cannot threaten me. You've known me too long to think just by pretending to call in the Secret Service to come in here and hurt me, you're going to turn me into a quivering puppy."

The President now had the phone receiver up to his ear and he was leaning his head to hold it against his shoulder.

"Oh, I'm not calling the Secret Service, Sonny. Actually, I'm dialing Helen Gandy. Do you know Helen? She's Hoover's old secretary. She kept all his secret files safe in an unknown location. Oh, she's as tough as they come, but the old biddy just loves me. I'm sure she'll open up some of the juicier ones about a certain young oil executive and a teenage Thai male prostitute in the wild days of the sixties in Bangkok."

"You wouldn't dare."

"Hmm, gee. I hope it's not too early to call her. She's an absolute bear before she drinks her first cup of tea. Oof. She may get so upset at this early intrusion she'll open one of those other files she has about you, too, Sonny. But since I don't have the time to wait for her to get calm and relaxed today, I guess we'll all just have to take our lumps, huh?"

The way the oilman sat down in the chair was as abrupt as if some invisible Secret Service agent had followed through with the threat to sweep his knees. He looked pleadingly at the President, who chuckled as he hung the phone up,

"Good boy, Sonny. Sit. Stay."

I was so stunned by what I was seeing and hearing, I leaned heavily on the desk. The President looked at me and said sharply, "It looks like you need to sit down too, Jim."

I went over to the other couch, across from Sonny Ferguson, and sat down. I'd never seen or heard the President talk or act like this before, and I was silently wondering if having sex with Eve had possessed the man with an alien phantasm. And, if so, what could I do about it?

The President began talking evenly.

"So, Sonny, yes, we knew the Altoonians were going to turn off the supply of their waste. They think we stole something from them. They want it back. They threatened us with not giving us any more of their crap until we return the item they want back. Obviously, they've followed through with their threat."

"And are you going to give it back to them, Mr. President?" Sonny Ferguson asked weakly.

"No, we are not."

The oilman's head snapped up with this news. He tried to stifle his reaction, but his voice came out steely and tight.

"Let me explain a few things to you. My company has invested an unfathomable amount of money into creating an infrastructure to process the Altoonian waste into the fuel at the three landing sites in the United States. I have, personally, offered my own funds to assist in the creation of similar facilities around the globe. The reason I've done all of this is because — after your initial personal invitation — I saw the unlimited potential of this situation and the unimaginable future it made possible. So, to be told the aliens are no longer going to be supplying us with the stuff is difficult for me to hear, let alone accept. And I am not alone. At all of the other sites similar arrangements have been made, with these same risks and rewards. So, if I am barely able to contain my rage with you, you can bet there's a handful of other individuals feeling equally as displeased with you."

"I understand all of that, Sonny."

"No, I don't think you do, Mr. President. I'm not merely reporting there are other oil executives around the planet who are entirely enraged with you at this moment. The impact of the loss of this waste products goes much, much deeper. The secret introduction of this alien fuel has altered the balance of the entire global petroleum market. As each country with an Altoonian ship within its borders has begun to reap the benefits of free fuel, they've all begun to cut back from their normal sources for the importing of petroleum products. As a result, the long-established global power structures are now in the middle of a rather quick and difficult change. To stop it cold now will have a catastrophic consequence on this process. To complete the metaphor, sir, if you do this, no one will be left standing!"

"Sonny, you might be overreacting here," the President said calmly.

"Are you kidding? Hell, even in our own case, we — the whole United States – now find ourselves suddenly free from Middle East oil for the first time in over four decades. OPEC is now entirely and completely impotent, and the camel fuckers are all scrambling to figure out how to keep control of their piece of the pie. But, while we might be ecstatic about this, those countries who have grown overly accustomed to keeping us on a short oil-soaked leash are discovering they don't control us anymore. I've even heard some of ‘em are so strained from this change, they are about to implode. The other day, I received an update about one Mediterranean country that’s on the verge of a civil war because they’re having to look into shifting their national identity into one involving the production of olive oil.”

Sonny paused to look directly at the President. Apparently he wanted to make sure that Ted was getting this. The President sat calmly, looking back at Sonny unemotionally as he adjusted the lapels of his bathrobe slightly.

“That’s how big this fucking paradigm shift has been!” Sonny continued. “Think about it – in only a matter of weeks, there’s been a complete and utter change in the power scheme on this whole planet, and I’m telling you there’s no way to just stop it now, back up and resume on the course we once were headed before the Altoonians arrived. So, when you tell me you understand about the impact the shutting off of the spigots of alien waste is going to have, I’m here to tell you you don’t have a goddamn clue about the real consequences! And I’ll give you fair warning here, Mr. President. If you can’t or won’t do anything to help us, we’ll take it upon ourselves to do it.”

“There’s no need to issue idle threats, Sonny.”

“Oh, I assure you, they’re not idle. You haven’t just kicked over a hive with this one, Ted. You’ve tossed an entire bee farm. If we don’t get those taps open soon, there’s gonna be a swarm of retribution raining down upon your ass!”

I leaned forward and spoke meekly.

"There's more to this than meets the eye on this issue, Mr. Ferguson. It's not all as simple as turning on and off of a tap."

"Seems pretty damn simple to me. Happy aliens, flowing fuel taps, and ringing cash registers – nothing's simpler than that!" the oil man muttered as he pursed his lips and then sighed heavily in frustration.

"Let me ask you something, Sonny." The President continued to speak in a smooth tone. "In '41, why did your father know he could swoop in and get all the oil rights from the Iranians after the British and the Russians had invaded their country?"

Sonny Ferguson regarded the President for a moment before answering carefully.

"He knew the Iranians didn't have the time to resist. The Allies had crushed their forces and were taking over. So, as soon as the Iranians saw how their defeat was imminent, they no longer had the time to defy any negotiations. My father said getting those rights was so easy, it was like taking candy from a baby."

"Yes, your old man was certainly shrewd. He knew those Iranians didn't have a leg to stand on. Well, I know the Altoonians are in a similar weakened position at the moment. Yes, they've shut us off, but they don't have the time to resist. You see, they're running out of food."

"They told you that?"

I looked at the President to see what he was going to say. The Altoonians had never mentioned anything to do with their food supplies. We only had guessed that from the shocking revelation by Eve about their eating of the Noosbits, but we had no idea of supply or demand in this issue. So, unless the two lovers had somehow been able to form some kind of deeper ways of communicating during their time together in bed to divulge that kind of fact, we had no idea how much or how little food the aliens had. But the President spoke with a straight face and a voice full of truth.

"Not in as many words. But I have a new source of information who tells me the Altoonians are definitely running out of food, and because of this, they're ripe for the plucking. So, here's what I need you to do, Sonny. Head right back to your office and pass this word on to the other energy syndicates involved with the Altoonian fuel production. The flow of waste will soon be resumed, increased and will never again be abated. As for me, I'm going to get in contact with the governmental leaders dealing directly with the aliens and let them know we need to hammer them with the fact we are aware that they're running out of food. When we've forced their hand on this issue, and the Altoonians know we know the truth, we will finally have some leverage to actually bargain with them about their waste. Up to this point, those bastards have been in the catbird seat. Now, we've got a chance to push back and get this whole relationship back to being an equal partnership. Any questions?"

Sonny Ferguson started to ask something, but it was clear the President's question was purely rhetorical in nature and he shut his mouth and looked down at his lap. The oil man glanced up at me and then over at the President, and then he stood up and walked out of the room.

"You ready, Jim? We need to head to talk to the other leaders and get the ball rolling on this one."

I grabbed his arm as he walked past me.

"For God's sake, Ted, what the hell's happening here?"

He smiled at me.

"Ah, to understand it all, Jim, I'll need to tell you more about making love to Grzzacka. The way her body opens up like a baby bird's beak wanting to eat..."

"Ach, never mind! Just…please, no more! Let's head to the Situation Room. But first, can you please put on some clothes? I don't think this bathrobe covers you up enough, Mr. President."

# A MEETING OF THE MINDS

Despite the surprising revelation of the President's theory about the dwindling food supply of the Altoonians, which he expressed in his confrontation with Sonny Ferguson, the next encounter with Moog and Haag was surprisingly short.

We watched as the two Altoonians lumbered slowly toward the meeting area and then remained standing as they asked, forcefully, "Have you requested this meeting to tell us you are returning our possession?"

The President stood and took a casual pose.

"No, we are not returning her to you. The reason we called for this meeting is to tell you the leaders of Earth are now fully aware you Altoonians are almost out of food. Our guest has informed us the population of Noosbits inside your ships are far too low to sustain your people for much longer, and we Earthlings are unified in our willingness to let you all starve to death, if it comes to that."

The aliens made a sound we'd never heard before. It sounded like a burp, but I think it was a gasp.

"What do you want?" Moog asked.

"We demand to be treated more fairly and to be given access to your ship. If we don't get this, we may have to terminate this relationship immediately. This same exact message is being given to the other Altoonian emissaries around our planet. We look forward to hearing back from you in the near future. Shall we go, Jim?"

I was so startled by how brusque he was, it took me a moment to realize he wanted me to walk off with him. When I stood up, the two Altoonians started sputtering complaints. When it was clear we weren't listening to their reprimands nor even looking back at them, they stopped and were silent. We continued on into the waiting vehicle and went directly to the Command Center without ever glancing back.

It was an excruciatingly long four hours before we received the request from the aliens to meet again. For me, the seconds ticked by too slowly while we waited, but President Kennedy seemed perfectly at ease with it all. I tried to plan some strategy with him to come up with proper responses to the different possible scenarios the next meeting was going to present, but he seemed resolute in his knowledge of exactly how he wanted this to play out.

Just like in the Oval Office, I could not help feel something was unnaturally wrong with him, but I could not risk talking to him about my fears. I just decided to watch him carefully, and I began to have my first seeds of doubt toward the man.

At the next meeting, for the first time all participants arrived simultaneously and sat down together. There was a moment of silence as each party waited for the other to speak first. Finally, the President spoke.

"I assume the Altoonians have had some time to digest what was brought up at the last meeting."

"Yes, we have." Moog replied curtly.

"Good. Then are we ready to really start negotiating this time as partners?"

The Altoonians made a noise more akin to a rumble, but Haag answered, "Yes."

"Good. We Earthlings would like to petition the Altoonians to immediately resume transferring their waste to us so we can restart our fuel production. What would the Altoonians like to request in return…other than the return of the one Noosbit who is now my personal guest?"

The way Haag glared at Moog told me the two aliens were now feeling as powerless as Sonny Ferguson had when President Kennedy threatened to expose the skeletons in his closet, and their simmering frustration was a subtle indication of the arrogance of their species. It was hard to see their mouths behind the Universal Translators, but I assumed they both had pouting frowns on them. Finally Moog breathed out heavily.

"Your assumption about our food situation is correct. Partly due to aspects out of our control and partly due to bad planning by the collective leadership of our species, we fled our self-destructing planet with too few Noosbits to nourish us for such an extended exodus. The calculations of our collective reproductive rates were incorrect. We Altoonians have been enjoying a higher birth rate than our main food supply. When this discovery was made, it was too late to readjust. We've been seeking a solution to our problem ever since."

This admission was far more revealing than anything we'd ever received from the alien visitors before, and I began to connect the dots and see some troubling conclusions. Even though the President seemed content to listen for further revelations, I needed to redirect the aliens to gain a greater understanding for myself.

"So what you're saying is you didn't come to our planet by accident? You actually sought us out!"

When the Altoonians replied with an affirmative answer, I looked over at President Kennedy to see if he was as shocked as I was, but he continued to sit in his recliner with a straight face. Inside my head, the synapses were firing faster than I could contain them and my thoughts were overflowing like a gushing well. I stood up and pointed my finger at the aliens.

"You came to our planet to *eat* us!"

The Altoonians looked at each other in confusion, and Moog turned to face the President.

"With the confidence you exhibited in the last meeting, we assumed all the Earthlings had come to this same understanding."

"No, it's happening at this very moment for my friend here," the President said.

"You tricked us into admitting it!"

"Yes, I did. And, in addition to the Vice President having this moment of self-discovery, all the other leaders of the planets are now coming to the same conclusion. We all know now that you came to this planet to find a new food source. I guess you could say the jig is up."

"You knew, Ted?"

"I had an inkling when they wouldn't ever discuss the specifics of their species' needs with us, but I began to grasp the truth as soon as we understood the Noosbits were their food supply. My time alone with Grzzacka only clarified the issue for me. Just like you did just now, Jim, I added everything up and came to the same answer you did. They scouted us to see if there were enough similarities between us Earthlings and the Noosbits for us to serve as an adequate substitute food source. The real reason they came to our planet is that they knew they had a new chow line here."

I sat back down heavily onto my chair because my legs were too weak to hold me up any more. The President nodded at my reaction, but he asked the Altoonians another question.

"Did you know your waste was going to have value as a source of fuel for us?"

"No, we had no idea. Before, as we've been traveling, we've just jettisoned the contents of our waste tanks into space. We assumed we would just dump them onto whatever planet we landed. We were excited when we discovered it might serve as some kind of connection for our two species."

President Kennedy frowned at this answer.

"So what was your plan?"

"In regards to what?" Haag inquired.

"In regards to how you planned to get us to help you with your food supply situation."

The two Altoonians looked at one another in what must have been a confusing moment for them.

"We figured we would overwhelm you with our technology, and, after we formed a rudimentary relationship, you would be happy to give us your outcasts to feed us ."

"Our what?" I shouted.

"It's okay, Jim."

"No, it's not *okay,* Ted. Did I just hear them correctly? Are they still requesting us to give them humans to eat?"

"Let's just stay calm here, Jim."

I'd been slow to figure out what was really being negotiated at this meeting, but now that I knew the real reason, I wasn't going to act like everything was okay. I stood up abruptly.

"Whoa! If you think we're going to start bargaining with the lives of our people, you've got another thing coming!"

"Sit down, Vice President Hunter. We need to hear them make a formal request before we jump to any conclusions. Let them continue."

I did as instructed, but it was clear the aliens were perplexed by our division. The President turned to give his full attention to the Altoonians, who shifted in their seats uneasily. Then Moog spoke up.

"We Altoonians request you Earthlings start bringing us members of your species for us to eat. In return, we will provide you with as much waste material as we produce, without interruption."

"If we accept this request, we need immediate access to more of your information and to your ship and crew. We need to...."

"Wait. We aren't *actually* going to consider this request, are we, Ted?" I blurted out, interrupting the President.

He gave me a disapproving look and then continued.

"As Vice President Hunter has pointed out, we cannot even think about accepting this request without some basic facts and figure like the numbers of Altoonians on each of your ships, the estimated amounts of projected food needed, and the specifics to the way the humans will be housed and harvested."

"Harvested?" I howled. "I cannot believe my ears! For the love of God, you're not seriously considering this insanity, are you?"

"Vice President Hunter, you will either become silent or I will have the M.P.'s come over and remove you from this meeting. This is not the time or place for such insubordination. If you want to continue to be part of this process, you need to shut the hell up…right now!"

The sting from his reprimand made me go silent. When I made eye contact with the Altoonians, I swear they were laughing at me. My face flushed with anger, but I'd heard the President's message loud and clear. I needed to remain silent for the rest of the meeting, but I'd be given the chance to express my displeasure about this deal later when the President and I were alone.

"Before we depart, I would like to know what your answer is to all of our requests. If we agree to consider the procurement of your food from our populations, will the waste transfer be immediately resumed?"

Moog nodded. "Yes."

"Good! And what about a tour of your ship? Such a thing would be a good show of faith for us, and it would be a good start to beginning the negotiations for any future endeavors between our two species."

President Kennedy stated his last comment far too evenly and calmly for my tastes.

The Altoonians stood up. Moog spat out his response in as cold a tone as the Universal Translator could relay.

"We will discuss the matter as a general council. I cannot confirm whether we'll agree to this request, but we'll let you know when we've made up our minds."

The President showed little emotion when he retorted, "We'll sit tight until you do."

# BETWEEN THE DEVIL AND THE DEEP BLUE SEA

The Altoonians did agree to all of the President's demands.

Even though I sat apart from him in the military transport on our way back to Washington D.C. like a brooding teenager, I was relieved when the aliens contacted us to let us know that they would be resuming the flow of their waste and that they would allow the two of us to board their ship in a few days.

I guess I believed that as soon as President Kennedy saw the inner workings of this sordid operation, he'd call an end to the proposed exchange of humans for fuel. Because of this naïve and overly optimistic belief, I felt a small level of excitement about being the first Earthlings allowed aboard an outer space traveling craft. However, the darker truth of the real reason for our being invited aboard eclipsed anything positive, and I was up in the air about how I truly felt.

When the day arrived for our tour, the Altoonians came up with a whole host of last-minute rules and regulations for us to follow during our visit. We were to come aboard in the middle of the night without the aid of any lighting and we were not allowed to use any recording devices during the visit.

The first request made a certain amount of sense, since the few members of the press still at the site might take notice of the Vice President and President of the United States of America entering the alien space ship, and the resulting news story would create far more inquiry than was needed at the moment.

The second request, however, made me uncomfortable, for it seemed to show both a lack of trust and an admission of guilt. Whereas we wouldn't be too thrilled, either, for the Altoonians to take any pictures while touring, say, our top secret Plant 42 in the Antelope Valley of California, I'm not sure we would issue such a strongly worded demand as they had given us. No matter what, the request revealed our two species still didn't fully trust one another. Even so, we still felt we needed to continue to jump through their hoops to satisfy their demands.

With the plan for our secret touring of the Altoonian ship set, the hour of ten o'clock at night was chosen for the meeting time. The President and I were to be guided by a black clothed sniper using a rifle with an AN/PVS-2 Starlight scope to the place where the Altoonian doorway would drop down, marked by an innocent looking blinking green light. While the rationale for coming during the cover of darkness of night made sense in helping evade any prying eyes of the press still watching, I began to formulate a conspiratorial belief that the Altoonians were really attempting to disorient and confuse the President and me so much that we wouldn't know exactly what we were looking at while on the tour.

Our guide to the site turned out to be none other than Gunnery Sergeant Bert Waldron II, the Marine sniper who'd taken out more nighttime targets than any other military sharpshooter in history. This young man was as talkative as a piece of granite, but he carefully guided us safely through the pitch dark to the blinking green light. Without any send-off he then vanished into the night.

When the chamber's sliding door finally opened for us, it revealed a dimly-lit and empty chamber, and we entered wordlessly. President Kennedy and I had not exchanged more than a few words in the last twenty four hours, but we both gasped a little when we felt the chamber shoot up toward the bottom of the ship.

What started out as a merely rapid ascent suddenly became a tumultuous ride. After enduring the crushing G's of a rocket launch in the initial ascent, the lights of the chamber suddenly flashed on with a wilting intensity as we came to an unexpected stop. The President and I struggled to recover from being thrown around like this, but then we started to shoot upward once more. When this happened still another time, I knew the Altoonians were trying to throw us off our game.

Due to the jarring experience, we entered the ship resembling a pair of drunks rather than visiting dignitaries. While we tried to regain our composure so we could make a strong impression on the aliens, we were unable to do so.

The interior lighting of the ship continued to cause us difficulties. The place was lit so dimly that our eyes, which were still recovering from the torture of the bright flashes in the chamber, now struggled mightily to make out any details of our new surroundings. We were greeted by Moog and Haag, who took a moment too long to look us over. Either they were crudely looking to see if we'd heeded their command not to bring recording devices or they were savoring the disorientation our jarring ascension had caused us. Either way, their lingering stare made me angry.

I sputtered, "Okay. Well, we're here now! Can the tour begin?"

"Come on, Vice President Hunter. Let's be gracious guests."

President Kennedy's voice was far too calm and even, and I glared at him in disbelief. However, the man did not return my look.

"Come this way," Moog deadpanned.

The immensity of the ship became evident by the distance we had to travel. The narrow and seemingly endless corridors had flashing and beeping machinery and electronics within their walls and ceilings, and innumerable passageways intersected one another and created an overwhelmingly complex and disorienting honeycomb of chambers and tunnels. We even had to use several automated moving walkways to get us across the vast distance between our starting point and our destination.

Then, as we turned a corner, we entered into a cavernous and empty hall. It was bigger in size than the inside of the Astrodome, and Haag informed us this was one of the main bays of the ship. We had up to this point seen perhaps half a dozen other Altoonians off in the distance as we'd walked by. It was overly apparent they were keeping us away from the rest of their population, and I concluded we were definitely on an official visit, not a social call.

This reminded me of my first international trip as Vice President, just after Ted and I had been elected. Although it was billed as an official visit to rebuild diplomatic ties between the U.S. and the new Nigerian government after their bloody civil war, the real reason I had been sent to the African country was to negotiate with General Yakubu "Jack" Dan-Yumma Gowon on behalf of several powerful American oil companies — especially Sonny Ferguson's Texas Oil & Gas — to help them wrest control of the country's rich oil fields away from the British oil companies. I was new to this type of diplomacy in those days, so while I resented being used as an international pawn, I balanced my negative feelings with my eagerness to see how the country had fared after their long and bloody struggle.

However, no matter where our motorcade traveled in the new capital city of Abuja, I saw no people. Even though we drove from the airport and through the city, no one was on the streets. Our motorcade route took us far away from the poorer slums and neighborhoods of the city, and all the downtown office buildings were oddly lifeless and clean – too clean. When I asked my host about this, he only smiled and pointed out the technological advancements his government had already put in place after the cease-fire. Then he sought praise for the inherent beauty of his country. I politely responded with the necessary flattery, but I knew what was really happening. I might have been new to the role, but it was obvious to me the Nigerian people had been trucked off to be away from my viewing. After all, out of sight, out of mind!

It was clear to me the Altoonians were doing the same thing now.

I snorted with contempt as I sneered, "Hmm, Imperialtate Moog, it must be a heck of an endeavor to steer such a big ship with only six crewmen. It makes me wonder how you accomplish this at all!"

The alien did not pick up on my sarcasm.

"There are more than six crewmen, Vice President Hunter."

"Ah, right. And exactly how many crewmen are aboard right now? I mean, we've asked for this detail before. Do you care to tell us *exactly* how many Altoonians are aboard this ship at the moment?"

"Jim!" The President hissed.

"I'm asking a legitimate question, President Kennedy, and one I think we need to know before we consider trading our citizens for fuel, right?"

"Of course, Vice President Hunter," Haag offered, "but could you tell us exactly how many Earthlings are currently living in New York City?"

"I could give you a ballpark figure!" I responded emotionally.

"Why," Moog interjected, "would we need to know the dimensions of one of your sports arenas?"

"No, I mean to say we could give you a rough estimate of the population of New York City. I think it is about eight million. What is your *estimate* of the population aboard this ship?"

"I do not think an estimate would be appropriate in this situation."

"Appropriate? I think knowing how many mouths will need to be fed is more than appropriate when we are discussing supplying them with our own people!"

"Jim!" President Kennedy hissed again.

"Here we are," Moog stated evenly.

An immense door slid open and we walked into a large room that was lighted better and was hotter than the corridors we'd been walking down. In front of us, a small group of several Altoonians attempted to appear welcoming, but they looked more like a herd of overprotective ungulates. Behind them, an endless row of cages stretched far out of sight. Inside the first few dozen we could see members of Eve's species.

The poor little blue naked creatures were grouped together in numbers of five or six within the metal mesh enclosures, and although they huddled together, their copper eyes looked at us with a piercing clarity. The shock of seeing them in these conditions and knowing what was going to happen to them was overwhelming to me.

"Do they ever get to walk around?" I asked quietly.

"Why would they want to do that? We let them live here to keep them safe until it is time to prepare them for consumption."

I looked over at President Kennedy, but the man's face was ashen with a similar shock from what we were seeing. He exhaled heavily.

"Are all of these cages full?" he asked.

Haag shook his massive head.

"No. That's the dilemma we face. See for yourselves. Look past these groups. You can see the rest of the cages are empty. That's why we need the Earthlings."

"And when you get those Earthlings, Imperialtate Haag, are they going to be put into these very cages?" I asked.

Moog and Haag looked at me like I had asked them the stupidest question ever, and then Moog said, patronizingly, "Of course. This is where we store our food."

"But they'll be in cages!"

Haag swept his arm behind him for us to look at the facilities.

"And fed and kept warm. They will be tended to until it is time to process them."

"You mean eaten."

"Yes."

"Well, do we get to see the processing area on this tour?"

Moog and Haag exchanged quick glances and then did an odd dance as they shuffled their feet quickly back and forth for a second.

"You want to watch an Altoonian eat?"

"Yes," I said. "I mean, no, I don't really want to. But I think it would be very instructive to see how the humans will end up. We have no idea how you prepare your food for consumption. Will you be cooking the humans? Will you be grilling them? Will you boil them? Don't you think we should know what our people can expect to have done to them?"

President Kennedy put his hand firmly on my arm.

"Now, I don't think we need to see that today, Jim, do you? Don't you think it would be odd if dinner guests demanded to watch their hosts cook their meal?"

"We didn't come here to eat, President Kennedy. We came here to tour this ship and learn more about the Altoonians. Don't you think we should see all aspects of their food preparation before we even consider sending other humans in to be eaten?"

The aliens started their quick little foot shuffle again, but then they turned together and addressed the President.

"According to our best calculations and our understanding of your measurements, we think each ship should ultimately be able to produce nearly two billion of your gallons of waste every thirty days of your planet's rotations around its sun, assuming we have a sustained food supply and an average population growth of our people."

President Kennedy gasped. He put his hand up to his chin and absent-mindedly scratched it. I saw how his mental calculation of profits was slowly pushing back his feelings of disgust from seeing the cages where our people would be held as they awaited to be eaten. I could barely contain my disdain for his overt greed.

I interjected as strongly as I could, and in the process I spit out each word I said.

"That doesn't matter, does it, President Kennedy? We're talking about people's lives. No amount of free fuel can equal a person's life, right?"

President Kennedy looked at me with a subtle expression on his face that clearly signaled me to shut up. I shook my head no.

"I won't stay quiet, Mr. President. I cannot, in good faith, negotiate the death of uncountable American people just for free fuel. I can't!"

Through clenched teeth, President Kennedy said, "We'll talk about it all later, Jim. Do you have any idea what our country could do without having to spend a cent to produce gasoline? Six billion gallons a month means the United States would get *all* of its gasoline from the Altoonians. Do the math! There are twenty other ships around the planet. If the Altoonians are all fed and able to reproduce, we'll have access to all the fuel we humans will need for years to come. Just think of the possibilities and the accomplishments our species would be capable of if we were completely autonomous and free from our needs of fuel production! So, let's keep all of our options open as we continue to be respectful guests on the rest of our tour."

Moog shuffled uneasily.

"Actually, this is the end of the tour. We thought you'd only want to see where the Earthlings will be stored before processing."

"Of course, Imperialtate Moog. We've seen this area, and now we can go back and tell the rest of our species we're making the right decision."

I was about to express my dissent when my eyes caught the expressions of the poor Noosbits in the cages. Now, no longer gazing at us and the Altoonians, they were all focused on the large doorway a short distance from where we stood. In that instant I knew that whatever I really needed to see was through there.

Without warning, I took off running. My hasty departure clearly caught both the President and the Altoonians completely off-guard, and I was into the next gigantic chamber before I heard the sounds of their shouting coming from behind me.

Because I figured I only had a few moments before I was stopped and detained, I was determined to continue jogging past anything I saw, without hesitating, even if they were the most disturbing sights. As ironic as it was, I began to run blindly through this section of the ship.

I came to an absolutely huge room with endless rows of small structures housing obviously immature Noosbits. These poor, pathetic, tiny creatures were chained by the neck in their small pens. Their little mournful faces stared back at me as I raced past.

The next room was smaller, and it only had about a hundred Noosbits inside it who were busy avoiding dangerous looking pendulums and rollers swinging from the walls and the ceiling. Even though the little creatures were spry, many of them had no way of escaping these projectiles and were hit by them and thrown violently into the air.

I was horrified by what I was looking at, but the shouts of my name and the sounds of heavy footsteps behind spurned me to keep going without stopping.

At the end of the hallway, I came to a dead end with an expansive pane of glass overlooking a large open space down below. Gasping for breath from the exertion of my escape, I bent over and looked down as a group of apparently sedated Noosbits were brought in on a rolling cart. There was a small group of thirty or so excited Altoonians on the other side of the room.

Seeing the little drugged Noosbits stagger off the cart and begin to weave their way around the room, the larger aliens moved quicker than they we'd ever witnessed at our meetings as they got ready to pounce upon their prey. Because of the Universal Translators, we'd never seen the mouths of the aliens before. Now, as they bared a set of shark-like teeth, any benevolence I continued to hold toward these creatures evaporated immediately.

As I watched, the Altoonians ambushed the Noosbits and began to devour them alive.

The scene was grisly. Instantly the white walls and floor of the feeding room were splashed with the magenta blood of the Noosbits. Watching this savagery, I nearly vomited from the gory – albeit colorful — scene in front of me.

When the President finally caught up to me, he grabbed my arm and flung me around.

"For God's sake, Jim. What an absolutely foolish and completely rude thing for you to do! Your behavior could undoubtedly have unspeakable consequences on the diplomatic efforts between our two...."

As he caught a glimpse of the scene down below us, he stopped talking and watched the ghastly feasting taking place. His mouth dropped open, but no more sounds came out. We were both standing there, with pained expressions of disgust on our faces, when the Altoonians finally caught up to us and began moving like skittish horses.

No one said anything for a moment, but then President Kennedy spoke from the side of his mouth.

"Excuse the Vice President's actions, gracious Altoonian hosts. He was most rude and unprofessional, and he will be punished accordingly when we return to our capital. However, now that we're here, what the hell are we looking at, exactly?"

Moog and Haag spoke blankly, "Feeding time."

Continuing to watch the spectacle down in front of us, the President sputtered his question.

"And what were those two other rooms we just went through?"

"The Room of the Young and the Room of the Preparation."

I turned to face the aliens, who continued to bob like the floor was red hot.

"So what exactly goes on in those rooms?" I asked,

The aliens seemed surprised at my question, but a tone of sappy patronization dripped from Moog's robotic reply.

"Altoonians have been feeding on the Noosbits for as long as time has been recorded by our species. And, in that time, we have made countless discoveries as to the different ways of raising them to enhance their flavor. For example, the tenderness of a young Noosbit is unparalleled by almost anything else we've tasted in any galaxy! Also, there are the subtlest of changes in texture and taste in a Noosbit who has been exposed to a purposeful stressful beating in the Room of Preparation. Without a doubt, the food prepared this way before feasting is considered by a vast majority of Altoonians to be far superior."

"I thought you were telling us the room with the cages was the storage area for the Noosbits!" I said.

"Whereas those creatures in the Big Room are well fed and are kept calm and happy to fatten them up, their very peaceful existence creates a fatty meat many Altoonians regard as overly bland in taste and greasy in texture. But the young and the tenderized ones…many find these the most delectable. There are many other ways we enhance the essence of the Noosbits, but we don't need to go into all of that today. That can be a topic for future conversations."

"Are the humans we are sending to you going to go through similar experiences?"

"We will see. Since we are not exactly sure what your species tastes like or how its meat responds to...."

The President interrupted Haag.

"Well, I think we've seen enough for today. If you two could be so kind as to escort us back to the chamber. We...I need to go back to Washington and talk with my advisors on how to start the process from our end. I think I'm ready to officially agree to this food for fuel trade deal. We just need to implement the means of obtaining and distributing your new supply of food in, shall I say, as discreetly and humanely a way as is possible. I will also pass along my observations from this outstanding tour to the other world leaders, and I will strongly recommend they also agree to this deal with their corresponding Altoonian ships. Thanks to what you two have shown us, I'm confident we Earthlings are making the right choice to trade you our outcasts for free fuel."

I tried to say something, but President Kennedy lifted up his index finger and glared at me with such animosity that I remained silent. I'd never seen the man so angry at me, and I knew I was in hot water with him. In spite of the fact I was the second most powerful person in the American government, the President was now reminding me he was, in fact, my boss, and if he was unhappy with me and was ordering me to be silent, I needed to do as I was told. So I merely nodded my assent.

In a surprisingly strong voice, the President then commanded, "Imperialtates Moog and Haag, please escort the Vice President and me to the exit."

We went back the exact same way we had come, but the walk was done in utter silence. It was hard to read the emotions of the Altoonians, but the President was still clearly fuming at me and I walked along without making eye contact with him or speaking to him. We made it back to the elevator and awkwardly put our hands atop theirs, and then the President and I entered the chamber and waited for the door to slide shut. When it did, he spoke in a voice as cold as a tomb.

"Vice President James F. Hunter, you've embarrassed your country today with your behavior. You will be, from this very moment, under my thumb, my friend. I expect you to remain silent and practice restraint through the next stages of this process. I know you're unhappy with what we saw today – I was, too – but the benefits this country will reap from a continuous and free fuel source are truly unimaginable and much more important than just the little bit of discomfort about the means of getting it. So, I want to make something clear. If you threaten these negotiations again, I will actively have you impeached...or worse."

"What?"

"I know a certain junior congressman from New Mexico who is chomping at the bit to prosecute you for accepting financial rewards and political favors when you helped your wife's father with his struggling mining business all those many years ago. If you don't do as you're told, Jim, or do anything I consider to be contrary to the good of this country, I will serve you up to him on a silver platter. Do I make myself clear?"

To have one of the skeletons in my own closet so freely brought into the spotlight made me gasp, but the fact that someone I considered a close friend was the one now threatening me made it even more painful. What else could I do but accept the validity of his threat and shut my mouth?

As the elevator let us out and we made our way toward the waiting helicopter, I remained absolutely silent. I understood what a truly dangerous position I was now in. As the President had just made painfully clear to me, I was, in fact, powerless to do anything about the situation at all.

I was surrounded by people who I couldn't trust and each and every one was a potential enemy to me. The realization of this made it hard for me to breathe. I'd only experienced this one other time in my life when it was also impossible to tell my enemies from my friends. In Vietnam.

▪ ▪ ▪

Upon our return to Washington, I figured the President would immediately send me away in disgrace, and I prepared myself for some kind of banishment. However, as soon as Army One landed on the South Lawn, the President informed me I was to join him for a series of nonstop, top-level meetings in the Oval Office to discuss the findings from the tour of the Altoonian ship and to plan strategies for fulfilling our part of the deal.

He was still clearly upset with me, but he was also inviting me to keep acting as the Vice President of the United States. Wordlessly, the man was challenging me to continue to faithfully discharge the duties of the office – so help me, God. I accepted this, but I was far from happy about it.

As he stalked off in the direction of the White House, he seemed entirely disinterested about whether I chose to follow him or not. After the briefest hesitation, I trudged after him to catch up.

▪ ▪ ▪

The first meeting we had was with Sonny Ferguson of Texas Oil & Gas. The oilman did a little dance – in fact, almost an Altoonian foot shuffle — as the President reported how the aliens were not only turning the taps back on, but promising an enormous quantity of waste from each ship on a monthly basis. Although it was risky to include Sonny in the specific details of the deal with the Altoonians, President Kennedy clearly understood the man's code of ethics was more than loose enough for him to overlook a tiny little element like genocide. Sonny Ferguson, it turned out, was a man who only had eyes for the profit margin, and this myopic quality only became stronger with his increased take from the promised flood of the almighty buck.

As instructed, I stayed silent through all of this. It was hard to watch the pure ecstasy of these two men as they planned how to manage and exploit the unrestrained flow of the wastes without mentioning once how many human lives would be lost in the process, but I bit my tongue and stayed quiet as a church mouse.

Our next meeting was with Felix Grandy, the United States Attorney General, Carlos Panzram, the Director of the Bureau of Prisons, Egan Moniz, the Director of the National Institute of Mental Health, and Thurston Nova III, the United States Secretary of Transportation. Once everyone was seated on the two couches in the Oval Office, the President began to spin a web of lies I could not believe the other men were so willing to accept.

With a completely straight face, he proudly reported the aliens had offered their advanced technology and great scientific knowledge to help us figure out how to completely eradicate crime and mental illness from our planet. Incredibly, no one balked at the absurdity of this statement, nor at the President's preposterous request for them to figure out the best way to transport the most dangerous inmates from our prisons, the most troubling patients from our country's insane asylums, and the overflowing contents of our homeless shelters to the Altoonian ships for "examination."

Because I had fully expected these governmental officials and health professionals to run screaming from the room as soon as they'd heard the details, you can imagine just how stunned I was when they all responded overwhelmingly and with great enthusiasm for the plan. They each began to blurt out their own ideas even before they'd heard the lucrative financial incentives the President began tossing around to their agencies like gaudy Mardi Gras bead throws.

■ ■ ■

Later, when we were alone in the Oval Office again, an uneasy silence hung over the room like smog. I watched the man furiously scratching down notes and memos onto a paper on his desk, before I cleared my throat loudly.

"Permission to speak, Mr. President?"

President Kennedy looked up from his work and smirked a salty-sweet grin at me.

"Of course, Jim. You should feel free to talk to me anytime, but especially between meetings."

The unspoken corrosiveness of his statement made me grimace, but I knew the window of time I had to express myself was closing while the scope of what I needed to say was becoming overwhelmingly huge. I calmed myself before speaking.

"I would love for you to tell me exactly what it is you think you're doing, Ted."

The man chuckled at my question.

"Oh, well, let's see…I'm making a deal with the Altoonians which will make everything so much better for this country, for this planet, and for our entire species."

"But at what cost?"

"I don't think it'd be an overstatement to say that I think our world is currently on the brink of one of the greatest moments of our entire existence, Jim. The chance to get our hands on a free fuel source like the Altoonian waste products and become completely self-sufficient is worth any minor sacrifice we must make. Just think about what we could accomplish if we no longer had to worry about the politics of petroleum products any more. We could put all of our efforts into achieving our almost unlimited potential. There'd be no limits to the scientific or societal developments we humans could attain. Think how amazing it will be. Nothing will be beyond our grasp."

"I'll repeat myself – at what cost, Mr. President? We're talking about feeding our own people to the Altoonians. To do as you are planning...well, it would be beyond unethical."

"Don't think of them as people, Jim. Think of them as a sustainable resource. We're talking about the undesirables here – those men and women who don't contribute to society anymore. In fact, these individuals actually take away from the rest of us. They suck us dry by forcing us to take care of them. Do you have any idea how much money we spend on our prisons? Do you want to wager a guess at how much we spend on taking care of crazy people? I'd estimate it to be several hundreds of millions of dollars a year! And guess what? Those prisons and jails and mental hospitals and street shelters aren't clearing themselves out. Quite the opposite. They're filling up and will soon overflow onto the streets! Don't you see? The Altoonians and Earthlings have the same problem. All the tanks holding our waste products are brimming and about to overflow!"

"For God's sake, President Kennedy, we're not talking about piss and shit here, we're talking about people! American people. Humans. When we offer up our prisoners, our mental patients, and our homeless to go into the alien ship, we're sacrificing human beings just for the chance to get some free fuel!"

"Again, Jim, you're not seeing the big picture. America is not alone in this dilemma. Just think about how full the prisons, the insane asylums, and the squatter's villages are around the entire globe. And some of these countries are so Third World in nature, they're too poor to afford even the basic necessities to help their own citizens survive. With this deal, we can offer them a way to get rid of these expensive drains on their societies *and* get an endless supply of fuel in return. Don't you see? It's a win-win-win situation."

"I cannot believe I'm hearing you say these things, Ted. I've always thought of you as a sane and compassionate human being, but now you are talking about people as if they are nothing but ears of corn. And — what's worse — you're acting as if this unholy deal with the Altoonians is like some kind of Mandate from Heaven! It's not. This is murder…on an unparalleled level!"

"You need to stay rational, Jim. Step back and look at the good before you dwell on the negative. Currently this entire world is dangerously — even viciously — divided by the need for fuel. When we go through with this deal with the Altoonians, we will get rid of all of those unhealthy relationships, once and for all. So, in the end, our prisons will be emptied of the un-rehabilitatable, our crowded mental institutions will be culled to remove the untreatable, and, as a result, both institutions will finally have the resources to be able to help those who really need it, those who are deserving. Not only that, but the streets of our cities, which are now rife with homeless crime and squalor, will be cleaned up and made safe again. And what's the reward in all this? A totally free fuel, unprecedented scientific and social advancements, and a happier population. The decision's a no-brainer, actually."

The way he looked at me, I thought for a second he was expecting me to applaud. When I didn't, he continued.

"And remember what Sonny was talking about. Some of the most prickly diplomatic relationships of this planet have been caused by the flammable petroleum industry. With this deal, we will have eradicated all the sources of this discord. The Earth will be left a much more harmonious and peaceful place by our decision. So let's face it, by making this deal we're helping the entire world become a better place. Truth is, it'd be insane for us to pass up on this simple agreement with the Altoonians."

"But how many Altoonians are there exactly, Ted? We still don't know how many humans they need. What happens if there are too many aliens and we eventually run out of these "undesirables," as you call them? What happens then?"

"Well, I guess we'll have to come up with some other process to choose who has to go."

The ease with which the President said this made me shudder with anger.

"Are you suggesting a lottery for the ultimate sacrifice?"

"Hey, that's not bad! Mind if I use your term there for the official label?"

"You cannot be serious, Mr. President. Who'd be responsible for the decision about which humans we send to the aliens next? Would the Israelis get to select the Palestinians? Would South African Whites get the opportunity to send those Blacks they felt were no longer essential? Would anti-Semitic leaders send the Jews to their deaths again? Are we willing to let the rich people sacrifice the poor? The young get to choose the old? The healthy choose the sick? Who gets to decide which people are desirable and which ones aren't, Mr. President? Are we really going to send them our orphans and foster children to be eaten as the most tender of Altoonian delicacies?"

"You're putting the cart before the horse, Jim. We don't even know...."

"And when the American levels for possible candidates for Altoonian consumption run low, Mr. President, are we really going to start importing humans from other over-populated and economically poor countries like Haiti or Sudan or Bangladesh…like chattel? Will we resurrect slave markets to process these people? How can we even fathom the asking of these questions, let alone face the answers to them?"

The President's face did not register any of the emotions I'd hoped to see, but rather he looked like he was trying to read the Japanese instruction manual for assembling a drum kit. When he spoke, his voice was too calm and calculating, and the coldness of it made me shudder again.

"No, you're absolutely right, Jim. Sooner than later, we'll need to create some kind of random selection process to make those choices completely mathematical. No one can argue against the fates when your number comes up. I'll meet with Adolphus Richter over at the Selective Service System so he can start working on this."

"That's not going to make a difference. If I'm not mistaken, whenever we've enacted a draft to send our people off to die, it's never been too popular. It's always created nothing but resentment, dissension and disobedience."

"Jim, the benefits of those wars weren't as obvious as the benefits of this deal."

"Before the government gets ready to sell our own people down the river and give them to these aliens, don't you think we should first have a public forum to discuss all the so-called costs and benefits of this deal? We need to make the populace part of this whole decision."

President Kennedy inhaled so deeply I thought he was trying to suck me into his mouth.

"What *we* need to do, Mr. Vice President, is figure out how to best serve the American people and our other fellow residents on this planet. Period. Our only role, at this point, is to design the safest and most efficient process to get humans into the Altoonian ships and the free fuel off them. I know you're not happy with this all, but that's the nature of leadership...going beyond your own selfish needs and comforts for the common good."

"Leadership? Leadership is not determining who lives and who dies!"

"Oh, really? When you and your sniper were shooting people left and right over there in Vietnam, who made the decision about who lived and died? You? No. You were only the second to the last step in a grand staircase of decisions which made up the process. There was a chain of command, Jim, which started up in these hallowed halls of the White House and headed down to you and your sniper. What I am proposing here is really no different. Our predecessors have done this same planning and execution of who is to live and who is to die...all in this very room.

"The truth is Presidents have always had the responsibility to lead this country in the best direction they saw fit. They've made the hard choices, not for individuals, but for the entire population. Come on now. Did LBJ call you up every time to check with your feelings whenever he was sending an order down to you to kill someone over there? Did he want to see if you were morally conflicted with the whole deal? Of course he didn't. He issued the orders, they came down to you, and you followed them…without hesitation and without argument. Well, that's how this world works!"

I shook my head and remained silent, looking like some kind of animated doll at Disneyland.

"As a soldier, I understood the reality I was in, Ted, and that it was my job to kill those individuals my government viewed as an enemy. But the people we're talking about turning into feed for the aliens, they aren't the enemy. They're actually the ones we've sworn to protect…not serve up as part of a six course meal. They trust us to keep them safe, not negotiate their lives away. And when they start noticing their family members and friends disappearing without any explanation, don't you think they're gonna start having some pretty damn big questions? And when those go unanswered, then what?"

"Naw, Jim. I don't think it'll be too hard to keep all of these details quiet. Think about it. When most Americans sidle up to the counter at McDonalds and order their hamburgers and Big Macs, they don't give a shit about the fact that the meat they're eating started with the braining of a bovine and then progressed through even more horrific machinery after that. They're just enjoying their food. And when it all comes out their other end, they couldn't care less with what we do with that foul stuff…as long as it just disappears. Most people are too busy with living life to worry about the specifics of mundane topics like waste treatment or food processing. As long as it all takes place and they get to live happy and easy lives, no one cares how it all happens. I think the same will be true with this deal with the aliens. When people start living lives full of the incredible benefits from the cheap alien fuel, they're not going to give another thought to where it is coming from. As long as it keeps flowing and they keep reaping the rewards, they'll all be as happy as a clam at high tide."

The man's cold certainty worried me. He was expressing no more emotions in his diatribes than someone discussing different linoleum options for the kitchen floor.

"No, Jim, the real trick will be figuring out who we can trust. Even as we continue to come up with ingenious versions of this truth, we need to be very careful who we include and who needs to be left out of the loop. As long as we can keep using the media to feed the public the necessary lies, I think it will run smoothly. Those little peons in the press are so starved for stories these days, they'll gobble up anything we tell them. Fact is, we're about as likely to run out of mistruths as the aliens are to run out of waste. So, truthfully, I don't think there's anything to worry about in regard to any upheaval from the American public."

"Okay, Mr. President, then how do you propose we decide who's trustworthy and who's not?"

"Well, I've enlisted the CIA to help in determining who in the government is an asset and who is a liability. The former will be included in the decision processes. The latter....well, they are going to go on a different pathway. From the line of these questions you're asking, I must admit I'm starting to have some grave concern about your status in this whole thing."

His blatant threat cause me to audibly draw in a stiff breath.

"So, President Kennedy, are you asking me to resign?"

"And alert the whole world that something is wrong? Oh, no, no, no. We definitely can't have such a public spectacle at this moment."

I felt the hairs on the back of my neck go up from the open-ended list of consequences the President had just inferred. If done properly by a pro, a tragic accident or mishap could befall me, and it would be an easy and quick way to get rid of me. I disappear, the nation mourns and comes together, which would only benefit the whole alien deal, and then there's no need for much inquiry or any fallout from my death. The implications of this gave me a cold sweat, and I knew I needed to do some quick damage control if I wanted to stay alive.

"Of course I wasn't offering to resign, Ted. I'm just a little overwhelmed by everything at this point and a little exhausted. I'm sure you are feeling the same way…on some level. I see exactly just how great an opportunity this deal with the Altoonians is, and I just want to know what role you need me to fulfill to help you implement it."

President Kennedy's expression went from one of grim resolve to a warm smile.

"I knew I could count on you, Jim. But I think the best thing for you to do now is head home and get some rest. I'm going to meet with the Joint Chiefs before I talk with the other world leaders. Due to the fact we're the only ones who know about Eve, the Noosbits, and why the Altoonians are really offering up the free fuel, we need to figure out a way to sweeten the idea of human offerings to the other leaders. The aliens have asked me to be the liaison in helping this take place. I think as soon as everyone understands the cost benefit analysis of the decision we are all making, they're going to jump at the chance to participate. I'm going to need your diplomatic abilities to accomplish all of this, so you need to head home and rest up for a couple of days. I need you to be as fresh as a daisy to help seal this deal and make this world a better place."

I was deeply stung by this apparent benching — not to mention by the open threats on my life I'd just received from the President. But I conceded defeat and quietly left the Oval Office. As I made my way down the North Hallway toward the staircase to the ground floor, I was surprised to see an unusual hustle and bustle of the White House staff. There was a renewed sense of urgency to the place, and it saddened me no end to think this excitement was all due to something many would never know the whole truth about. These drones of government were hard at work to enact something terribly heinous, yet many of them were being kept in the dark about its true purpose. If they'd known that they were working on trading human lives for free fuel, I'd like to think most would have walked out the door and down the street without another word.

I made my way down the stairs, through the West Wing Lobby, and into the foyer to wait for my car. I was in quite a somber mood. When it pulled up, I got in and took my seat in the back. At first, I wistfully watched the White House disappear from view as we drove away, but then I turned to face forward and I closed my eyes. In a world gone mad, I was unable to do anything to make things right again. I felt as helpless as a baby.

▪ ▪ ▪

Inside my residence, I could not stop shivering from the contrast between the completely lifeless feel of my deserted home and the current state of frenzied excitement at the White House. The difficulties of the previous days had finally worn me down, and all I wanted was a stiff drink at my desk. I figured the alcohol would wash away all of the toxic thoughts and feelings overcoming me, thus allowing me to actually rest.

After I had decanted out some bourbon and sat down in my familiar chair, something hit me with the force of the great Mazu Daoyi's staff. Just when my spirits were lowest and I seemed entirely lost, I had a moment of sudden enlightenment about how I could help stop this madness. The realization literally took my breath away.

I had a talent no one knew I had.

Actually, I had hidden it completely since my days in the military. The concept of using it now to help stop the humans for fuel trade made me sit up in my chair with a sudden sense of hope, and I nearly tripped over my own feet as I stood up too quickly and started looking around for a pen and some paper to draw out a map of the interior of the Altoonian ship.

When I was being considered for the U.S. Marine Scout Sniper School at Camp Pendleton, I stood out from the rest of the candidate pool because of my ability to make a mental map of my surroundings from a single visit and then transcribe this information to be used later. I wasn't even aware I could do any of this, but I'd discovered I could as soon as I was sent out on a training mission to simulate a recon for a snipe. Almost instantly, I was able to learn the terrain and store this info in my memory.

As I practiced using this skill more, I soon discovered I could even map out escape routes while in new and unfamiliar locations and produce a handwritten map with the detail of a printed atlas. Because of this, I was rushed into USMC Sniper School. I was not only an excellent marksman with a rifle and could hit any target from any required distance, I was nearly flawless in maneuvering around in the geography. The combination of these qualities made me the most advantageous member of any sniper team.

The military psychologists identified me as having an enhanced ability to create a cognitive map of my metaphorical spatial environment. They came to the inevitable conclusion I'd be an ideal sniper spotter because I could identify potential targets quickly and correctly ascertain the conditions of the shoot for the main shooter, and, at the same time, subconsciously keep a detailed record of the geographical layout of the terrain in my head. Because of my mental mapping acuity, after the shot was taken, I could get the team home without issue. This freed my sniper from having to worry about these details of where to go and how to navigate, and this allowed him to fully concentrate on the accuracy of his shot. We made for an effective and lethal assassination duo.

Due to the development of this skill, my codename became AMS because I knew exactly where we were at all times…even better than the Army Map Service, the branch responsible for the creation of all the military maps of Vietnam. It was not uncommon for officers outside my regiment to come and ask me to give them details for the terrain into which they were about to lead their troops.

Now, as I sat in my chair in my residence, my nearly-forgotten ability had suddenly flashed into my mind once more. I grabbed a random briefing on my desk, flipped it over, and instantly began to draw out the layout of the inside of the Altoonian ship on the back of the paper. Some of the details and their scale were harder to reproduce because the mechanized walkways shortened some of the distances and therefore altered those parts of my recollection. But the facts flowed straight to the pen in my hand. By the time I'd finished, I had a comprehensive map of the interior of the alien ship in front of me.

I wanted to do something with this information, but I didn't know what that was.

I stared down at my map like it was a scattered pile of divination bones from some ancient and foreign oracle. While it didn't take away all the troubling feelings I had from seeing the Noosbits in cages, being tortured, and being eaten, the simple act of creating it allowed me to take hold of these recent unpleasant experiences and turn them into something positive. The fact that my map could be a guide for a force to maneuver successfully inside of an Altoonian ship and strike at the aliens caused the neurons inside my brain to spit and spark like a shorting out transformer. To gather my wits, I looked up at the ceiling of my office.

Even though I still wasn't sure how to use it, my drawing suddenly felt like an all-powerful tool in search of a purpose.

With this thought, I became so instantly exhausted that I nearly put my head down on my desk and fell asleep. Because I didn't want to damage the map in any way, I carefully stowed it within my filing cabinet for future use. I finished my drink and then headed upstairs to get some sleep. When the nightmarish sights and sounds of the day continued to haunt me, I took two Nembutals and then slept like a log!

# IT WAS NO LAUGHING MATTER

After resting up at home and puzzling over what I should do with my map of the inside of the Altoonian ship, I had to strive to keep my wits about me when I found myself back again at the White House, surrounded by people who'd apparently checked their sanity at the door.

The President continued to utter his outlandish claims and bold-faced lies to an all-too-willing audience, and I kept waiting for someone to step forward and take umbrage with his proposals and plans, but no one did. In fact, people I'd known and revered as being fundamentally good, kind and God-fearing were now leapfrogging over one another to get onto his bandwagon to support the deal with the Altoonians. I should've been shocked by it all, but I'd been involved in politics long enough to know more swallowing than spitting happens in Washington.

However, even I was surprised by their complete willingness to accept this unholy alliance without any apparent reservations.

While the President and his advisors eagerly worked to put together the complex pieces of the food for fuel deal, I marveled at the ease with which they undertook the process. Not only did they have to design the most efficient ways to transport human beings to the alien ships, they needed to figure out how they were going to continue to guide the press to mislead the American people about the whole situation while quietly establishing a completely new market around the globe for the new alien fuel. With the skill and precision of a well-choreographed bourrée, the many participants in the White House tried to keep in step with one another.

Even though I sat next to the President during these meetings and appeared enthusiastic about all the planning, I continued to feel the whole food for fuel trade was unforgivably unethical and the way we were keeping the details from the public made me beyond uncomfortable. There was no way I could convince myself to endorse the idea in any way, but I wanted to keep my job and stay alive, so I went along with it. All I could hope for was someone to break away from the pack and stop the whole thing. Since I knew this could not be me, I naively waited for someone else to volunteer. There didn't seem to be any takers.

While the United States government usually moves forward with its new policies and plans so slowly as to make a glacier appear speedy, the tidal wave of enthusiasm for the secret agreement with the aliens had hurried each new development right along with an unprecedented rapidity. Literally overnight, special trains and railways for transporting humans in and alien waste out had been engineered, designed, built and staffed. Special mobile refineries were set up close to the sites, and the whole food for fuel process commenced without any fanfare or dissent. With no obvious glitches in the first few days of the operation, the President boastfully announced that the endeavor was taking on its own momentum.

As the updates continued to stream into the White House about everything appearing to be running perfectly at the landing sites, a real sense of contentment began to settle onto everybody involved. The Altoonians were ecstatic to be getting supplied with new food, the business leaders and governments were getting more free fuel than they could use, the world's press was satisfied with the copious, but fake stories of the mutually beneficial interspecies relationships they were being fed – pardon the pun — by the government, the majority of the Earthlings were just happy to still be around after the alien invasion and to get on with living their lives, and the President was thoroughly enjoying the nightly company of Eve in the White House.

Life on this planet, although irrevocably and irreversibly changed by the alien presence, now went along smoothly on its new track as we all pretended everything was good and fine. And, since no one wanted to rock the boat, it all seemed like it was.

With President Kennedy, Sonny Ferguson and the rest of the White House insiders each looking as smug as the cat who swallowed the canary, I felt the need to go take a closer look at things for myself. When the President made the most innocent comment about wishing the Altoonians weren't still keeping us at a distance from the whole process, I volunteered to go to the Pennsylvania landing site to monitor the situation and see if I could help bring us a little closer. The President seemed pleased by my new support of the whole deal, and he enthusiastically granted my request. Without a moment of hesitation, I set off immediately.

Once at the Command Center in Pennsylvania, I contacted the Altoonians to set up the unprecedented one-on-one meeting. I knew this was going to cause the aliens some uneasiness, so to calm them I told them President Kennedy was merely sending me as an emissary to make sure all of their needs were being met perfectly. I made it a point to say I wasn't coming to officially meet or negotiate with them, so we didn't need to follow routine meeting procedures. The aliens were at first a little hesitant, but they eventually invited me to proceed right to the transfer site to meet alone with Haag.

Directly underneath the center of the Altoonian ship, I walked amid the newly constructed area just as a transport train was slowly moving into place. As I gingerly made my way around the new tracks and junctions, I was met by a solitary Haag. The alien was pleasant in his greeting, but he was obviously troubled to be meeting with me alone. He was all thumbs as he awkwardly attempted to get his bearings in our tête-à-tête, and I personally enjoyed his moments of discomfort more than I should have.

When Haag began to show me how the supply train was divided up, he displayed some uncharacteristic giddiness. The original idea of building a pipeline had been scrapped once we knew we were exchanging fresh humans for alien shit, since we needed a way to bring in these "supplies" and take out the waste at the very same time. The setup of these trains was done in a predictable pattern based on each car's contents to ensure the most efficient loading and unloading procedure. It was essential to have the unloading and loading of the train cars happen simultaneously, all the while carefully camouflaging the true goings-on from any onlookers .

The first Pullman was full of prisoners. The car's windows were securely barred and the single door in the middle looked exactly like a thick bank vault door. When this swung open, those prisoners who hadn't been shanked from being cooped together on the train ride were funneled directly into the ship by several severe looking Altoonian handlers holding what appeared to be some kind of laser rifles. I'd never seen the aliens' weapons before, so I took a particularly good look at them before the approach of the next rail car. This one turned out to be an empty tanker intended to be filled up with alien waste products, so it bypassed the entrance the prisoners had gone into and went directly to the massive spigot just down the line.

Perfectly spaced, the next train car pulled up to the same entrance the prisoners had entered and began to disgorge its human contents of mental hospital patients. These unsuspecting men and women came out cautiously and then whooped and gawked as they walked toward the alien ship like trained monkeys. As they did, the train moved forward again, and another empty tanker car went to be positioned under the spigot.

Haag proudly announced the next train car was full of those lost humans from the streets of our cities. He spread his arms wide as he counted off the pattern.

"It is all a beautiful rhythm, Vice President Hunter! First it's prisoners, then tanker, then insane ones, then tanker, then street people, then tanker and repeat. And repeat. And repeat! It never stops! Your world gets cleaner and cleaner — fueled to do its great things — while we

Altoonians are happy, well fed and content to be here with you."

It was hard for me to pretend this sight didn't upset me greatly, but I nodded like someone who is getting the details of a car accident involving a loved one. As I craned my neck to look at the endless line of cars in this one train, which went back as far as the eye could see, the scope of the operation now hit home.

As my mind whirled with its own calculations, I had to ask, "And this process goes on twenty four hours a day?"

Haag said as enthusiastically as his computerized Universal Translator would allow, "No. At nighttime, the trains are made up of only empty tanker cars to ensure our tanks of waste are actually getting drained adequately enough. Think of all the free fuel, Vice President Hunter!"

And that was when I finally reached my saturation point in regards to the Altoonians. I wish I could say it had happened far sooner, but I had been able to maintain enough separation between my personal feelings of outrage and my official duties as Vice President. Throughout all the most unpleasant interactions with the Altoonians and even in the midst of the President's free fuel-laced inebriation and his new sexual relationship with Eve, I was able to feel like I wasn't getting my hands dirty – I was just doing my job. I could look the other way, and it would not get to me. But now, seeing the endless train cars and feeling the gut-wrenching pain as I came to grips with the true impact of this fuel for food arrangement, I was unable to remain complacent anymore.

I just didn't know what I could do. It sounds silly for the Vice President of the United States of America to admit to feeling impotent, but I did. I was almost willing to accept I could do nothing to change anything.

When you're waiting for some kind of portent for what to do next, you often find yourself spending lots of time hoping you'll recognize the form of this specific notification when it finally comes. Not to sound too irreverent, but throughout my life I'd wondered if the prophets and saints in the Bible ever lost hope as they waited for their personal sign from God. I mean, they must have been wondering if it was going to be a burning bush, an archangel, a talking frog, or a farting camel, right? Who knew what it would be? God surely did, but He wasn't going to spill all His secrets, was He? So, those poor patient men and women had to wait and wait for the real thing to come along.

Well, the signal intended for me at that moment turned out to be a combination of both the spectacular and the mundane. While I watched the load of scruffy, dirty and ill-smelling street people amble toward the Altoonian ship, no one seemed to take special notice of the overweight man wearing a filthy McDonalds sweatshirt and ripped blue jeans. He was shuffling along with the rest of this mass of a marred humanity, but, oddly, he held onto a single red balloon on a string. This was tied innocently to his wrist, and the ridiculousness of the sight of a grown man with a balloon in such a dark scene of human livestock heading toward their doom was something to see.

Then, without warning, the balloon popped.

To this day, I'm not sure what caused this to happen, but the all-too-familiar sound of a popping balloon was almost instantly followed by Haag falling to the ground and by the alien equivalent of an alarm howling out loudly from the bottom of the ship. Several Altoonians, wearing much different headwear, rushed from the ship and grabbed the unconscious Haag and carried him inside. The street people, who'd been fueled with promises of whatever they desired, continued to stream unguided into the portal before it slammed shut. Their alien handlers were nowhere to be seen. The popping of the balloon had literally cleared the decks.

In the following uneasy and unsettled moments, the scene around the train remained frozen in time. As I found myself standing alone in the midst of this incredible sight, I was unable to fully comprehend what I was witnessing. With no open entrances or available alien guards, the train remained stopped in position, unable to continue with its mission. The other humans around, both the soldiers and the special uniformed porters, all looked at me to see what they were supposed to do next. Although it was not too dignified, I merely shrugged my shoulders as if to say, beats me.

I waited a little longer for someone to come out of the alien ship, but when no one did, I turned and started walking back to the Command Center. As I made my way, I tried to digest what had just occurred. My initial conclusion was that Haag must have fainted from fear as a result of the explosive sound of the popping balloon. But this seemed utterly ridiculous. For a veteran space traveler to overreact to such a mundane sound was so silly, it seemed completely impossible.

If Haag hadn't been frightened by the popping balloon, he'd definitely been incapacitated by it. And not only him. All the aliens around the place closed up shop and immediately abandoned their posts. Such a response certainly seemed like an overreaction to the popping of a child's tiny balloon. If it wasn't the noise that caused this all to happen, what else could it be, I wondered.

That's when it hit me. The red balloon had been floating in mid-air, so it must have been filled with helium. If the aliens had not been reacting to the noise of the popping balloon, perhaps they were responding to its contents. I stopped in my tracks. There was no other conclusion to come to: Haag's incapacitation and the sealing of the ship had been due to the helium inside the balloon.

Helium was poisonous for the Altoonians!

I looked around to see if anyone else was watching me, but no one seemed to notice my presence anymore. I felt the powerful tingle go up and down my spinal column because I now knew the aliens had a weakness. With my map and some helium, a force could strike back and stop all of this madness.

If someone would just make themselves known and be willing to lead this force, I could give them the bonafide weapons for defeating the Altoonians.

▪ ▪ ▪

Once back inside the Command Center, I attempted to reach out to the Altoonians.

When they finally responded to my inquiries, they remained completely mum about the balloon incident. Instead, they apologized for running a routine safety drill in the middle of a food/fuel transfer. When I asked if Haag was okay, I was told, forcefully, that he was fine. When I pushed the issue, they pretty much demanded that I head back to the meeting area so I could see with my own eyes that he was okay. Even though they were quite incensed when I said such a meeting was not necessary, I politely declined their invitation. Instead, I sent along a get-well message for Haag. They curtly told me they'd pass along my unnecessary sentiments to him, but then they got very tightlipped and began another prolonged period of radio silence.

Why didn't I take them up on their offer to meet with Haag? Here's the thing. As improper as it is to say, the truth was I couldn't tell one Altoonian apart from another. While Haag seemed a little smaller than Moog, there didn't seem to be any obvious way to differentiate the genders of the aliens or even their separate, individual identities. As a matter of fact, I had my doubts that we were always speaking to the same two aliens in our meetings with Moog and Haag. Part of the problem was the way the Universal Translator blocked a clear view at their faces. With no certifiable way to tell who was who, any switcheroo was not only possible, but most likely.

With the Altoonians now as silent as the dead, I headed back to Washington on Marine One. I wanted to go to the President and tell him about my map and the devastating effects of helium on the Altoonians just to see if he would come out of his stupor long enough to show he was still salvageable as the leader of the Free World. If the man remained committed to continuing the arrangement with the Altoonians, I'd have no choice but to look for some other person to lead the rebellion against the aliens. But I needed to give my friend, President Ted Kennedy, one last chance to come to his senses before I did.

I needed to be sure he was truly a lost cause.

▪ ▪ ▪

Instead of going into the White House after the helicopter landed, though, I went to my residence. Before I talked with the President, I needed to freshen up and grab my map. Once ready, I put this and some other vital supplies into the Marine backpack I had kept from the war, and then asked my driver to take me straight over to the Old Executive Office Building.

I went into my office and picked up the intelligence files the FBI had dropped off about the various extremist groups in the country. I put these into my backpack and went out to talk with my secretaries before I left. Mrs. Pretlowsky, Nancy Bliss, and Sarah Deminson gave me all of my messages and reminded me about scheduled events and meetings, and then we chatted politely about the weather and the baseball standings.

I know I should've told them about the devastating storm I was preparing to stir up, but I could not afford to show my hand to anyone. It certainly wasn't because I didn't trust these women – they were loyal to me to the very end. But I worried if I told them even an iota of the truth, I'd be endangering them more. Knowing what I know now, this thinking was not only completely erroneous, it probably resulted in their gruesome deaths at the hands of The Army of Christ. But, at the time, I was overprotective of these ladies and I didn't want to be the one who put their lives in danger.

Ach, never has a more contradictory statement been uttered by me before!

When I walked inside the Foyer of the West Wing of the White House and went up the stairway to head to the Oval Office, I was grabbed at the elbow by Morty Brahmson in the hallway and pulled inside the bathroom. He was surprisingly strong for a man his size, and he blocked the door in such a way as to indicate I had no choice but to stay and talk with him. His face looked pale and sweaty.

"What the hell is going on, Jim?"

I was rather put off by his virtual abduction into this restroom, but I was more than a little sore by the overly familiar tone of his question. I was about to remind him I was the Vice President, after all.

"I'm sorry, Mr. Vice President. I'm just freaking out a little here. I thought I could live with the whole food for fuel trade with the Altoonians, but the way the President continues to act these days makes me wonder what we're doing. You seem like the one person in this place with their head screwed on straight. I just need to find someone else who might share some of my outrage and my concern."

Not wanting to over-commit, I answered in the vaguest of terms, a la the Altoonians.

"What are your main concerns, Morty?"

The man opened his eyes wide. He shook his head like he was trying to get water out of his ears.

"For the last twenty four hours, the President has been locked within the Master Bedroom of the White House with Eve. He's put the place under Romeo Protocol again, even though we have a lot of things to take care of. He's given strict orders not to be disturbed, no matter what. I am telling you, people are starting to talk, Mr. Vice President."

I rolled my eyes.

"Who's talking, Morty?"

"I'm not at liberty to say. But take it from me, there's a dissension beginning to brew, and I am afraid if the President continues his bizarre behavior and does not address this back room chatter, this whole enchilada could blow up in our face."

I sighed heavily and leaned against one of the sinks. I grimaced as I nodded absently to my reflection in the wall mirror.

"I'm headed to the Oval Office right now, Morty, to talk some sense into the President. Or try to. I think it is time to take the gloves off and stop this madness with the aliens. I just hope he'll listen to reason."

"What if he doesn't?"

Morty's question was the same one I'd been asking myself since returning to D.C.. I shook my head as I answered him.

"I really don't know, Morty. I guess I'll look for someone who will take charge."

"I know who should take charge. You should. As I've been trying to stop the bleeding around this place, more and more people have confessed to me that they're looking to you to stop this madness. You have a lot of support out there, Jim."

"Whoa. Let's not get ahead of ourselves, okay? I am not about to commit treason any time soon, Morty. I'm just hoping that President Kennedy will listen to what I have to say, and we can start to right this ship."

Morty grabbed my arm again and leaned in close to me.

"I mean, you have *a lot* of support, Jim. And they are just waiting for you to take charge. You have a sworn duty to uphold the laws of the Constitution so you have a legal right — and the political backing — to declare President Kennedy incapable of leading any more. You could, you know, just take over. You can end this crazy situation, Vice President Hunter."

I recoiled at his comment and backed up a step away from the man. I shook my head vigorously.

"No, I cannot do any of that, Morty. And I will not even think a thought like that."

"There are a lot of powerful people who have been watching your career with interest, Jim. They are ready for you to accept your destiny and become President of this great country."

"Even if that's so, they'll have to wait for the next election."

"If things keep going the way they are, there won't ever be another election. You are the only hope we have, Jim. You just haven't realized it fully yet. How does it sound to be called President Hunter?"

It sounded good.

I am mortified to say just how good it sounded to me. But I had enough wherewithal not to allow myself to be duped into a false reality in the midst of a White House loo, so I gave Morty a sharp look and pointed at the door.

"Mr. Brahmson, you need to move out of my way and let me out of this bathroom right now. I am scheduled to meet the President soon. Please allow me to leave, and I will not remember ever having this conversation with you."

Morty slid to the side and, making a grand gesture of a matador, he spoke out of the corner of his mouth.

"Oh, here you go, Mr. Vice President. But we did have this conversation, and I know you heard some of what I was trying to say to you."

I pushed past him and hurried down the hallway. My heart was thumping loudly from the whole affair, and I hurried over to the Oval Office as quickly as if I were eluding pursuers nipping at my heels.

There was a Secret Service agent I did not recognize standing right outside the Oval Office, blocking the door. He gruffly asked where I was headed, and when I told him I needed to see the President, he ordered me to wait in the Outer Office until the President was ready to see me. When I added that the reason for needing to talk with the President involved national security *and* the survival of our species, the agent was so completely unmoved by this assertion, he responded that those issues could definitely wait.

As I sat down, my anger at the agent's message and my malaise from the discussion with Morty made it almost impossible for me to remain seated in the chair. There was the muzak version of Elvis' "It's Now or Never" playing on the speaker system, and I could not help but feel like I was waiting for a root canal appointment at the dentist's office. To calm myself, I decided while I waited to look at the reports I'd picked up about all the insurgent organizations in our country.

I took them out of my backpack and began to leaf through them. They were very thorough and very boring. Soon I grew overwhelmed from reading about these whack-jobs and smalltime hoods. There seemed to be no end to the dissension out there in America, and I became disenchanted with looking at the countless foes of the government. Just as I had put most of these folders back into my backpack, Jocko the squirrel came loping down the hallway towards me. As I've said, it wasn't uncommon to see the president's pet scampering around the White House, and I really didn't give his approach much attention. Without warning, the rodent leaped at my leg and sank its incisors into my calf.

I howled in pain from the bite and reached down to grab Jocko, but the squirrel let go and fell to the floor. I could instantly see the wound was bleeding, and I was in a state of shock over what had just transpired. In my moment of inaction, the little bastard grabbed my backpack and started dragging it toward the pet door leading into the Oval Office.

I watched in horror as Jocko and my backpack disappeared from sight. I made a mad dash toward the pet door, but the Secret Service agent took up a defensive stance to keep me where I was.

"You did see that, right?" I bellowed. "The damn rodent bit me on the leg and then stole my backpack. It was full of very sensitive information. I need to get inside the Oval Office to retrieve it."

"Not until the President calls for you, sir. You need to wait."

"You've got to be kidding me!"

The man's stern silence was an indication that he was not, in fact, kidding at all. I sat down in a huff and rubbed the bleeding wound. It hurt. As I shook my head and got ready to confront President Kennedy about his pet's attack on me, I noticed there was a single folder sitting on the chair next to mine. On top of it was my hand-drawn map. I picked it up and carefully put it inside the folder.

I glanced, too, at the report within, and it contained all our information about The Army of Christ. By the time the President finally called me to come inside the Oval Office, I was not only familiar with the contents of the file, I was also well aware this meeting was going to be a waste of time.

It came as no surprise to find the President awash in another one of his blissful post-coital hazes. To be blunt, he acted as high as a kite. The man still wore nothing but a bathrobe and slippers, and he was reclined in his chair with his hands behind his head and his elbows leisurely pointed straight out.

I marched right up to his desk and forcefully put my hands down on the wooden surface.

"I've been waiting for a couple of hours out there, President Kennedy."

"You don't say. I had no idea it was that long."

"Well, it was. And, guess what else? Jocko attacked me. The little bastard bit me and pulled my backpack with the intelligence about insurgent groups through the pet door into this office!"

"You don't say. He's just having some fun, Jim. We all are."

With this he pulled his beloved squirrel Jocko out of his bathrobe pocket and began to scratch his pet's belly. He looked down at the animal and addressed it directly.

"Vice President Hunter says you've been a naughty boy again, Jocko. Naughty, naughty. No ice cream for you."

"Where's my backpack, Ted? I need the information inside it."

"Oh, Jocko hides things all over this place. Kissinger thinks it is his attempt to act like a normal squirrel by hiding stolen items in the White House instead of nuts in the park. I think Kissinger steals things from the White House and hides them in the park. Ha-ha. I don't know why I pulled Kissinger out of retirement. He's probably senile, but if he won a Nobel Peace Prize for Vietnam, maybe he can handle the Altoonians, as well, if we need him. But your backpack will turn up eventually, Jim. Don't you worry."

With his belt being too loose and the opening of his bathrobe now revealing more of him than I wanted to see, President Kennedy kept on scratching his beloved squirrel. Finally he asked me what I was there to talk about with him. When I responded I needed to chat with him about what I'd seen at the landing site, he interrupted me and calmly assured me everything in regards to the Altoonians was happening as it was supposed to.

He continued to restate how the whole situation was the best thing for both Altoonians and Earthlings, but his voice was slurred with an intoxicated hubris. Finally, he suggested – audaciously — I needed to spend some time with one of the other female Noosbits he'd recently traded for with the Altoonians to fully see just how happy all Earthlings could be with the present arrangement. With that, I knew our conversation was at an end.

Without another word I stood up and got ready to leave. In the midst of his seeming euphoria, the President was barely capable of speaking coherently to me, but just continued to scratch Jocko. I looked at the man as he reclined back in his chair and closed his eyes. In spite of the chance of not being heard, I needed to say something meaningful in this moment, but all my words failed me. I wanted to say something magnanimous and profound, something historical and sentimental, something to echo throughout the future eons with a powerful significance, but all I could muster was one short phrase.

"Well, it's been fun, Mr. President."

As I'd expected, the man did not react to my bizarre salutation other than to nod absently to no one in particular. I stood there for an awkward second in embarrassment over my failed attempt to say anything important, but then I grabbed my lone file and headed to leave.

The President opened his left eye and said enthusiastically, "Oh, hey, Jim! One last thing."

"Yes, Mr. President," I whispered hopefully.

"Could you tell Morty on your way out I'd kill for a pepperoni pizza from Famous Luigis?"

"Sure."

His right eye popped open, "Oh…and Jim?"

"Yes, Ted?"

"Could you ask Morty to get extra cheese on it this time? Seems Eve can't get enough of the stuff these days!"

▪ ▪ ▪

As I walked out of the Oval Office and down to my waiting car outside the White House, my feet felt like they were each a hundred pounds. I was so discouraged that I contemplated going back to my residence to drink scotch until I passed out, but I knew I needed to stay sober a little longer. I had my driver take me to the offices and residences of those top officials of our government who were aware of the deal we had struck with the aliens. I was hoping I could find some of the support Morty had been talking about and I could sway one of them into leading an insurrection against the President.

Instead, I found each and every one of them so completely blissful from the new Noosbit concubines the President had presented to them as gifts that they were unable to complete a single lucid sentence, and I knew I was going to be an army of one. Whatever happened, I needed to bite the bullet and take the leadership role in the rebellion.

With the sun setting, I dragged myself back to my residence, filled my largest tumbler with scotch and drank it down. After doing this six more times, I headed over to the couch to pass out. I was inebriated enough to be able to accept the fact there was no turning back for me now, but sober enough to know that once the dominoes started falling, they were more than likely going to fall right on top of me.

Either way, tomorrow would be the start of my resistance movement against the Altoonians and President Kennedy.

If, by chance, I was somehow able to stop them, I might get enough of the American people behind me to be elected as their next president in the next election. As I thought about this, I was unsure if the exact source of the resulting nausea was from the alcohol or just my conscience.

▪ ▪ ▪

I woke up the next morning bright-eyed and bushy-tailed. From the amount of enthusiasm and energy I was feeling, I knew my body was now creating a biochemical cocktail of hormones to get itself primed for what was coming next. This had happened frequently during my time in Vietnam, and I savored the warm return of these feelings.

However, I knew too much of a good thing was dangerous too, so, as my driver took me directly to the White House, I kept reminding myself to stay calm. Even with that effort to subdue myself, though, I nearly skipped like a character from *The Sound of Music* on my way to the door of the White House and down the halls toward the Situation Room.

As I'd hoped, the room was entirely empty when I arrived. I locked the door and set about making contact with the other governmental leaders around the globe dealing directly with the Altoonians. Bluntly, I asked them how they were all feeling about the current human lives for alien waste deal President Kennedy was brokering for them. I was pleasantly surprised by their unified response of disgust and disgruntlement about it.

Because they were still not aware of the existence of Eve and the other Noosbits, and they were not, therefore, currently receiving any sexual benefits from these aliens, their displeasure over the trade of human lives for fuel ran deep. I was pleased to learn the world's leaders were actually a sympathetic audience in regard to my desire to put the kibosh on the Altoonians.

Even though it put me in immediate danger by confiding so much with them, I outlined some of the specific steps I was preparing to take. While it was shameful to hear myself utter the treasonous plan of enlisting an extremist group to assist me in my act of rebellion, if the other world leaders were judging me in any way, they didn't show it. In fact, after they listened intently to everything I had to say, they seemed to be raring to go to get the whole bloody event started.

# IN THE FACE OF DANGER

According to the FBI file, outside of Hillsboro, West Virginia, in the mountainous landscape of Pocahontas County, there was an unassuming hamburger joint called Blanco's. Looking like some kind of solitary snowman standing guard outside the George Washington and Jefferson National Forest, the starkly white, painted cinderblock walls and the strangely white shingled roof of this small eatery both made it stand out and disappear at the same time. For most patrons, the place served the best hamburgers this side of the Appalachian Mountains. However, to those few trusted individuals in the know, the strange, tiny restaurant was actually the gatehouse to the headquarters of The Army of Christ.

Thanks to Jocko, the only choice I had left for an ally in my fight against the Altoonians came down to the organization highlighted in that one remaining file, so I set about to figure out a way to get myself to Blanco's, make contact with the extremist organization, entice them to take on both an alien race and quite possibly the U.S. military, and, somehow, then get out of there alive. After all, there was no point in even attempting this errand if I did not get to live to tell the tale, right?

But I needed to figure out some way to get from my residency in Washington D.C. to Blanco's in the mountains of West Virginia without being detected. I certainly could not just hop aboard any of the presidential helicopters or military choppers to fly there. The last FBI briefings guaranteed such a preposterous frontal approach would result in a ground-to-air missile being used like some kind of suppository. And that was a result I wanted to avoid like the plague.

Since my mission was secret — and secret from *everybody* — I could not have my driver involved in any way. I certainly couldn't ask him to take me to Dulles Airport to rent a car since there'd be no way I could sidle up to the Hertz desk without the world knowing Vice President James Fenimore Hunter was renting a car. Even taking a Greyhound bus or an Amtrak train down to West Virginia could not be done with a shred of anonymity, so I was at a loss of how to get myself to meet with The Army of Christ.

Then I thought about Mrs. Pretlowsky's dead-beat son, Justin. Although I'd be the first to admit I didn't always give my secretaries my undivided attention – let alone give them their just due — I can say I did listen to them whenever they needed to talk to someone about all the painful aspects of their private lives. I was, without a doubt, a horrible boss, but when one of those women was having troubles with their spouse, their children, their house, their car, their cats, even their plants, I tried hard to help them when I could.

So, almost more times than I can count, I'd heard about Justin Pretlowsky and the trouble he'd gotten into...again. Through the years, I'd even attempted to intercede several times to get his charges lessened or cleared all together. It was the least I could do for the dear woman, his poor mother.

I knew that the boy was out of jail and living at home these days and that he was having a hard time finding any legitimate work. With his rap sheet now having more pages to it than the Washington D.C. telephone book, Justin was all but unemployable. Mrs. Pretlowsky was more than aware that when her boy ran out of money and needed more, he was going to do something stupid enough to get another free ride to jail. He'd certainly become far too risky by now for me to try to get him gainful employment, but I realized he and I could actually help one another.

I needed to clandestinely get my hands on a nondescript car to get myself to West Virginia, and Justin would be pleased as punch to get a thousand bucks to give me his orange 1977 Ford Pinto and look the other way.

After Justin Pretlowsky had accepted my offer over the phone and met me at the secret exit hole I had already made in the fence around my residence to sneak out whenever I wanted to get away without an escort, I started driving his orange jalopy to find Blanco's.

As I drove, I took stock of my current situation. The battered and rusting car I was currently driving looked like some kind of a diseased and rotten citrus fruit. Inside, the cloth of the sagging and ripped ceiling liner billowed and fluttered in the wind from the never-closing driver's window, and empty cans of Natty Boh tinkled like wind chimes as they rolled around in the passenger side foot well. The whole car smelled strongly of reefer. In fact, the semi-circle of roaches laying around the rim of the car's ashtray were like Scouts in front of a campfire.

As for me — due to the fact I had donned the disguise I'd used to escape from the July 4th celebration — the unrecognizable reflection looking back at me from the rearview mirror looked like a stranger who was more likely going to some kind of rainy outdoor rock concert than a high-ranking official of the U.S. government. I was suddenly almost too distracted by the look of utter disbelief in my eyes to keep the sputtering and backfiring Pinto in its lane.

When I finally came to the tiny white hamburger shack and its enormous parking lot, I pulled in and parked well away from the other cars there. I took off my silly disguise – it would only get me into more trouble if I continued to wear it during my attempt to have an audience with the extremist group's leader – and I got ready for what was coming next.

As soon as I exited the car and began walking toward the strange white structure, I realized all bets were off. Either I was going to be shot by the poorly hidden sniper I'd spotted high in the pine tree in front of me before I even reached the shack or I was going to make it all the way to the headquarters and make a deal with the Devil.

Regardless, I was crossing a point of no return.

I'd reread the FBI file extensively the night before, and I knew what I was up against. The Army of Christ was considered by the intelligence community the most formidable of all the extremist groups on the list because they were a highly organized, well-led, and widespread organization. It was clear their name was not a cute moniker, but indicative of the size of the organization's membership and its preparedness. They were no club. They were a real fighting army.

Their leader was a mysterious man by the name of George Franklin Buchanan. He'd been surprisingly innovative in the recruitment of a broad spectrum of people. Not only did he go after the religious right, the white supremacists and the conspiracy theorists that made up most hate groups, he courted disgruntled ex-military veterans as well as common citizens fed up with governmental corruption.

It was the veterans that the FBI worried the most about. Fresh from the fetid sea of discontent about Vietnam and the other recently failed and undeclared wars that the United States government had undertaken in the preceding decades, these men still had their usable military training and skills. Angry people are always dangerous for governments to deal with, but those who can shoot straight, pilot helicopters and jets, and use explosive ordinances are the ones who really keep up at night those agencies designed to maintain the national peace.

Aside from its makeup of military veterans, the other big reason the Army of Christ had risen to the top of the intelligence community's watch list was their vast geographical range. These guys weren't just a bunch of backwater rabble-rousers ready to cause some trouble in a circle of activity just a few miles from Appalachia. No, this was a highly organized and trained paramilitary group that had branches throughout the length and breadth of our country. Sure, their headquarters was hidden behind

Blanco's in rural West Virginia, but their reach extended from sea to shining sea, so to speak.

Unlike other extremist groups, The Army of Christ had wisely chosen its central message to be less antagonistic and attention-getting. While they did preach about keeping the white man in power, they also sought to preserve religion's prominence in society, to keep the United States government from getting too bureaucratic and controlling, to support a stronger and better led national military force, to maintain a secure national border, to fund better public schools, and to protect the environment. In fact, their platform was so broad that many of their middle class supporters would have been downright shocked to find out the organization with which they'd aligned themselves had any racial agenda at all. Case in point was the high number of the Vietnam vets joining who were black, Hispanic and Native American soldiers and who felt wronged by their unrecognized sacrifices in Southeast Asia.

As I walked, I straightened my shirt and prepared my presentation. The FBI infiltrators of the organization all had reported the same thing. If you were to get anywhere with The Army of Christ, you had to make it past this hamburger joint. Rejection at Blanco's was usually, quite literally, a kiss of death. So, as I made my way, I rehearsed what I was going to say. I didn't want to waste this opportunity because of something I wasn't ready for. As a former military man, I still operated under the "Six P's" rule: Proper Planning Prevents Piss-Poor Performance.

Once I got up to the counter, I was greeted by the unfriendly gazes of three rugged men. They wore no discernible uniforms, but it was clear from their overly confident movements they all had guns nearby their persons. Even though their menacing looks made me worried they'd shoot first and then ask questions later, the man standing closest to the counter talked to me like I was any other customer in line.

"We're closed for the season, bub."

I nodded, but replied evenly, "I am here to see the Man."

The FBI had lost several agents because they had not used the correct terminology when approaching the members of this organization. I guess, to The Army of Christ, if you exhibited too much familiarity, they shot you for your condescension. But if you showed too much diffidence, they shot you for your lack of directness. So, taking the middle road, I forged ahead with my mission knowing full well I could, at any moment, make a fatal mistake.

I stared back at the three men as they now tried to process my request, but I remained silent. I knew if I attempted to elaborate or clarify at this point it would be seen as a sign of weakness.

Finally, the man at the counter broke the silence by saying, "The Man's schedule is all booked up today."

"Tell him the Vice President of the United States, James Fenimore Hunter, is here to see him. I'm betting he might find an opening for me."

One of the other men went to a telephone on the wall and dialed a number. He spoke into the receiver quietly and listened carefully to the other end.

"Are you alone?" the man on the telephone suddenly barked at me.

"I am alone."

"Are you unarmed?" he bellowed at me again.

"I am unarmed."

I waited for him to follow this up with, "Are you stupid?" but he didn't.

He then resumed speaking quietly into the phone before hanging it up. He pointed over to the side of the shack.

"Mr. Hunter, walk around the building with your arms up in the air. One of us will come out to frisk you before taking you up to HQ. Just remember, there are a shitload of guns trained on you at this very moment, so no funny business, right?"

"Well, there certainly will be no *funny* business from me."

"Even if you were to try some, sir, you wouldn't make it far. It'd be like you'd run into a 'two-step snake.'"

I did not like the man's arrogance. His reference to the poisonous krait the American soldiers in Vietnam had come to fear made me angry enough to be snippy.

"Yeah?" I said. "Well, you might want to tell your shooter at six o'clock that his position in the pine tree has been compromised. Tell him that when you're hunting deer, it's okay to wear a blaze orange vest because deer are pretty much color-blind, but when you're hunting people, you can be seen pretty easily."

The man looked up involuntarily. Because of the vest, I'd spotted the sniper as soon as I had gotten out of the car. Snatching up the military grade walkie-talkie near his hand, the man pushed the button to speak and then practically spit into it with his disdain.

I didn't wait for some kind of acknowledgement, and I walked around to the edge of the building, as I'd been instructed. A man came out of a fortified door and proceeded to pat me down. Finding no weapons, he pushed me forward and started to walk behind me. He guided me with the tip of a rifle, though, and we walked past my car and up a well-hidden driveway.

After we had left the burger shack far behind, the thought that I was headed right to a quick execution and a shallow grave sent a shiver up my spine. Then we came to a well-concealed concrete bunker in the undergrowth of the forest, and I knew I was actually being taken to the Man.

The design and construction of this formidable building spoke volumes as to the intent and preparedness of the organization to take military action against its perceived enemies. As ridiculous as it must sound, I also felt a sense of satisfaction that Jocko had picked the right card for selecting the allies I'd need to take on the Altoonians.

I entered the bunker and let my eyes adjust to its dimmer light. A man with a beer belly, long hair, and a beard came up in front of me with his hands on his hips.

"Hello, Mr. Hunter. I am the Man. Why have you requested a meeting with me today?"

The FBI files had been comprehensive and they included multiple photos of George Franklin Buchanan, so I knew right off the bat that this man was an imposter. I appreciated the half-hearted attempt to deceive me, but I also felt a wave of irritation go over me.

"Well, you are definitely *a* man," I said, "just not *the* Man. I came here to meet with the leader of The Army of Christ, but if he's going to waste my time with this charade, please just tell him that I stopped by. Good day."

The man scoffed, “And where exactly do you think you could go, Mr. Vice President? You’re kinda standing in the middle of enemy territory right now. It’s not like you have a whole helluva lot of options other than to stay and talk with me.”

“Well, that may be true, but a squadron of MC-130E Combat Talon bombers with full payloads of “daisy cutters” is just waiting for the transmitter sewn inside the lining of my stomach to get tripped. When it does, we’ll all be crispy briquettes before you can French braid that mop of hair on top of your head.”

The strength of my partial bluff was enough to cause the man’s face to go a little ashen — which told me it had actually worked — and I grinned proudly.

“Of course, I didn’t come here today to die. I just want to meet with George Franklin Buchanan.”

“Hello, Mr. Hunter. I am he,” a calm voice uttered benignly behind me.

I spun around and there was the man in the intelligence photos. George Franklin Buchanan looked more like a Sunday school teacher or benevolent uncle than the leader of a dangerous paramilitary organization. He was tall and lithe, and his white hair was neatly parted on the left side of his head. He wore a dark blue business suit with a well-matched tie and had black plastic framed eyeglasses, identical to the pair worn by Senator Barry Goldwater, pushed high up on the bridge of his nose.

“I am George Franklin Buchanan,” he said, almost kindly.

“Nice to meet you, Mr. Buchanan, I am James Fenimore Hunter.”

"Oh, Mr. Vice President, I know very well who you are. Even though I'm sorry to say I didn't vote for you in the last election, I can honestly say this had more to do with the man you ran with than any dislike I have for you, sir. A man with such a distinguished military record as yours and such a clean political record is someone I can definitely get behind. But as true as that may be, I must ask you now why you've put yourself at so much risk just to meet with me today?"

"Is there a more private place to talk, Mr. Buchanan? I have some sensitive issues I'd like to discuss with you...alone."

"Ah, I see," the man replied with the same unease a car salesman might have if the customer asked for bucket seats as opposed to a bench seat. "Well, yes, we should go into my private study, Mr. Hunter."

To alleviate my discomfort, I decided to exchange pleasantries.

"This is quite a facility, Mr. Buchanan. I had no idea you were so well set up."

The man glanced back and gave me a look to indicate he knew full well I'd been fully briefed about the bunker and the organization's capabilities. But he nodded softly.

"It *is* pretty impressive, Mr. Vice President. And — not to totally debunk the threat you made to my man just now — it could easily protect us from anything a squadron of aircraft with conventional weapons could throw at us. Theoretically speaking, that is."

We entered his office and he politely ushered me in and shut the door. He sat behind a cluttered desk more closely resembling a college professor's, and he looked back at me impassively. I sat down in a metal framed military surplus chair in front of the desk and gazed back silently at him. We stared at one another for another awkward moment or two before he spoke.

"So, Mr. Hunter, what exactly is on your mind today?"

"The Altoonians."

"Ah, the alien invaders. Never has our planet faced such a threat as them, and never has our oppressor — that which calls itself the government — been so complacent. It's given in to all their demands. Even the Jewish owned media is allowing these uninvited visitors to have complete *carte blanche* as they saunter into our midst and do whatever the hell they want. Usually, when something of this magnitude is being kept completely hidden from the common people, it's been my experience nothing good is happening. These creatures definitely do not fit into the picture of the new world we are seeking to create, Mr. Hunter, so I am curious as to what you have to add to my assessment of their current presence on our troubled country."

Although his voice continued to be kind in tone, he'd used his words and phrases like razor blades to slash and cut at what he was talking about, and I knew instantly I needed to be careful with whatever information I revealed to him in this conversation if I wanted his organization's help in my endeavor. I couldn't afford for him to become another enemy against me. I coughed into my hand and then spoke.

"Perhaps we have failed our people by the way we've handled some aspects of this encounter, Mr. Buchanan, but the truth is the Altoonians haven't been completely honest with us Earthlings. And I know why. They're not here to help us."

"A blind man riding a wild pig could see that, Mr. Hunter. But what new information do you have that might shed some new light on the true nature of the Altoonians?"

I closed my eyes and shook my head.

"They're eating humans, Mr. Buchanan. We've become their new food supply."

The older man's expression didn't change at first, but then his eyes grew large as he began to wag his head. He looked down at his desk and struck it with his fists.

"I knew there was some big secret to it all. I just had no idea it was *that* big! Well, well, that's certainly a hard pill to swallow, Mr. Hunter. A hard pill to swallow indeed. But why doesn't the almighty United States just flex its military muscle and do what it's supposed to – protect its people?"

"For many reasons, Mr. Buchanan. But mostly because we know if we attack them, we'll be facing an enemy who's far more technologically superior than the Russians and Chinese put together. Our analysts have calculated the potential casualties and damage of a direct military assault on the aliens, and, indeed, their reports have included the very effective phrase, 'Attacking the aliens would undoubtedly result in the debilitating destruction of the entire planet with unseen and unequaled carnage.'"

Buchanan clucked his tongue.

"Sounds like you and the other false leaders of our world have a real problem on your hands. I've yet to hear how any of this makes an iota of difference to me or to this organization. As a matter of fact, I think the old proverb fits here. 'An enemy of my enemy is my friend.' In truth, I'm now jealous of the aliens because I'd love to have the misguided and impure government of the United States of America by the balls as tightly as they do now."

The way he delivered his last bit was like a kindly looking Santa Claus at the mall saying he wanted to slit a child's throat. I felt a rush of adrenaline at the possibility of losing the edge to the meeting, and I knew I needed to throw him something enticing enough to help me…even if it wasn't quite true.

"They're only eating white people."

"What?"

"The Altoonians don't want to eat any other ethnicities or races. Only the flesh of pure white people tastes good enough to them."

"Good God!"

To this day, I have no idea where my horrendous lie came from. Although I had frequently visited those darker places of my soul which had been exposed during my involvement in war and in politics over the years, I'd never before ventured to its very nadir as easily. And what's worse, once I'd tapped into it, more malicious and inciting mistruths began to flow freely from my mouth like I was spitting watermelon seeds.

"The truth is, Mr. Buchanan, if the aliens' behavior isn't put into check, there's a very good chance they will quickly decimate the white population until it no longer holds a majority anymore."

The man slammed his fists onto his desk again and stood up.

"And what about you and the rest of the U.S. puppet government? Why the hell won't you do *something* to protect your people?"

"We can't. Not alone. That's why I am here today – to enlist The Army of Christ's help to stop these aliens."

The man sat slowly back down into his chair, apparently mulling over my last request.

"Naw, something doesn't smell right here, Mr. Hunter. It doesn't make any sense for you to come here alone today and walk into this lion's den to ask for our help. If you were an ordinary citizen, maybe, but not the Vice President of the United States of America. You ain't telling me the whole story!"

"No, I am. We need help to stop the aliens."

Mr. Buchanan sat back and stared at me. Clearly he was not convinced. He leaned forward.

"What about the President? Why isn't he doing anything?"

Knowing I needed to be careful here and not have these disintegrating negotiations come apart at the seams, I tried to be somewhat vague.

"The President appears to be getting some kind of compensation from the aliens that I am not, so he's happy with the arrangement. Other top officials in the government also seem to be in bed with the aliens, so to speak, and they are all determined to block my attempts to stop this travesty from happening."

Making President Kennedy the scapegoat of the whole thing was, perhaps, wrong of me, but I needed to sell my idea completely. Since the man I was appealing to for help had an abhorrence of both the aliens and the government, I needed to make him want to attack both of those perceived foes at once.

The man scratched his chin.

"But why The Army of Christ?"

"I cannot risk approaching any of the leaders of the United States military since they must remain loyal to their commander in chief. And I cannot ask a foreign army to intervene, for that'd be seen as an invasion of our country. No, only a highly organized and armed group on the fringe of society can be the answer to this problem. I've done my research, Mr. Buchanan, and of all of the extremist, anarchistic and agitator-led organizations currently under surveillance by the U.S. Intelligence Community, The Army of Christ is generally regarded as the most powerful. You are well-led and well-armed. I believe you can tip the balance in a fight against the aliens."

"Let me get this straight, Mr. Hunter. As the acting Vice President of the United States, you not only willingly participated in extending an open-armed invitation to a population of cannibalistic space invaders to come to our planet and feast upon our own people, but now you're having some kind of change of heart on the matter and you've decided to come and enlist a radical group — with many members whom view the government you represent as the *true* enemy — to fight these aliens…who you've already defined as being so technologically superior that they've got the most advanced and equipped armies of this world shaking in their boots, too scared to fight."

The man stopped talking and stared straight into my eyes. His gaze was piercing, and I knew I needed to answer him with the right response. But the fact was, I didn't have one. When I tried to think up another creative fib, I drew a complete blank. So I just told the truth.

"Yes, Mr. Buchanan, everything you stated just now is absolutely true. I don't have time to even attempt a half-assed defense of myself from all your hurtful indictments of my past sins, so I'll just say I came to you today to ask The Army of Christ to be the lever and fulcrum to dislodge the rock sitting atop and crushing this world at the moment…the Altoonians. If we can loosen their hold on our planet, the resulting short maelstrom might clean up the mess that — as you just accurately pointed out — I've been so instrumental in creating."

The older man spun his chair around and stared at the back wall. Silence permeated the room until I could hear the rhythm of his breathing. When he slowly swung his chair back again to face me again, his voice was taut with anger.

"You do realize you're asking me to lead my men right into a suicide mission, don't you?"

"No, I don't think so, Mr. Buchanan. If I were asking you to take on the aliens in a head-to-head kind of traditional military action, it definitely would not end well for The Army of Christ. However, I've got a plan to hit them hard when they aren't looking, and I've some secret intel to give the upper hand to whomever is fighting them. With this, the Altoonians will be knocked so far back on their heels, their vulnerabilities will be exposed, and then we can strike at their weak underbellies. It won't take too much to finish them off once we get them in a compromised position. It certainly won't be a walk in the park, but it won't be suicide either."

"Well, I certainly cannot ask my men to sacrifice their lives for the very thing we've been fighting against…the government of this country! Not with a clear conscience, I couldn't. No, I'd need some real reason to join this fray."

"Well, Mr. Buchanan, what do you want?"

"Oh, come on now, Vice President Hunter. You've no doubt read my manifestos in your intelligence briefings. You know exactly what I want."

I did know what he wanted...a racially pure world with him as the king. I most definitely could never give him what he really wanted. However, because I needed his help if my plan was going to work, I put my hands together like I was praying and I pleaded with him.

"Mr. Buchanan, my only goal is the removal of the Altoonians from America and getting them to stop eating our people. I didn't come here today to broker the end of the United States. I came to find an ally in the fight against a mutual enemy."

I would come to regret ever uttering those words, for never was a self-fulfilling prophecy with such clarity spoken aloud before. Just looking out my hotel room at the devastated and charred remains of Washington D.C. these days tells me I was, in fact, brokering the end of the United States when I met with Mr. Buchanan in his bunker. At that moment I just didn't see the forest through the trees.

"Quebec."

The man abruptly spit out the name of the Canadian province like he was answering a question on a television quiz show.

"Pardon me?"

"I want Quebec."

"Um, I can't give you Quebec, Mr. Buchanan."

"If you want me to send my men into this doomed fight with these aliens, I want some kind of guaranteed reward for them and for me. I want the province of Quebec."

I looked at the man to see if he was kidding, but he was staring back at me with the same intensity he'd had all along. I shook my head at his demand.

"I don't have the authority to give you something that doesn't belong to me. Quebec is an integral part of the sovereign nation of Canada, and I am in no position to offer it up to you."

"You could tell me you wouldn't try to stop me if I attempted to take it, I guess."

"I think Canada would try to stop you if you attempted to take over one of their provinces."

"I can handle them. What I'm asking from you, Mr. Vice President, is your assurance the United States won't intervene when my men begin to take it."

"You're serious?"

"As a heart attack, Mr. Vice President."

The man's startling request had completely thrown me for a loop. I tried to regain my composure, but his ridiculous counter-offer had completely unsettled me.

"Well, I think I can agree to state that if The Army of Christ helps drive the Altoonians from this planet, the United States government and military will not directly attempt to stop you from trying to take the Province of Quebec from the country of Canada."

"That was quite well put, Mr. Hunter. Are you a politician by any chance?"

I smiled at his retort.

"But why Quebec?" I asked,

The man's eyes narrowed with menace.

"Is the reason any of your business?"

"No, of course not, Mr. Buchanan. I ask out of curiosity, not judgment."

"Uh-huh." The way the man smiled let me know that he knew that I was, in fact, judging him. He pointed at me with his finger. "Did you know the Quebecois have repeatedly tried to leave the Canadian Confederacy? They are the only French speaking province and they have more of their roots in France than in England, so they don't feel like they're part of the rest of the Anglophile establishment that runs the country of Canada. I think, at this point, the people of Quebec would see me as a savior if I could get them free from the grasps of those thuggish English-based goons in Ottawa!"

The arrogance of the man and his clear insanity caused me to laugh nervously and I responded quickly.

"Well, it certainly is beautiful country up there."

The man looked at me as if I'd just started reading the ingredients on the side of an oatmeal box. He pursed his lips.

"Beautiful? The hell with beauty, Mr. Vice President! The province of Quebec has a superior location right across the St. Lawrence from this country. They have unlimited natural resources, including an almost endless supply of timber and hydroelectric power. They have a willingly rebellious population. Being the King of Quebec would be an enviable position of power."

I was nodding nonstop now because the man's voice had risen and his high pitch only highlighted the craziness behind his desire to trade a Canadian province for his help with dislodging the alien invaders. I was hoping my agreeable nodding would end his tirade and refocus our conversation back to planning my rebellion, but the man suddenly sat erect in his chair and put his hands squarely on his desk. He cleared his throat and then spoke with a calmer and gentler voice.

"There *is* a personal reason for wanting to rule Quebec. My great, great, great, great grandfather was none other than General Richard Montgomery, the infamous Irishman who fought for the American Colonies during the Revolutionary War. In 1775, he and Benedict Arnold led two armies as part of an invasion of Canada. They met up at Quebec City and their combined forces attempted to conquer the city. Unfortunately, they were unsuccessful. The army was repulsed and Montgomery was killed on the Plains of Abraham. This shameful defeat has been passed down to each generation of my family, and even though my ancestors have since then prospered, our failure to take Quebec has been an ugly legacy to our blood that I've longed to wash away for my entire life. So, it may sound strange to hear me ask for the chance to take Quebec, but now you know why it's so important to me. If I finally take the land my ancestor, Brigadier General Richard Montgomery, failed to, I will once and for all erase the deep familial sense of failure which has plagued us for over two centuries. In one single act I could purify our entire lineage! Surely a man with your own tainted familial history can understand such a rational request as this."

I arched my eyebrows and looked hard at the man across the desk from me. The inference about my relative, General David Hunter, and his scorched earth attack on the Shenandoah Valley during the Civil War, should have given me more insight into the type of adversary George Franklin

Buchanan actually was, but I only thought he'd made a lucky guess.

When I saw that the man now expected a final answer to his request for Quebec, I quickly went over the deal in my head. Since I had lied earlier and knew Mr. Buchanan and most of the members of The Army of Christ were either going to be killed off in the initial attack against the Altoonians — or by the U.S. Army in the counterattack of my plan — I assented.

"Okay, Mr. Buchanan. You can try to take Quebec after we've successfully defeated the Altoonians."

"Splendid! It's a deal. Now, just tell me your 'big plan' for how we're going to defeat the Altoonians, and we can set this whole thing into motion."

"Uh-uh," I said with a negative shake of my head. "I want you to have your lawyer — who I know is in the next room and probably listening in and recording our conversation at this very moment — to write up a proper treaty so we both can sign the document. In clear and legally concise language, I want it to document your offer for The Army of Christ to help in defeating the Altoonians, and in return for you to have the freedom to attempt to take the Province of Quebec from the nation of Canada."

Now it was time for Buchanan to show surprise. The FBI's reports had identified the man as having an unnatural hang-up with legal representation and documentation on all official decisions and agreements, and I had just used this information to hook him like a muskie. After the man continued to stare at me for a minute, he finally laughed softly and then spoke up toward the ceiling.

"Well, Cecil, you heard the man. Draw up a doggone treaty right quick and we'll sign the thing and make this whole deal official. Then we can get to the business at hand of stopping those despicable aliens from eating good, God-fearing white people."

We made some small talk while we waited, but eventually the lawyer — dressed more like a hunter ready to go out on a fall deer hunt — came in and placed the neatly typed documents, one in front of each of us, and gave us both a pen. We signed on the assigned lines and then switched papers and signed those.

With the legality of the treaty in place, I requested Mr. Buchanan to assemble his commanders so I could outline my plan to them. The man seemed initially perturbed to do this, but he eventually consented and gathered the men I'd asked for in a large board room in the bunker.

I've never had the experience of addressing such a hostile audience before. Sure, I'd faced angry voters and the like in my career, but I'd never stood in front of a unified body of people with such a shared hatred and personal distrust of me. So, as I carefully and thoroughly divulged all of my observations about the aliens, showed them my map, and went over the schemes for defeating the Altoonians, many of the gathered men whistled so loudly and scowled so fiercely that I worried there was going to be open dissent amongst them.

However, when I noticed Mr. Buchanan, sitting at the other end of the table, his eyes glowing like they were electrified, I knew my plan for getting rid of the Altoonians was going to be followed exactly as I'd laid it out. I now had a hate group as a willing ally in my fight against the

Altoonians. This reality suddenly terrified me more than I could say.

As soon as I finished talking, Mr. Buchanan stood up and started barking orders with more energy and aggression than I had seen from him. He commanded some of his men to go and make connections with all of the sympathetic co-conspiring agencies, clubs and militias to assemble a vast and unified armed force to pull off the proposed synchronized attacks at the three alien landing sites on American soil. He then ordered three other men to spare no expense to acquire all the necessary weaponry and ordinance needed for such an assault on the Altoonian ships. Then, after he sent the remaining men scrambling to assemble and prepare of their forces, he turned to me and boldly directed me to give him my hand-drawn map of the alien ship's interior layout.

I took it out of my pant's back pocket and looked down at it. I wasn't sure it was the best idea to give it to him, but since I knew I could draw more copies from memory and because I had already shown it to the world leaders for them to copy for their troops, I felt it would be best to have this copy in the hands of the attacking soldiers who would need to know their way around the ship if my plan of defeating the aliens was going to work. I timidly slid it across the table toward George Franklin Buchanan as if I were passing a contraband note in school.

The man snatched it up and told me to head directly back to Washington to keep up appearances and to organize the other foreign powers to synchronize their assaults on the aliens to coincide with his insurrection. The last thing he wanted, he said, was for The Army of Christ to be standing alone with its pants down around its ankles when the attack started in this country.

Without waiting for a response from me, the man shook my hand and rushed out of the room issuing orders without even another glance back.

My walk back to the orange car in the parking lot was the longest and loneliest moment of my life. I felt as if I'd just taken a shit on the altar of St. Peter's Basilica while the place was filled to capacity with an audience of grandmotherly nuns. I mean, when you commit an act of treason as big, as nefarious, and as destructive as I just had, there's no one else on the entire planet who can possibly understand the unfathomable depth of your despair. And, even though I knew my intentions were good and just, I had, in theory and treaty, just sold out the United States of America. And Canada. And Quebec.

There was nothing else to do, really, other than to pray for God to have mercy on my soul…even though I felt as if I had just sold that item to Satan himself.

# THROWING A WRENCH IN THE PLANS

I returned to Washington, but the city seemed more like the Saigon opium dens of my memory than a center of power in the Free World. President Kennedy and all the high ranking government officials were now enjoying the companionship of the Noosbits. I'm not proud to report that a series of new, unofficial brothels had been established around town for those with enough security clearance to warrant the confidentiality to share the experience of having sex with one of these provocative aliens, and because of this, it seemed as if the entire government was either languishing in a euphoric state or impatiently waiting their turn to do so.

Watching this made me feel like we were all back in Roman times. How many sordid tales were there about the emperor and his cohorts in the Senate being too busy participating in their orgies to actually govern the Empire? That hadn't worked out too well for them, so I knew we were cruising for the same kind of downfall if something didn't change. I still held out hope that President Kennedy and the rest of the men in power could be brought back to their senses, but nothing I saw gave me any optimism to believe that was going to be true.

Just as I had been instructed by Buchanan, I drove the orange Pinto back to Washington and snuck into my residence to make it seem like I'd never left.

Later, I had my driver take me over to the White House. I couldn't find the President, so I snuck down to the Situation Room to make contact with the other world leaders and check on their preparations. Before I got there, however, Morty Brahmson intercepted me again. He wanted to know where I'd been, and he seemed to know that my excuse of having had a bout of stomach flu wasn't entirely true.

"How are your plans going, Jim?" he asked me. "My efforts to drum up support for you have been going like gangbusters, but the proof is in the pudding. With President Kennedy and his cohorts all acting like they're at a Grateful Dead concert, everyone is looking for you to take charge. Are you ready for that?"

"President Kennedy is just letting down his hair, Morty. He's been under some major stress since the landing of the Altoonians, and this is his way of blowing off some steam, I guess."

Morty forcefully shook his head no.

"With the entire government seemingly on vacation, right now, the American people are starting to take notice. They're asking questions, Jim. And not the kinds of questions you want asked either. I mean, what starts with unanswered inquiries from agitated groups of concerned citizens can very quickly lead to rocks and bullets, almost overnight. But you've got a plan, right? I'd guess you were off busily working on that. Maybe you need to call a press conference and announce your bid to take the reins. Then you can outline your plan to get the aliens in line, too. Perhaps a series of financial sanctions directed against them – you know, so it looks like we are trying to brush them back off the plate."

Morty's proposal to go public with a potential takeover of the executive office and an overt offensive against the aliens was such a bad idea, it was beyond ludicrous. Alerting the President, the aliens and my new-found allies, The Army of Christ, about my schemes at this point would be certain suicide – both political and actual physical suicide.

"Oof, Morty, let's not jump the gun on this one. I do have a plan in play, but it requires some patience to get all our ducks in a row. Plus, I'm sure the President will eventually come to his senses after he's done enjoying himself. We cannot rush off, half-cocked, and make the situation worse, right?"

"Jim, there's actually more danger out there now than ever. There are forces at work, especially in the media who are enjoying their role as pot-stirrers, and they're riling up an unsettled public. If they're allowed to continue for much longer, their opposition may grow too strong to contain. It is essential that anything that's going to happen starts immediately, like in the next few days."

"It will, Morty," I said flatly.

"Well, where were you headed just now, Jim?"

Even though I didn't like the fact I was being challenged by a White House Chief of Staff who had grown too big for his britches, I calmly reported a little of my plan to calm the man.

"I was on my way to speak with the other world leaders to see if they're facing similar situations in their countries. Once I know this, we can plan on some internationally coordinated responses."

"What can I do to help, Mr. Vice President?"

"Why don't you continue to be vigilant about the press-led dissension you mentioned. If you could put it all into a report and get a copy to me in about five hours, that'd be great."

"I can definitely do that. I'm sure the people are going to get behind you when they see you acting like you're in control around here. Everyone just wants some good leadership, Jim, and I think you will bring that to this place."

"Well, thank you, Morty. I appreciate your dedication and your loyalty, and I think all Americans feel the same way about you."

I might have been laying it on too thick, but Morty Brahmson walked away with much more confidence than before. I felt a pang of regret in my gut from my continuing acts of deception, but I did honestly believe I was working to fix the problem of the Altoonians. At that time, the process seemed somewhat simple – start an armed rebellion to dislodge the aliens, survive the small upheaval that followed, and start putting back together the pieces afterward.

I did worry, though, about my being ostracized as a result of some of my treacherous actions. Now I know it was ridiculously naïve for me to think the biggest thing I had to worry about in the post-apocalyptic world I was so busy creating would be surviving some kind of social shunning or damaged friendships.

As I would discover when things truly flew out of the frying pan and into the fire, my apparent lack of friends in the future would have less to do with some kind of moral outrage over what I'd done, and more to do with them all getting gruesomely killed in the rampant genocide I'd personally unleashed upon them.

▪ ▪ ▪

I sealed myself inside the Situation Room, and continued to reach out to friends and foes alike for the next five hours. By the time I had finished with these seemingly endless communications and negotiations, I was fairly confident all the Altoonian ships on our planet were going to face some kind of opposition at the very same moment the Army of Christ attacked the three ships in the United States. Whether all of the foreign governments would implement such a radical and violent plan as mine in their assault on the aliens, I couldn't be sure, but it was clear they were going to try to do something.

While some leaders were so irate about the deal with the aliens to trade their own citizens for free fuel that they were gnashing their teeth and cracking their knuckles to get into a fight, other leaders were seemingly more swayed by the immense profits and benefits from the arrangement to do more than just slap the aliens' hands. Regardless, I came away from my phone calls feeling there'd be some form of resistance, but I wouldn't really know how effective all this would be until after the moment came and went, and that gave me a bad case of the heebie-jeebies.

Before I let Morty into the room to give me his report, I needed to have one last conversation with George Franklin Buchanan. My phone call to him turned out to be like petting a coiled poisonous snake.

He coldly informed me his army was now ready. They were armed with the weapons I had predicted would work best against the Altoonians and his troops were moving into position to wait for the agreed time to commence their synchronized attacks. When I expressed some concern about them having an ample enough supply of ammunition, the man said two things that gave me a moment of pause. First, with a bravado seemingly too confident — considering the circumstances — he proudly bragged no army of his was going to be relying on just peashooters and potato guns to fight a battle this big. When the time came, they'd have access to the biggest and best weapons out there! Then he brusquely ordered me to immediately meet with the Altoonians again to set the plan into motion.

Looking back now, I should've known the man was more than just being cocky; he was enacting his own plan.

When I finally let Morty into the room, he reported his findings to me. I listened intently, but did not offer him any new insights from the information he was sharing with me. Instead, I surprised him by inviting him to join me on a trip to the Pennsylvania landing site to talk directly with the Altoonians. When he asked why, I lied right to his face and said the aliens had expressed their own concerns about the current state of President Kennedy and the dissolving quality of the current affairs of this world. We just needed to assure them all was fine and dandy. As I hurried him out to the South Lawn and pushed him aboard the waiting helicopter, he was too stunned to resist.

During our flight I described the format of the meetings with the aliens, and I strongly urged him to remain quiet throughout the negotiations, no matter what was said. His silence would reflect the confidence the Altoonians required in a human leader. If he talked, they'd definitely take notice and smell a rat. Then we'd have two problems to deal with. He nodded solemnly, but his eyes were as troubled as a steer being led down the chute to the slaughter house.

As we flew over the countryside on our way to Pennsylvania, I will fully admit I was overwhelmed by Morty's report. He had indisputable evidence our American society was close to an open insurrection. Because everyone in a position of leadership at the capital was now acting like they were sniffing glue, there was a highly unstable environment of deep discord and discontent growing among the American people.

Due to the current tightlipped silence of their politicians, the people looked to the press more than ever to get information. These newshounds were on the scent, and their stories and media pieces only seemed to inflame the crowd. It was so bad at the moment that the only release valve for a buildup of this kind was a violent, popular uprising against their apparently impassive and uncaring government.

As ludicrous as it sounds now, I thought this news about a people's revolution could actually be useful in the attack on the aliens. After all, if this discord intensified to an unhealthy level at the right moment, that firestorm could actually finish off the deed...if The Army of Christ was somehow not successful in its attempt to dislodge our unwelcome visitors. Even if the extremist group was fried to a crisp by the aliens' laser weapons, a united rebellion by the citizens of our country could turn into a concerted effort against the Altoonians.

As a fan of proper military strategy, I knew the timing of it all was essential. If the people revolted too soon, it would totally derail everything. So I silently prayed the impending social upheaval would simply have the goodwill to wait until our violent attack on the aliens was already underway.

I can now see how this prayer must have gone over like a lead balloon with God.

▪ ▪ ▪

Morty Brahmson had never been to a meeting with the Altoonians before, so he remained in a state of awe during all the proceedings. I needed him to be a silent partner during my presentation to the aliens, so his being tongue-tied and wide-eyed worked out perfectly for me. If he'd been a seasoned veteran of these meetings and not so impressed with the gigantic size of the immense ship overhead, and the two menacingly large creatures lumbering toward the meeting area, he might have had the courage to say something contrary to the countless deceptions I began telling Moog and Haag as soon as we all sat down to meet. But, thankfully, he was unable to do anything more than stand up, walk, and nod when he was told to.

He was, in fact, the perfect patsy to accompany me on the mission to set the end of the world into motion.

The one thing about the Altoonians that still shocks me to this day – despite the fact that they were a technologically advanced population of veteran space travelers — was that they often exhibited the innocent gullibility of mere children. When I told them President Kennedy was so thrilled with his "gifts" from them that he wanted to return the favor and give something back to his Altoonian friends, they seemed almost like ecstatic kids waiting around the Christmas tree to open their presents.

As I continued on, in great detail, about the fictional process of choosing truly superior tasting individuals from the population to be brought to the Altoonian ships, Haag and Moog seemed to be drooling into their Universal Translators. They rubbed their hands together and made sounds I'd never heard them utter before, and I had the feeling I was causing the same reaction as if I were promising to bring delicious Wagyu steaks from Japan to two starving men. They were in such a swoon they barely acknowledged the announcement that each of these gourmet human presentations was going to be accompanied by ridiculously opulent gifts to represent the love of the earth and sky our two species now shared with one another.

I found myself speaking with the rising and falling timbre of a mesmerizing A.M.E. Zion Church minister, and my confidence grew the more I felt the inner warmth of having the two aliens in the palm of my hands as I made my spiel.

When our meeting was finally over and we parted ways, I had to herd Morty towards the helicopter like I was ushering an elderly man to the bathroom. Even though he was still too overwhelmed by the meeting to know what was happening, I knew the Altoonians had bought my phony story hook, line, and sinker.

Somewhere over Maryland, Morty finally came to his senses and began asking about the things I had just offered the aliens. I was able to brush off his newfound questions with a false sense of authority, and I reposted him to the duty of monitoring the discontent within the population to make sure the pot didn't boil over too quickly. As soon as we landed, I sent him off with the task of capping any vents seemingly ready to blow. In spite of his own awakening curiosity about my grandiose offerings to the aliens, the critical aspects of the duty I'd assigned him eclipsed any of his own personal need to know the truth. Isn't it sad to say it is those people who are the most focused on doing something positive for the greater good who are the easiest to bamboozle and lead astray?

As I walked through the White House Diplomatic Reception Room and into the vaulted Center Hall, I was struck by how eerily quiet the building still was. With the outside world currently in such a state of hue and cry, the deserted and lifeless hallways of the place more resembled a mausoleum situated next to a busy road than the residency of the President.

Seeing no one was around, I turned left to head toward the kitchen to make myself a meal. I was famished. I'm well aware how bad this sounds. In spite of just setting the country on a collision course with its own demise, I still had a healthy appetite. No, this definitely does not shed a good light on me, but I've never claimed to be anything but a flawed human being.

Hey…nobody's perfect.

I had a hankering for a good Reuben sandwich. There was a precedent for this type of craving from another crucial time in my life. When I returned home from Vietnam, all I wanted was some thinly sliced corned beef, smothered with Swiss cheese, sauerkraut, Russian dressing, all settled gently upon perfectly grilled slices of real rye bread. So, instead of reuniting with my family members and friends immediately after disembarking the military transport, I snuck over to the Old Ebbit Grill in Washington and ordered one of their infamous Reuben sandwiches. Interestingly, the noises I made while I ate this sandwich all those years ago were surprisingly similar to the sounds the Altoonians made upon hearing about the newly tasty human offerings we were going to give them as presents.

As I now went about preparing my sandwich in the White House Kitchen, I noticed some motion in my periphery. I had grown so at ease with the serenity and solitude of the empty building under Romeo Protocol that I spun around defensively at the sudden intrusion into my space. It was Eve. She was naked as a jaybird, and through some hand signs and pigeon English, she explained she'd come to get a bite of food to eat while the sated President slept.

The dwarfish alien was obviously a quick study of our language and human conversation for she was now more than capable to convey the details and the emotions behind whatever she was saying. It was quite clear, for example, that she was as relieved to be free of the lustful grasp of the President as she was hungry for something to eat. She was so comfortable with me, after we'd made our greeting to one another, she set about searching for something to eat without another word.

Eve looked different to me. Even though it's not overly polite to say, I thought she looked like she'd put on a few pounds since I first met her in the hanger at the Command Center. I didn't spend too much time pondering this since I was wholly focused on making my Reuben. For her part, Eve seemed too preoccupied with her own search for food to take much notice of me either.

She proceeded over to the ever-present Boston Cream pie in the crystal pie stand and took the White House Pfaltzgraff Holiday Cake knife to cut herself a substantial slice. She must have been famished for she crammed one piece into her mouth in while she cut another, which she devoured equally quickly. When she cut herself a third slice, I smiled to myself because I now knew why she'd appeared to gain so much weight. A minute on the lips, forever on the hips, right?

After Eve ate her pie, she slowly made her way over toward me.

"Vice President Jim, why you not around? Why I not see you any more?"

For the second moment in too recent a time, I was transported back to Vietnam. This time I was haggling with the *nuoc cham* smelling child prostitutes of Saigon, as they used their broken English and freshly pubescent bodies to lure us American servicemen into their clutches. I'd love to say I had always been an upstanding Christian man and turned them all away, but I had the medical bills to prove otherwise. As repugnant as it is to say, their sales pitches had brought them immense profits at my expense.

Even now, as I stared back at Eve as she hopped up onto the metallic prep table I was using, I have to say her nakedness and her proximity to me was causing me a moment of arousal. She was close enough that I was able to reach out with my hand and stroke her, but I refrained. I needed to remain focused on enacting my plan, not fulfilling any sudden lustful urges. Plus, I was too excited to simply enjoy my nearly perfect Reuben sandwich sizzling in the pan in front of me.

Then Eve innocently brought her feet up onto the table. Oh, those muscular and substantial feet! Everything had been happening so quickly from the moment we'd first set eyes upon her that I'd forgotten how impressive her feet were! Now, like a cobra swaying to the movements of its charmer, I found myself completely mesmerized by them. My eyes — which had just been solely focused on the sandwich grilling in front of me — now strayed over to those feet, and I was helpless to fight from falling under their spell. The way her toes were beautifully stubby, yet silent with power. And her arches…they looked more like the supportive architectural elements in the crypt of a mighty cathedral. And the way her robust and muscular ankles commanded and connected those powerful calves to those gorgeous feet.

As I stared at every little detail of those magnificent feet, the concupiscence I'd been feeling since remembering the memories of sexual escapades in Southeast Asia now built to an unhealthy level and I ogled and leered at those supple yet powerful alien appendages next to me. I'm not going to lie – I was too close to indulging in satisfying my desires. I had to hold my hands down at my sides to prevent myself from instinctively reaching out and touching Eve's gorgeous, gorgeous feet.

Now might be the right time to confess I've always loved feet. Women's feet. There may be men who desire nothing more than to see other parts of a naked woman, but my heart belongs to their feet. There have been many instances when my love of feet has taken on an obsessive quality during my life, and that causes me some major guilty feelings. Truth be told, I've always held the belief it was my special interest in feet which played the major role in driving my poor wife Geraldine to drink.

My attraction to feet was well within the normal realm during the early courtship with my future wife, and even during those first years of our new marriage. However, as soon as it was obvious we were two highly flawed people bound together in an unhealthy relationship, my increasing preoccupation with Geraldine's feet still didn't help her own devastating feelings of inadequacy. I was so focused on what was going on below her boot line that I lost sight of the rest of her…until she was spiraling out of control.

Poor Geraldine! My dear wife grew to understand I didn't care if she hated me, hated herself, and drank as much as she could to provide some analgesic to the pain from both of those emotions…just as long as her feet were pampered with washing and pedicures. Even though I was an upright husband who was in love with his wife — especially those lowest parts of her — I now know my insensitivity about my wife's emotional and mental state contributed to her ultimate downfall and institutionalization.

I am also somewhat ashamed to admit I haven't been fully faithful to my wife since our separation. While I've never engaged in sexual intercourse with another woman, I have asked those women I consider closest to me to allow me to enjoy their feet...on a purely platonic level, of course. Mrs. Pretlowsky, Ms. Bliss, and Ms. Deminson have all indulged me by letting me savor their feet at some point during my Vice Presidency. There were those thinly veiled, religion-based pleas for the ritual of washing their feet and those pedicures given under the auspices of helping the healing of the early onset of bunions, but my hands never moved above their ankles. There wasn't ever anything overtly erotic – for them, anyway — involved. They all understood I needed to merely satisfy my foot longings – not have sexual relations. To their credit, these saintly women were all wonderful and supportive in their fulfillment of my needs.

However, as I now watched Eve's magnificent feet provocatively flip and flop in the air like the tantalizing movements of a cat's tail, I started to comprehend I was in real danger of allowing my own foot desires to consume me and distract me from the gravely important tasks at hand. I wanted nothing more than to run my forefinger up between the toes of her right foot and up the slope of the bridge, circle her gloriously stout ankle joint like it was the fine rim of a salted Margarita glass, and then seductively trace the curves of her enticing arch. I wanted to kiss her heel and then bring my tongue down the length of her sole. I wanted to suck on each of her twelve toes....

It was this anatomical fact that instantly dispersed my sexual fantasy by fanning out the inebriating mists of my libido-filled stupor. For, as delectable and irresistible as Eve's feet were — and, as God is my witness, they were! — the fact that she had twelve toes reminded me all too well she wasn't human!

The realization I was about to allow myself to succumb to the feet of an alien creature who had, unintentionally, contributed to the horrendous situation our species now found itself in was too much to ignore. It suddenly didn't seem right to be dreaming of doing all those pleasurable and sensuous things — even to those beautiful, beautiful feet of Eve — just as I was about to lead the rest of the world in front of an oncoming bus. To give in to my powerfully carnal desires would have belittled the cause I was fighting for…freeing our entire race from the clutches of an evil alien presence.

As if I had snorted some smelling salts, I immediately jerked back and stood as far away from Eve as I could in the confines of the kitchen. If she had any disappointment from failing in her seduction of me, none registered on her face. She remained implacably stoic sitting up there on the prep table.

Another movement now caught my eye, and I broke my gaze away from the alien in front of me to see what it was. There was a flash, like the movement of an individual fish in a school of herring, and my brain quickly processed that something threatening was approaching me. My military training took over my body as I prepared to intercept my attacker, but it was no one other than President Ted Kennedy.

He had the Pfaltzgraff Holiday Cake knife in his right hand, and he came straight at me yelling, "You can't have her! I won't share her with you! Get your own!"

Without thinking, I grabbed his wrists roughly and wrenched them like I had been taught at Parris Island to take control of an assailant. But the man seemed possessed, and he continued to yell out how Eve was his and no one else was going to have her. He began to fight against me as if his life depended upon defeating me.

While the two of us struggled, I looked over at Eve. She looked bored with everything, and her apathy shocked me enough to momentarily loosen my grip on President Kennedy. He immediately exploited this to get the upper hand on me, and he actually cut my arm with the cake knife. He was too enraged with jealousy over his alien lover for me to talk him down.

I tried to, but he wouldn't listen to me, and he now resumed his attack with his fury-fueled strength. I sought to defend myself. Even though I didn't want to hurt my friend, my own self-preservation instinct and my military training kicked in and I savagely elbowed the man in the nose and then drove the Pfaltzgraff blade deep into his neck.

The image of this moment is like some kind of horrifying black and white daguerreotype branded inside my head. As the man backed away and put his hands up to the cake knife lodged in his trachea, he gargled out his last words.

"Oh, Jim, how could you?"

Then, before I could stop him, he pulled the knife out. When he did, it must have severed an artery for his ruby red blood began spurting over me, over the tables and over the kitchen floor. As he sank to the floor like a torpedoed ship, I knelt down and cradled his head tenderly. I had the all-too-sudden understanding I'd just killed the 37th President of the United States of America!

Not only was I committing an unforgivable act of treason in my efforts to start the violent confrontation to purge our country of our alien invaders, I had also just killed my friend and the Chief Executive in a stupid fight over an interstellar love interest in the kitchen of the White House with a cake knife!

There'd never been a sillier moment in my life, nor one so rife with greater implications.

I glanced up at Eve. She continued to look bored, and this only made the rage in my gut corrode the building fear about what I'd just done. I stood up and stalked over toward her.

She seemed so unthreatened by my movements she even waved her feet tantalizingly in front of me a couple of times, but I was undeterred. I grabbed her by her hair and began dragging her, kicking and screaming, over to the broom closet. I threw her inside, shut the door and locked it. I could hear her making a racket in there, but I turned to clean up the mess. With my insurrection about to commence, I did not need the fallout of the discovery of the President's lifeless body in the White House Kitchen to cause an unneeded whirlwind while I orchestrated my plan.

I lugged President Kennedy's naked body into the walk-in cooler and then tried to wipe up as much of his pooled blood as I could with his bathrobe, but this made the situation worse, so I stopped. My clothes were now saturated with the President's blood, so I shed them and threw them into the trash can. Hung up next to the cooler was a cook's coat and pants, and I grabbed these and put them on. Time was of the essence, and I quickly snatched my now badly burnt Reuben sandwich and hurried off toward the Situation Room trying to appear as nonchalant as I could.

I scurried down the West Colonnade and through the deserted corridor to the overly quiet West Wing Lobby. Despite my ridiculous outfit, my uneaten sandwich on a plate, and the stress-filled palpitations of my heart, I tried to appear as if I wasn't doing anything out of the ordinary. Luckily for me, I was able to make it all the way to my destination completely undetected.

I locked the doors from within and moved the large meeting tables and chairs against the door. Safely ensconced within my den of treason, I sat down to eat my sandwich. The sublimity of the moment hit me like one of those giant ocean swells overwhelming the swimmers at a beach. I found myself involuntarily being flung from a calm state into a blissful one and then finally into one of core-shaking sobs…all in a matter of seconds.

Once I had gathered my wits enough to finish my sandwich, I tried to video-phone the other leaders around the globe to have some kind of last minute communication with them. But no one was there. I don't know if they were entrenched deep inside their own government bunkers or were busy prepping their troops for the upcoming assaults, but no one answered any of my hailings.

Well, one person did – George Franklin Buchanan. Oddly, he only sang the last verse of the "Notre Dame Victory March" in a sing-song voice,

*"Cheer, cheer for old Notre Dame,*
*Wake up the echoes cheering her name,*
*Send a volley cheer on high,*
*Shake down the thunder from the sky.*
*What though the odds be great or small*
*Old Notre Dame will win over all,*
*While her loyal sons are marching*
*Onward to victory.*"

With no further clarifying statement as to why he was singing that school's fight song, Buchanan simply stated, "Drop your cocks and grab your socks. We're gonna set the spurs to the horse! Thanks for *all* your help, VP Hunter."

The muted black screen seemed to suck me into it. There, in the onyx-like glass, was the reflection of me. I was wearing a cook's outfit, I looked like I hadn't slept for several days, and my face, which still had the stains of President Kennedy's blood on it, was etched with nothing but doubt and uncertainty. I wasn't sure whether to laugh or feel pity for the poor soul in that reflection, but the intimate moment was vaporized when my finger inadvertently hit a button and streamed the nightly newscasts of the network media outlets.

There, in the central-most screen, the glowing light of the news studio caught my attention. At his iconic news desk sat the venerable Walter Cronkite. His stature in American culture was now irrefutably established as the one and only trustworthy mouthpiece for the truth. All of us in politics knew that when we wanted — really wanted — any messages to be directly injected into the hearts and brains of the American people, we needed to have Mr. Cronkite read it.

Forget the presidential press conferences or televised speeches. Those were listened to and watched with such thick filters of cynicism that they were as effective as humming into wax paper on a comb. No, if you wanted all of America to know, think about, understand or just believe in something, it needed to be read by Walter Cronkite on the nightly news.

So, when I saw the familiar snow white hair, eyebrows and mustache and the impish grin of the man as he readied himself to read the Top Story of the night, I prepared myself to experience the purity of what the man was going to say and let it singe my soul. But when he said he was saddened beyond all belief to be reporting that he had learned the Altoonians were trading their waste to be turned into fuel in exchange for an endless supply of human offerings for their food, the Reuben sandwich in my gut became a Bouncing Betty.

Somehow the cat had not only been let out of the bag, it was licking its claws and getting ready to pounce on all of us!

# THE TROJAN HORSE

Walter Cronkite's revelation was the perfect definition of a bombshell. His status as the most trustworthy news reporter and beloved national icon made his utterances about the deal with the Altoonians seem like he was Moses descending from the top of Mt. Sinai to read a tell-all book to the American people.

I didn't know how he'd gotten hold of the information, but it didn't matter. The damage had been done. With everyone knowing the ugly truth, I was certain the swirling undertones of a popular uprising were going to ignite and consume everything in their path. If so, this was going to be a major threat to everything I'd set into motion. Suddenly, my plan felt like a half-assed piece of origami.

Not only was a ruthless extremist group supposed to attack the aliens at the very moment the people of the country learned about their government betraying them, but the President lay dead in a walk-in cooler while his murderer, the Vice President, sat completely alone and pretended to pull the strings like he was still in control. It was a moment of pure chicken shit!

Just as the truth of the matter began to fully soak in to my now reeling mind, the wall of screens in front of me blazed instantly to life with news reports from around the country. From one of them, Colonel Archibald Simmons began to give me a play by play of the events currently happening at the landing site in Pennsylvania. When I warned him about the news story just aired, he told me he was well aware of the backlash and that there was already a noticeable amassing of both press and protestors at the landing site almost instantly after the newscast.

I reminded him his men needed to be hyper-vigilant to prevent any kind of assault by the citizens, other than the already described arrival of the special visitors I had outlined in my last briefing with him. The commander nodded knowingly, but then shook his head and grimaced as he apologized for letting those members of the press whom the President had put on ice at the Command Center escape. He didn't know how they'd gotten out, but they had, and they had somehow found out what was really happening at the Altoonian ship and had sent their story to Walter Cronkite. I told him the fault in the matter was not his, but fell on the President and myself. But he wouldn't hear of it, and he continued to hold himself personally responsible for the leak. He was a good man.

Of course, I knew what had really happened and who was really to blame. The whole damn situation had gotten completely out of control because the President had become obsessed with Eve and because I had become so preoccupied with my plan to drive the aliens out. Of course, it was ridiculous to assume those reporters were just going to sit in a conference room forever and twiddle their thumbs while they waited for us to get back to them and give them everything we'd promised.

Those veteran newspeople, such as they were, must have smelled the lies we were serving them and the bigger story begging to be uncovered at the landing site. When it was clear we weren't coming back to give them any information, they'd set off to get the real scoop. We could have prevented the current calamity if we'd only steered them in a less dangerous direction — with misdirecting stories and fake exposés — but we'd gotten too consumed with our own schemes to get out of our own ways. And now our failures were going to ruin everything.

When Colonel Simmons then announced a massive parade of people was arriving at the site, I knew it was The Army of Christ, and they were right on time. Simultaneously, the live feeds from the other news networks also began showing the approach of this odd gathering of people, and I sat back into the chair. I had an overwhelming sense the attack was going to fail miserably, but the spectacle was going to be worth the price of admission anyway, and I just wanted to sit back and watch how everything played out.

I was suddenly struck by the funny notion that the day's actions were going to be like a tap-dancing faerie in golf shoes atop the pimple on a giant's ass, and the inanity of this thought made me laugh out loud. My audible guffaw caused the commander to ask if I were alright.

"Just getting myself ready for the show, Colonel," I answered.

While I continued to watch the news reports of the approaching procession, Colonel Simmons kept reporting exactly what he was seeing. At first, he couldn't make out what was coming toward the base of the Altoonian ship, but as it came closer, he saw it was vast columns of men slowly walking toward the ship holding the ropes of five Macy's Thanksgiving Day Parade balloons. There was Mickey & Minnie Mouse, Felix the Cat, Popeye, and Mighty Mouse…all inflated fully and being pulled gently toward the scene by men in unobtrusive khaki trench coats. The scene on the screens looked like the famous New York City parade had somehow made a wrong turn and gone two hundred miles out of its way.

TV news reporters were beside themselves to either explain or describe exactly what they were seeing, but they were so caught up in trying, they spoke as fast as auctioneers. Truthfully, I didn't hear their words anymore, for the way the sunshine hit the undulating balloons and made them shimmer like primordial jellyfish was enough to make me sigh with contentment. It was as if each of the monitors I was looking at had become a framed work of art on the walls.

Everything seemed like it was going according to my plan, but then Colonel Simmons grumbled deeply, and I knew something wasn't right. He cleared his throat before speaking.

"Sir, I'm not sure why this is happening, but I think we may have a real problem here. I just got a report of some unauthorized aircraft circling the site and several units on the ground moving their positions closer to the alien ship without any proper orders. I've tried to raise them, but I'm not getting any response back. We may need to consider the possibility there are some rogue military forces working against us at the moment."

I looked up at the ceiling as I painfully comprehended something that I hadn't thought was plausible, but that was actually coming to pass. The FBI reports had been clear in their warning about The Army of Christ. The organization had a dangerous ability to recruit discontented members of the military, both those in active service and those of the veteran status. Because of this, they posed a duel threat. They could not only appeal to veterans to join their ranks, they also had the ability to entice soldiers already in the military to fight against the country. I hadn't completely disregarded these advisories, but I'd held out hope that any current servicemen who were even tempted to join The Army of Christ would stay loyal to the country, no matter what.

Hearing from Colonel Simmons that there were now military hardware and units freewheeling around the situation, I knew The Army of Christ had called for their people on the inside to grab the necessary planes, weapons and soldiers needed to defeat the Altoonians. Somehow, to do so, they would've had to obtain all of the top secret access codes, and that was classified information they could not have gotten their hands on. Even Colonel Simmons seemed more than a little perplexed when I brought that up to him.

"There's no way," he said, "that they could have done that without getting ahold of the Pickett's Briefing."

Pickett's Briefing?

I had seen it. It was a very dense, very fact-filled document the military had assembled with all the codes and information needed for a direct assault on the aliens. The leadership of the various branches, in an attempt to create a ready-to-use implement for a worst case scenario, had compiled the document to be a one-stop source for any military action against the Altoonians…if it ultimately became necessary. I'd received the briefing and had tried to read it, but I was overwhelmed by the extent of the material and the minutiae of the details and I'd left it on my desk at my residency unread.

I slammed my palms down on the counter in front of me! Was there a chance I'd drawn my map on the back of Pickett's Briefing?

I was so driven to regurgitate my mental image of the inside of the Altoonian ship, I'd just grabbed the first loose piece of paper I could find; I never once checked what was on it. If such a super sensitive briefing was on the back of that piece of paper, that meant I had simultaneously given my map *and* confidential information to the leader of an anti-government extremist group with delusions of world domination. In effect, I had handed over all the information Buchanan and The Army of Christ needed to defeat the aliens and the U.S. military too.

I had inadvertently given the keys to the kingdom to a lunatic.

As I comprehended just how much I had underestimated George Franklin Buchanan, I knew who was now really in charge. I was nearly sick to my stomach. I wasn't the controller of the situation. I was the one being controlled by it. With my plan no longer the main play in motion, I was forced to watch those screens just to see what unexpected turn the whole thing was going to take next.

As the Thanksgiving balloons were brought ceremoniously toward the alien ship, the craft's skin opened up with its usual liquid metallic movement, revealing a humongous bay. This continued to widen until it looked like an expectant mouth. A huge gathering of the Altoonians had come outside to receive the "gifts" they'd been promised by the President, and I knew the trap had now been set.

I quickly gazed at the screens showing the two other landing sites in the United States to see if things were going as smoothly at those locations. In Nevada, the Goodyear blimp, hijacked from its scheduled coverage of the USC/UCLA football game, was being carefully guided underneath that Altoonian ship by a similar army of trench coat wearing men. It looked like they were carrying a foil covered sausage to an awaiting and hungry eater.

In Louisiana, an endless convoy of tanker trucks parked underneath the alien ship now made the space look like the largest truck stop on the planet. The Altoonians, their eyes all growing large with the anticipation of receiving such a offering of the choicest tasting humans stood out in the open in large groups and showed their eagerness with their familiar foot shuffling.

In the next instant, the trap was sprung and the screens all instantly changed.

The fairly impressive detonations of the parade balloons and the blimp were flashier than the high-pressure purging of the tanker trucks, but the lethal impact of the massive release of helium on the Altoonians was instantaneous. As the aliens all crumpled to the ground, the men of The Army of Christ surged forward onto the fallen aliens and into their ships. I was transfixed as I watched the screens all show what looked like ants swarming onto and then overcoming a large beetle.

Just as I had envisioned, the helium instantly disabled the Altoonians and gave the soldiers of The Army of Christ the opening they needed to get into the ships and use the map I had created to get at the ship's vulnerable insides. From the ensuing and impressive laser weapon battle, I knew the men of Buchanan's forces had already been able to get their hands on the alien armaments and figure out how to use them. Although the thought of an army of madmen with space-age weaponry was another level of this nightmare come true, if The Army of Christ force was going to have any chance of defeating the aliens, they needed every advantage they could get.

Then all hell broke out.

"Incoming!" Colonel Simmons barked loudly into his microphone.

The unmistakable sounds of approaching bombers, the hiss of Super Walleye missiles, and what could only be called some kind of garbled rebel yell was followed by all of the screens going black at the same time.

I frantically tried to hail the colonel again, but all I heard him utter before the line went totally dead was, "You better run for the hills, sir. They're coming your way!"

In a panic, I tried every frequency I could, but there were no responses from the landing sites. Then, in a bombastic flash, the screens came back to life again with the cacophony of the reports from the Pentagon and the simultaneous newscasts from the headquarters of various news agencies around the country. Although it was overwhelming to hear them all talking at the same time, they were generally saying the same exact thing.

Apparently the massive army made up of The Army of Christ — and almost every other extremist group and revolutionary organization in the United States — had quickly overwhelmed the Altoonians, and then, with the aliens quickly defeated, had immediately turned their attention on going on the offensive in almost every direction. This burgeoning military force, growing ever larger as they assimilated the huge number of military defectors into their ranks, was fanning out from victory to victory.

According to interviewed survivors, The Army of Christ soldiers gave everyone they met a simple choice: join or die. The televised violence of the early massacres was enough evidence to make the decision an easy one for most Americans. It was clear from the growing size of this force and its swath of destruction that the cresting tsunami of anarchy was about to smash down upon our civilization and wash the streets with its violence.

Before signing off, I contacted all surviving American military leaders to give them *carte blanche* to fight back against this insurgence with any means necessary. Over the years, as part of many bi-partisan strategic planning sessions, the American government had put several plans in place for last-ditch efforts to defend our country in doomsday scenarios such as this one. When I told them we were now in a *Betwixt Scylla & Charybdis* situation, I was giving the acting leadership of the Army, Navy, Air Force, Marines, and Coast Guard permission to fight an all-out war against The Army of Christ and its allies.

I felt compelled then to add how they could expect to have a little less leadership coming from the White House, since an assassin had apparently killed the President. By the time I began to assure them I was going to make one last televised speech to the people of America to tell them what had happened and what we were doing in response, it was clear these fighting men didn't care about anything other than just getting into the brawl at hand.

Then, all the screens in the room went blank. As I sat in the darkened room, I had a moment to begin to contemplate my role in creating this cataclysm. But before I could delve too deeply into that matter, however, the displays blazed to life again, all filled with the same image of George Franklin Buchanan standing with two glum-looking Altoonians.

Buchanan identified himself and then he introduced the two aliens to the American people as Moog and Haag, the alien leaders with whom the President and Vice President had negotiated away the lives of thousands and thousands of Americans to line their own pockets with riches. I gulped audibly because the broadcast was being televised on every channel, every frequency. Whatever was going to be disclosed in this telecast would now be known by as many people as still had access to a television, radio, shortwave radio, citizen band radio, uhf radio, or "ham" radio.

Buchanan physically prodded the two creatures with the butt of an Altoonian laser rifle and forced them to tell all the details of the secret meetings, the horrific truth of the food for fuel trade, and even the shady exchange of the sex slaves from Eve's people for the titillating exploits of our high-ranking governmental officials.

The two aliens glumly continued to spill their guts, leaving nothing to the imagination. When Moog and Haag had nothing left to reveal, Buchanan shrugged his shoulders and spoke with no emotion to his now vast audience.

"Say goodnight, Gracie."

"Goodnight, Gracie," the Altoonians repeated dryly through their Universal Translators.

Buchanan then fired his rifle rapidly into both their heads and spewed the camera with their yam colored blood. While the cameraman futilely attempted to swipe the goo off his lens, Buchanan began yelling loudly at the now blurred camera.

"American People, we, The Army of Christ and its allies, have purged this scourge of alien invaders from our land, and we are now ready to get rid of the real enemy living in our midst. The United States government. Where *are* President Kennedy and Vice President Hunter? While these alien monsters have been given license to feast upon our species in a government sanctioned butchery, those two 'leaders' have remained awfully silent on the matter. Are they hiding? If so, why? Well, brothers and sisters of this failed noble experiment, my men and I are going to find them and make them atone for their sins. I am giving you a fair warning not to get in our way. We are a vengeful wave of justice and we will stop at nothing until we have routed out the traitors from our nation. Join or die, America!"

The screens all went back to their original broadcasts, but I didn't look at the confused and angry expressions of the newscasters nor at the images of the violent maelstrom raging out of control across the country on those multiple screens. Instead, I frantically started to remove the barricade blocking the door.

If I was now in the midst of a battle of information and misinformation, I needed to get myself on air as quickly as I could to somehow give my own press conference. In it I would try to right some of the wrongs, calm the dissent, alert the country their President was dead, and prepare everyone for what horrors were coming our way. I still wasn't sure how I was going to exactly do all of this with one broadcast, but I had to give it a go.

The world I found outside was in complete disarray. The skeleton staff of the White House were all acting like a bunch of teenagers trying to frantically extinguish the fires started during the party they'd had while their parents were away.

My sudden appearance seemed to comfort them and give them the necessary focus, though, in spite of the damning revelations Buchanan had made over the air. I assumed control of the situation, and I demanded to be taken right to the Press Briefing Room to get on the air and talk with the American people.

While the crews fired up all of the cameras and sound equipment, those few members of the press who were still at the White House came out of the Press Corps Office with such dazed expressions that they resembled bears awakening after a winter-long hibernation. I tried to look authoritative and calm, but my disheveled cook's outfit gave me the appearance of some kind of street person, and I noticed how the assembled members of the press not only simultaneously avoided my gaze, but gave me back such intense looks of pity.

When the red light atop the camera went on, I was initially surprised by the similarity of its hue and the blood of President Kennedy on the floor of the White House

Kitchen. That slight hesitation gave the press conference an air of seriousness, so when I nodded and began to speak, I felt a power surge within me.

"People of the United States of America, I come to you today with a message of unprecedented importance. Truly, as I think back, I cannot come up with any other speech given to the entire country by a President with a subject so grave, a message so dour, as the one I must give today. From Abraham Lincoln's Second Inauguration speech of 1865 before a completely divided country, to Franklin Delano Roosevelt's Pearl Harbor Address and the resulting declaration of yet another World War, to Lyndon B. Johnson's 'Let Us Continue' speech after JFK's assassination, no other President has had to present such an overwhelming series of disclosures as I do to you today. It would be an understatement to say I've got a lot on my plate to relay to you!"

"As you are well aware, George Franklin Buchanan just broadcast an appalling and lie-filled message accusing the leadership of this country of having sold out the human species for free fuel and calling for a revolution against the government of the United States. His libel charges are completely and utterly false! From the moment they touched down on the planet, the Altoonians threatened the human species with annihilation if we didn't comply with all of their wishes. President Kennedy and I were forced to negotiate an exchange of prisoners for free fuel, but we did so unwillingly. The aliens had us over a barrel, and we had no choice other than to accept their conditions.

"However, the Altoonians had a second, nefarious part to their plan. They infiltrated the government with a mind-controlling alien we code-named Eve. What initially looked like an escape by one of their adorable-looking captive creatures turned out to be a well-crafted scheme to send a traitor into our midst. And once it was brought into our confidences and shown true compassion and hospitality by President Kennedy, it began to alter his thoughts. He tried to fight against that clandestine mind control, but I am beyond sad to announce that it was the alien Eve who killed President Ted Kennedy with a knife in the kitchen of the White House last night. I arrived too late to save him, but I was able to disarm the alien and contain her in the broom closet of the same kitchen."

"These two announcements are earth-shaking, in and of themselves, but there is more, my fellow Americans. To break out of the yoke the Altoonians had put on us, I enlisted the help of The Army of Christ, led by Mr. George Franklin Buchanan, to lead a surprise attack to drive off the alien population. The outcome of that action against the Altoonians was successful, but now it appears Buchanan and his followers have broken the terms of our agreement to take this opportunity to pursue their own twisted and heinous agenda to violently attack this wonderful country of ours. Sometimes the cure can be worse than the disease, I guess."

"But Mr. Buchanan's actions give me, as the current acting President of these United States, no other recourse than to hereby declare war upon The Army of Christ and its supporting militias. They may have liberated us from the Altoonians, but they now threaten to overrun this country with their own racist and nationalistic agendas, and we must defeat this enemy with our unity and our steadfast love of country!"

"American People, I beseech you today to prepare yourself and your families for the oncoming violence. It's about to descend onto us all, but we can defeat it by standing up and fighting! They may appear strong, but they are a loosely connected coalition of antagonists who will not survive the infighting bound to happen very soon. It is time for the common people of this country to strike back and...."

When all the lights and cameras in the room suddenly went off, I knew The Army of Christ had gotten hold of the Westinghouse Electromagnetic Pulse weapon being stored in the secret armory in Cleveland Park and attacked the power grid of the city. The shock of being cut off in mid-sentence was replaced by the pang of resignation that the devastating attack upon the capital had already commenced, and I loudly told everyone in the room they needed to get the hell out of Dodge.

I certainly was on my way out. But as soon as I came from behind the podium, I was forcefully gathered up by none other than Jim Richardson, Harvey Sanderborn and the rest of my Secret Service detail. They'd been searching frantically to find the President somewhere in the White House, but after hearing my announcement of his death, they now sought to protect me, the acting President of the United States.

We fought our way through the complete bedlam within the hallways and finally reached the Oval Office to plan the next steps of my escape. As they whisked me through the President's Conference Room, I saw, outside in the Rose Garden, the unmistakable silhouette of Henry Kissinger as he hustled a small naked figure toward the shrubs and the hidden exit. I could see that little bastard, Jocko, too, loping right behind that procession. I knew Kissinger was taking Eve for his own, and, in light of the oncoming and unstoppable horrors, I didn't fault the old man for being so selfish at such a chaotic moment.

But I did mourn the loss of those feet, those perfect, perfect feet of Eve!

# TOO MANY COOKS SPOIL THE BROTH

I've already described what happened next. Those brave Secret Service men snuck me into the Willard Hotel to hide me in the secret top floor suite, left me alone to search for food, and got themselves killed and beheaded. Then I snuck down to the hotel's kitchen to get my own food, and I found the copy of Youzhong's highly flawed book about English idioms, and this led me to write an account of the events leading to the horrific and horrifying situation in which we now find ourselves.

After I finished bringing this testimonial up to date, I collapsed in exhaustion and slept soundly. When I awoke, I could tell from the relative peace outside the suite windows that the world had lulled itself into a temporary moment of post-devastation calm. Even though I knew I should do something to take advantage of this brief respite in order to escape, I found myself unable to resist rereading my account and to start some minor editing and sprucing up of the journal entries. As I did, I was shocked to the core by the story I'd written down.

Far from an absolution, it was nearly an indictment. If I'd set out to make it seem like I was one of the good guys and was free from guilt from creating this mess, I had seemingly produced a far different document. No, in fact, it read more like *The Three Pigs and the Wolf* fairy tale, except I was playing the role of the wolf!

Unable to believe my eyes, I began to peruse the whole thing again. I was wholly convinced this second examination of the document would allow me to find some parts to the story I might have missed the first time, like all the scenes that would exonerate me. Underneath the bed, within the safety of my tin can corral, I forced myself to scrutinize each word of the text slowly and purposefully in hopes I could find some of those profound things I'd said and those good decisions I'd made during the entire chapter with the aliens. If I could just locate a few of these, I knew I'd be happier. After all, a story in which you play the hero certainly has a nicer ring to it.

Alas, that's not what I found. Stunned beyond words by the dismal portrayal of me and my actions, I put my chronicle gently down onto the carpeted floor like it was made from the thinnest rice paper. There was nothing in any of my words which cast me in a good light. When I wasn't acting in a cowardly manner, I was making the worst decisions possible. I mean, who in their right mind allows the President of the United States — who was clearly under the narcotic-like influence of Eve – to run around and make unethical deals between a bunch of anthropophagous aliens and a group of money-hungry capitalists? Who in their right mind then enlists an extremist group led by a madman to fix the problem?

Only a fool like me.

I came out from under the bed, stood up, and sat down wearily on the soft mattress and put my head in my hands. The real villain in the story I'd written down wasn't the Altoonians, Buchanan, Eve, or President Kennedy – they, of course, all played their part – no, the real villain was none other than yours truly. I'd thought my journal was going to make me out to be a hero, but instead it only highlighted the fact that I was the one who helped funnel the world straight into this catastrophic culminating event. Clearly, I'd failed to live up to expectations.

Then I spotted Youzhong's book, down on the floor, just under me, and the golden calligraphy on the apple red cover grabbed my attention once more. I picked it up and opened it, hoping to find some misguided idiom to describe the depths of my despair.

As I flipped through the pages, Youzhong's introduction came up in front of me. I scanned the words again, but this time Richard Nixon's name triggered a memory. After I had first told my father about my decision to enter politics, he recommended I take on none other than "Tricky Dick" as one of my role models. I argued I didn't think the president who was in charge when our country fled Vietnam like a dog with its tail between its legs, and who had become the first president in United States history to resign, was exactly the type of politician I needed to emulate.

My father responded by saying it was the way the man worked so diligently during the years after his resignation to clear his name and improve his image that I needed to remember. For, in his continued efforts in this regard, Nixon showed the world he was certainly no quitter. I began to point out the direct correlation between the act of resigning and the very definition of quitting, but my father waved me off.

"No one remembers who's winning the race through the first or second turns, Jimbo," he said to me, "but they *do* remember the ones making the mad dash down the final stretch to win the race. Don't ever forget that!"

The whole conversation and his strong message now rushed back to me, and his words lifted my spirits. Sure, reading my journal could lead a reader to extrapolate that I might have been a main ingredient in the downfall of this country – and, in fact, this entire world — but by finishing strong and righting as many wrongs as I could, I had the possibility of making the final judgment of me, as a person and a politician, a more favorable one for future generations.

Even though I could admit my performance as Vice President might have left a lot to be desired up to this point, I could remedy that by doing things to show I was a better man than my chronicle made me out to be. If I could record myself as I was doing some inspirational or meaningful acts, maybe I wouldn't go down in the annals of history as such a total schmuck. I might have lost this specific race in the first few turns, but I knew I could still win it in the final stretch. After all, church ain't out 'til they quit singing.

The real importance of my journal began to make itself known to me. Beyond being a device to clear my name, it could be a vital tool for much more. If I kept updating the entries, the book could actually be used as an essential document to help with the rebuilding of our world. Like an inverted road map showing how we all got here – how a chosen few had led the way by jumping off the cliff and into an abyss of absurdity – it would be a testimony of how to avoid such similar societal jack-knifings in the future. If I could pull this world out of the swan dive I had been so apparently instrumental in setting into motion, this chronicle might just have a happy ending.

But what could I do? In the middle of a world which had devolved entirely into anarchy, what kind of rebellion could a lone man, armed with a single pistol and an extra clip, hope to instigate from the fortified and secret suite of an abandoned hotel in the middle of a devastated city? As far as I could tell, there were no more organized institutions of our former country left. The government, the military, and most of our society all seemed to have been disbanded and dispersed to the four winds. If so, there was not a single force at my disposal to either enlist for help to make some kind of strike against The Army of Christ or to rally and form some kind of insurrection. In fact, other than heading out the front door with my gun blazing — which would be definitely an act of futility — I didn't see too many options for me. I certainly was not spoilt for choice in this matter.

Before I could figure out what to do, I heard an amplified voice coming from the street, its message repeated, over and over.

"The glorious coronation of King George Franklin Buchanan is going to be held on the South Lawn of the house of wickedness and oppression — previously called the White House — at sunrise tomorrow morning. All citizens who want to keep on living must come to the event and witness the beginning of the new era. Join or die!"

I made my way to the nearest window to sneak a look at where this message was coming from. Down on what was left of 14th Street, a lone police car with a giant set of speakers attached to its roof slowly made its way around and over the charred remains of our society as the message blared out and echoed off the pocked buildings of the downtown area. I watched the vehicle as it came to the end of the block, stopped, and — ridiculously — used its turn signal before turning onto F Street and heading out of sight.

Some movement atop the National Press Club Building across the street caught my eye. Over on the roof, in the orange-tinted sky of dusk, I saw a person hopping and leaping in the air like someone being forced to dance by having bullets shot at their feet. It didn't take me too long to ascertain it was none other than Morty Brahmson!

I went into the bathroom, grabbed the heavy porcelain lid off the toilet and threw it through the glass hotel window. Morty was yelling something as he danced, and I waved my arms to get his attention as I stuck my head out of the gaping hole I had just created. When he finally saw me and recognized me, he started waving his hands frantically at me. I knew, with this kind of activity, the hidden sniper out there would make us pay for our stupidity. But Morty seemed completely unafraid, and he continued to wave his arms about as he shouted at me.

"Don't fear, Jim! All is not lost!"

I called back, "Get down, Morty! There's a sniper out there! For God's sake, get down!"

But he was too excited to have my warning register with him.

"She had a litter, Jim!"

"Get down, Morty!"

"She had six babies, Jim. Do you know what that means?"

It sounded like nothing but the ramblings of a crazy man, and since it was clear he was about to get shot, my next request for him to get down was done half-heartedly and he merely waved me off.

"Don't you see, Jim? This isn't the end. It's the beginning!"

"Good God, Morty!" I screamed. "Get down and stop your insane jabbering!"

"No, Jim, I need to shout it from the rooftops. Eve had a litter of six healthy babies! That old goat Kissinger got her safely to the hidden government bunkers at the Raven Rock Mountain Complex with the other Noosbits. The Army of Christ dummies spent all their energy on killing the Altoonians and going on their rampage, but they didn't bother with gathering up the insignificant Noosbits. All of them were freed and now are in hiding. And guess what? All those females previously given as gifts in the government are pregnant. Jim, their gestation period is amazingly short and they have large litters of babies at a time. Do you know what this means? Our two species not only can mate together, but with their amazingly high birth rates, we can build a new species to populate the Earth faster than you can say Jack Robinson. Isn't that so exciting!'

I felt bad for the guy. In the middle of this wasteland, this once proud capital city of a great country, he was sounding more like some kind of prophet on nitrous oxide than a supposedly sane man heralding a true new beginning. Although my prior attempts had failed, I once again shouted out that he really needed to get down.

"But the people need to know there are pockets of resistance everywhere. Our troops and even some loosely organized local militia have made successful stands, here and there, and they have stopped these assholes in several major and heroic battles. And now there's such terrible infighting in Buchanan's company of clowns, the man is in real danger of losing it all!"

"This world is dissolving into dust, Morty. It's our own fault. Just get down before you get shot."

"No. Now that I've found you, Jim, I have more hope than ever. Don't you see? *You* can lead us toward this new beginning for our planet. When the forces of good see that their leader is here, ready to fight, they will know not all is lost. Just like you always wanted, Jim, you're the President now. You can give them the signal they need to win this war!"

"Morty, don't you see? I'm the cause of all of this! Me! I did this. I set it all into motion, and then I threw the necessary fuel onto it all to watch everything burn down to the ground. I can't be the author of both its devastation and its rebirth, Morty. It just doesn't work that way!"

"Hey, you have to break a few eggs to make an omelet, Jim."

"I didn't *break* some eggs, Morty. I blew up the whole goddamn henhouse!"

"Don't look at it like you destroyed anything, Jim. Think of yourself as a poultice. You just drew all the poisons and toxins to the surface where they now can be dealt with. Don't you see? You can now be the leader who takes us toward a perfect society, a better...."

As the man's brains sneezed out the side of his skull and his body fell like a puppet whose strings had been severed with a razor-sharp samurai sword, I instinctively dropped down to the floor as I listened to the echoing of the rifle shot bouncing from one building to another like some kind of hopscotching kid.

My heart mourned poor Morty, and the insanity he was spouting in his final moments on this planet, but anger flashed within me. The brave men of my security detail. Morty. How many more innocent and good people had to die needlessly? I could no longer lie down and let this all happen. I needed to personally strike back.

The deaths of the stranger and of Morty Brahmson told me the hidden sniper was probably situated atop the Willard Hotel, facing the National Press Building. The exchange between Morty and myself had been animated and loud, yet the sniper hadn't tried to take me out. That indicated the gunman wasn't in a good position to shoot at my room. Maybe he was right above me. So, if I could get myself up to the roof, I might get the jump on the guy. I certainly couldn't stay in my suite any longer.

I gathered up a few essentials and took the show on the road. I grabbed a flashlight, two cans of SPAM, the Chinese/English idiom book, my own chronicle, and I threw them into a pillowcase. After I stuck the pistol back into my belt, I headed once more through the secret door in the back of the closet. I made my way slowly back to the staircase, but this time I crept up the stairs toward the roof access. By the time I had reached the door at the top of the stairs, I listened for any sounds coming from the roof, but did not hear anything.

Hoping the door wasn't sabotaged in any way, I slowly opened it and silently squirted out into the evening air without detection.

The darkness of night greeted me. The moonless sky was filled with the pinpricks of thousands and thousands of stars, but due to the fact that the city's street lights were still off, the nocturnal blackness lay heavy on everything like a thick fog. As I began to creep toward where I thought the hidden sniper was nested up, the concussive crunching of the gravel of the hotel's roof from my slow and deliberate pace was as deafening to me as if I were attempting to silently cross a layer of bubble wrap.

A sudden explosion nearby provided a flash of light to see the silhouette of someone near the edge of the roof—exactly where I figured the sniper to be. I got down and began to crawl closer just as another explosion relit the person. Now I could see the man's head and neck, and I swear I saw that the man was smeared with the green camouflage paint snipers wear. Before he became engulfed by the darkness again, my eye caught the sight of something pointing downward, which I assumed was his sniper rifle. Whoever he was, he was doing a superb job at remaining absolutely still and hidden on this rooftop, but somehow he hadn't sensed my presence.

I slowed my breathing and waited for the right moment to strike.

Since I couldn't use my pistol to dispatch the man because the muzzle blast would immediately disclose my location if I missed and leave me a sitting duck, I needed to figure out an effective way to kill him while making no sound. Other than President Kennedy, I hadn't murdered another human being in a long time, and the current version of me was a faded and over-washed imitation of the honed and skilled soldier of my past. Point of fact, the only times of late I'd been given to move around so stealthily was when I'd attempted to sneak bottles of liquor out of my house and away from my dear alcoholic wife.

This unpleasant recollection triggered me thinking about the current status of my dear Geraldine. I know it must seem strange to hear me admit this was one of the first times I'd thought about her throughout this whole ordeal, but since she was safely ensconced in the posh rehabilitation clinic near Taos, New Mexico, I was fairly certain the horrors now threatening to overwhelm our species weren't probably going to seep into her peaceful neck of the desert. First off, there weren't enough people or any viable targets around it to warrant any attention. Secondly, as calloused as it makes me sound, there seemed to be little reason for The Army of Christ to attack such a tranquil and innocent place. What would the gain be to disturb the walking narcotic-induced zombies of such an institution? I imagined if someone did knock on the door of that place, the off-putting reply would be, "No one's here but us chickens."

Then I remembered the violin string in my wallet. It could be used as a garrote. This technique of killing someone was wholly unpleasant, but it was as effective and silent way to do the deed. I removed my wallet from my pant's pocket and slipped the wire out of it and wrapped it securely around my hands. Another flash gave me a clear view of the man again, and I moved up beside him and silently got ready to put the wire over his head and I aimed my knee toward the small of the man's back to get the best leverage point to choke the life out of him.

Then, with the lethal speed of a bamboo viper strike, I struck.

Just like those great white sharks that attack the surfers wearing wet suits and only realize too late they haven't bitten into a seal, by the time I knew I'd begun to garrote a statue, the damage was already done. As soon as my wire struck stone and my knee had touched cold jade, it was too late to stop the momentum of my attack. The additional weight of my body on the statue and my yanking motion caused the entire sculpture to tip, snap its anchors and topple over with me still clinging to it.

I then heard the sounds of a southern-drawled voice garble out right beneath me and the statue, "Aw, what in the hail...."

The crashing sound of the falling statue and the sickening noise of it landing on the sniper in his prone position on the roof, crushing him like a bug, were followed by a silence filled with outright surprise. Even though I was unharmed by the whole event, I clung to the neck of the statue and waited for what was going to happen next. Inexplicably, nothing did.

Only the sounds of the devastated capital and the nighttime rustling of a breeze filled the air.

I slowly disentangled myself from the statue, and because I was curious as to what it was, I took out my lighter to shed some light on it all. It was risky to do so, but I figured if no one knew I was there after such a loud event as the knocking down of the statue, I didn't have to worry too much about revealing my location with the flames of my lighter.

It took me a couple of passes to fully ascertain what had happened. To make a long story short, I had mistakenly attacked a smaller jade version of a Statue of Liberty that was atop the Willard Hotel and caused it to topple onto The Army of Christ sniper I had been stalking. The man had been squished by the weight of the statue, and the whole grisly scene — thanks in part to a smashed handle of bourbon next to the man — had the smell of piss and shit and Jack Daniels.

I was thoroughly confused. I took my lighter over to the base of the statue, still standing where my attack had started. There I found a commemorative bronze plaque that read:

*This statue is given to the American*
*People as a gift from Kim Il-Sung and the people of the*
*Democratic People's Republic of Korea after the*
*assassination of President John F. Kennedy.*
*1963*
*A newborn baby has no fear of tigers – North Korean*
*proverb*

I was completely taken aback. I certainly never knew North Korea had ever given the United States a statue after JFK's assassination, and I was further perplexed by what it was doing on the roof of the Willard Hotel. Unable to process any of what had just happened, I hopped over the sniper's body to make one more pass with my lighter across the statue itself.

As I carefully avoided the leaking messes from the dead sniper, I illuminated the sculpture to get a better look at its features. Oddly, the artist of the work had not only decided to make the face of the statue Jane Fonda's, he had left one of her substantial breasts exposed out of a fold in her robe. These rather inappropriate features and the source of the statue itself gave me more than enough clues about why the statue had secretly been put atop a random hotel roof to be forgotten about. Obviously the artist hadn't been quite right in the head.

As I extinguished my lighter by closing its top, I inadvertently kicked the sniper's rifle. I reached down and felt around about the darkness for it. As my hands found the wooden stock of the weapon and moved over its length, my brain was able to figure out it was a thirty-aught-six Winchester Model 70 Super Grade hunting rifle with a Leupold 6×42 scope.

This was the same model hunting rifle my father had given me as a kid, and that recognition brought back warm memories of going out into the woods with him. When I was sixteen, I shot so many squirrels with my Winchester that my old man had made me eat nothing but squirrel stew until I decided to stop my indiscriminate killing of the vermin. Holding the familiar weapon in my hands now, I knew exactly what I would do with it.

I slung the rifle over my shoulder and began to head toward the far end of the Willard roof. If I could find the iron ladder down to the lower roof of the neighboring hotel, just below me, I knew I'd have a pretty good view of the South Lawn of the White House when the sun rose. My night vision was not as good as it once was, so I had to make a few misguided attempts, but I was finally able to find the top of the ladder curled over the low wall at the edge of the roof.

Once I'd climbed down, I made my way over to the southwest corner of the roof below. I lowered myself behind a parapet and lay down. It was too dark to see anything, and I figured if I catnapped, I'd be fresher for taking a shot at Buchanan the next morning.

▪ ▪ ▪

As the eastern horizon lit the world with the bruise-colored precursors of the morning's sunrise, the police car with the loudspeakers made another pass on the streets down below to announce the imminent coronation of King George Franklin Buchanan and the mandatory attendance for all citizens choosing to remain living. This woke me up, and I lay there and listened to what was happening around me while I got my bearings. I could hear the sounds of shuffling feet and the involuntary grunts and groans of the groups of people being herded down the streets by armed men toward the site of the ceremony.

Ever so slowly and cautiously, I raised myself up so I could see their approach. Even though a thick haze from the countless fires still burning out of control hung low in the sky just over the tops of the ravaged buildings of the downtown area, the dawn's light revealed the depth of the devastation inflicted upon Washington D.C.. The smoldering wreckage where the White House and the Capitol Building had once stood continued to give off smoke like huge smudge sticks proffering their twisted prayers to the heavens. In the distance, I could see the remaining stub of the amputated Washington Monument.

There was nothing that hadn't been marred by the violence.

While the damage inflicted upon our once glorious city was horrendous to witness, I could see that some of the destruction afforded me a unique opportunity. Because all of the trees on the Ellipse and the South Lawn had been obliterated by the various explosions in the assault by The Army of Christ, I now had an unobstructed view to the makeshift stage that had been hastily constructed at the spot the President's helicopter once landed. I would have a clear shot at where Buchanan would soon be standing.

I estimated the distance between me and there to be about four hundred yards, and I lay back slowly knowing, even as rusty as I was as a sniper, that I had the necessary skills to make such a shot.

As I rested there for a moment or two, I cleared my mind of all of its thoughts. This was no easy task to do, but it was essential for what needed to happen next. When I was finally ready, I sat back up and brought the scope of the rifle up to my eye.

I could clearly see there was now a gathering of people standing around the stage that sat in the midst of a grotesque scene straight from one of Hieronymus Bosch's paintings. There was a circle of crucified men and women stationed so they resembled the undifferentiated graduations of an analogue clock face. Even though this sight was too horrifying to fathom, I knew I could not waste the moment it would take to feel outraged by this painful and public humiliation.

Instead, I took aim at the microphones where I knew Buchanan would soon be standing for his coronation and steadied my nerves.

Accompanied by an escort made up of various military and municipal vehicles, including the now familiar police car with it speakers blaring triumphant music at the loudest levels, the impressive presidential Cadillac limo made its way toward the stage. It stopped there and a battery of ill-matching bodyguards took up positions to lend protection to the passengers.

The driver popped out of the front door and scurried to open the rear door. A large group of men exited the vehicle, so many, in fact, it looked like a clown car disgorging its swollen contents. Led by none other than George Franklin Buchanan himself, the solemn procession of men walked the short distance and ascended the steps of the platform to take up their position around the microphone, facing the crowd.

Even though he wore the same plain outfit of a Sunday school teacher, Buchanan now had the silver Universal Translator sitting akimbo on top of his head, a strange image indeed. I guess he was thinking the device would instantly make his words understood by anyone who was listening to him – making him the undisputed king of this new world – but he looked as ridiculous as someone who had chosen to wear a French horn over their head.

I began to worry I wouldn't be able to pull this shot off. If I missed, there'd be no second chance. I laid the scope's crosshairs onto the section of the exposed face now showing itself through the wide opening in the Universal Translator. With my self-doubt pooling up within me and beads of sweat forming on my forehead, I hesitated for just a moment. Then the familiar feel of the rifle from my childhood calmed me and the memories from my many squirrel hunting days came back to me.

I imagined Jocko the squirrel being in the opening of the Universal Translator, and I pulled the trigger and the rifle went off.

I immediately ducked back down behind the rooftop parapet. I did not need to see what was going to happen. My shot was undoubtedly going to hit its target. My bullet was going to fly straight as an arrow into the left eye of George Franklin Buchanan, shatter the lens of his eyeglasses, and turn the man's brain into scrambled eggs.

As I rested my head comfortably on the pebbles of the Hotel Washington roof, I knew the man was as good as dead.

There was momentary silence after my shot, but then a confused cacophony broke out. The chorus of curses and epitaphs coming from the stage area was only drowned out by a series of violent explosions that rocked the buildings and by the ear-piercing shrieks of fighter jets from the skies. I sat up to see what was taking place, and it was clear as day the counteroffensive against The Army of Christ had officially begun.

As Morty had predicted, there was a force just waiting to start an upheaval. My assassination of the nearly coronated king had been the signal for the beginning of the true rebellion. Far from a omen of death, my lone rifle shot had been like a starter pistol and now the race for the finish line was underway.

The sky was filled with the unmistakable howling of the approaching fighter-bombers and the droning turbofans of the high altitude flying B-52's, and I knew they were about to carpet bomb the entire area around the White House. I'd been a part of the military enough — both in the planning and the participatory stages of various strategies — to understand that when dealing with a violent extremist group who's taken over your country, you have to take off the kid gloves and make a statement.

The Air Force was about to enact a scorched-earth campaign that would make my relative, General David Hunter, proud. I knew if I wanted to survive the deadly onslaught about to rain down on us, I should immediately take cover. But as I got ready to run for the hills, I had an epiphany. The only way to atone for what I'd done was to stay put. Because I was more than part of the problem, I needed to let the military's bombastic solution take me out too. If you'll excuse the pun, this sudden revelation blew me away.

You see, I knew now that I'd been totally correct when I'd told Morty I couldn't play any role in the possible rebirth of the world I had just helped destroy. My killing of George Franklin Buchanan had righted only one of my wrongs. The list of other transgressions was far too vast to fit onto a Chinese imperial scroll. My sniping of Buchanan — albeit only a feeble and long-overdue attempt for some reparation for the horrible decisions I'd made — would have to suffice for me. The rest of the cleanup from the mess I'd been so elemental in making was going to fall to others, hopefully much better people than I.

No, there was no escaping for me. I needed to stay where I was and pay the piper.

I climbed back up onto the parapet, sat down, swung my feet over so they hung off the side, and grabbed my pen to update the chronicle by adding these final scenes to it. Nobody would really be impacted by my death, but the lessons from my journal would be the guide with which any future society could usher itself away from the precipice of any self-destruction like this one. I set about to just keep the words flowing until the very last moment.

▪ ▪ ▪

So, now, as I'm watching the squadrons of these impressive bombers beginning their runs, I know my death is imminent. Even though I'm filled with regret for putting the future in jeopardy, it's not my problem. I'll be dead.

Actually, everyone who's had a hand in this train wreck is dead. President Kennedy is dead. George Franklin Buchanan is dead. Morty Brahmson is dead. Haag, Moog, and most of the Altoonians are dead. Countless other human beings are dead, and even more will die as this madness plays itself out.

But as long as the sun rises up in the East and sets in the West, as long as good men and women of this planet continue to fight against forces of wickedness, as long as we retain those good qualities of hope, justice and love, our species will go on living. If such a miracle can happen, there's the chance humanity will rebuild.

I'm just sad I'm not going to see it.

The finality of this moment is causing me to hyperventilate a little. While I struggle to stay calm, the innocent question of what exactly is going to happen next has yet again popped into my head. And as the guided bombs now fill the air like a horde of attacking banshees calling out my name, and I know my own fate is sealed, I find peace in repeating the wisdom of that street person eating a human limb in the Willard Hotel kitchen.

"Aw, it beats the shit out of me."

Signed,

"*"

Former Vice President of the United States of America
Acting President of the United States of Amer....

# A DAY LATE AND A DOLLAR SHORT

*(Transcription of the speech given by Dr. Bishop to the Emergency Session of the United Scientists of the United Nations at The Hague and broadcast to the citizens of planet Earth on the first day of the second year of the Post Altoonian Adventum.)*

As seemingly contradictory as it is for a formerly agnostic scientist to begin his presentation to a large gathering of the scientists who have been charged with rebuilding the societies and cultures of Earth by quoting from a couple of passages of the King James Version of the Christian Bible, I think it is the right thing to do. For, as we all are entreated to fix an entire planet which, at the moment, still languishes in a state of shock over having endured such a large-scale apocalyptic event, we may need to use the most profound and perverse tools available to us to help guide us along the process. So, with that aim in mind, I would like to launch my speech today with a selection from Genesis Chapter 7, Verse 23:

*"And every living substance was destroyed which was upon the face of the ground, both man, and cattle, and the creeping things, and the fowl of the heaven; and they were*

*destroyed from the earth: and Noah only remained alive, and they that were with him in the ark."*

And then a little later, in Genesis Chapter 8, Verses 9-11:

*"But the dove found no rest for the sole of her foot, and she returned unto him into the ark, for the waters were on the face of the whole earth: then he put forth his hand, and took her, and pulled her in unto him into the ark.*

*And he stayed yet another seven days; and again he sent forth the dove out of the ark;*

*And the dove came in to him in the evening; and, lo, in her mouth was an olive leaf plucked off: so Noah knew that the waters were abated from off the earth."*

Honored colleagues, I do not share these passages whimsically. Because we are the remnants of a species who has survived the rather traumatic ordeal thrust upon this planet, it is my belief we must continue to act like Noah and his family on the ark. After all, we all gathered together to weather the storm, waiting for someone or something to tell us the bad times are finally over, and we still today seek a sign telling us that we can have hope, that we can start to rebuild. Well, to continue this metaphor, ladies and gentlemen of the scientific community and the survivors of the planetary community, I feel like I'm the dove with the olive leaf in her mouth as I present my findings to you all today.

For our world has definitely faced a similar destruction to the one Noah's world underwent in the Bible flood story. It's hard to look out onto what is left these days and see anything recognizable. The cost of it all upon humanity is almost immeasurable, yet humans *have* survived. Our dear planet was nearly destroyed, yet here we all are. It will be we survivors who will be the architects of the future we are going to build.

That's not to say I think we should just reconstruct what was lost. We would be completely remiss, in my opinion, to just start churning out a duplicate of what was present before the arrival of the Altoonian ships upon this planet. No, I don't think we should build facsimiles or only slightly updated versions of what we once had. We have the chance to take this cataclysmic event and use it to send ourselves off in a new and inspiring direction. One day, hopefully soon, we will be able to look back upon the horrors we've all lived through and see the beneficial results they've allowed the human race to take advantage of.

I am, in no way, stating we should celebrate the horrific days we've all been forced to ride out, but we have the opportunity to do so much good at this moment. The reset button was hit as soon as the aliens were attacked and our world imploded. We are blessed to have this second chance to make something even better than we had before!

Now that Vice President Hunter's revealing journal is available for all to see, we're fully aware of the plethora of faulty decisions and hedonistic undertakings which led to the destruction of the United States of America as well as most of the Planet Earth. Although we can't sweep all the man's great flaws as a person under the carpet, I do wish Mr. Hunter had survived the victorious counterattack on The Army of Christ in Washington D.C.. I think he would have been relieved to see that his good friend Morty Brahmson had been spot-on about the future.

But while he didn't live, his chronicle did. And I'm here today to say I think we should use it as a recipe for the new mixture we are going to start concocting for our future. We might need to use it to define the negative space of the changes we are inspired to make, but we should use it nonetheless. It is an extraordinary document.

You see, we shouldn't think of Vice President Hunter's testimonial as only a description of our sketchy past. It's also a blueprint to our future. It documents the exact moment when the solution to our species' survival was unknowingly presented to me by the former President Kennedy. When he commanded me to continue on my research of the alien waste products and the metallic cube they were enclosed in for transportation, he may have been giving me these tasks just to keep me too busy to cause any trouble, but he also unwittingly allowed me to find some shocking discoveries.

For, even as the fires of destruction burned out of control all around me, I continued to do my research as instructed. As painful as it was to put the blinders on and ignore the travesties occurring throughout our world, I quickly identified some things I knew would be essential for rebuilding our future. And I want to report these findings to you all today. So, you see, from the dusts of our world, I want to offer up some optimism to the human race.

I will not go into the specifics of my methods today, but you will be able to read about those in my future scientific publications. Suffice it to say I've put those Altoonian wastes and their metallic cube through a battery of tests to better understand their chemical makeup, properties and reactive natures. At first, this research went nowhere. After all, the substances I was testing are not from this planet, so I had no way to set any kind of baseline by which to judge the results. While I modified and improved the refinement process for turning the aliens' waste materials into higher grade fuels and set up my entire scientific compound to reap the benefits from this source, I was unable to make any new discoveries in regards to the waste storage cube or the chemistry of the waste products themselves.

Truth be told, I was at a complete dead end – until Vice President Hunter and The Army of Christ showed the world the devastating effects helium had upon the Altoonians. It was the impressive impact from the introduction of this earthly element on the aliens which led me toward the first insights into unlocking the incredible discoveries I'm about to reveal to the world.

Again, if you want the specifics as to my methods, you will get a chance to review my research findings in a series of scientific publications in the not-so-distant future. Simply, I can tell you that helium unlocks the elemental natures of all Altoonian substances. It is true I haven't figured out exactly why this is so, but for our current purposes let me say it happens on a molecular level. Helium gas was not only fatal to the Altoonians, but it also breaks the very bonds of the alien chemistry. While this quality allowed the human fighters to get the jump on the aliens in their battle, it will also allow us to reap untold benefits to help with the rebuilding of our world and our species.

I'm here today, making this impassioned speech to you, to let you know that as much as our planet currently resembles nothing more than a pile of ashes these days, the combination of helium with the remaining supplies of the alien presence – their wastes, dead bodies, and all twenty three of their derelict space ships – will provide us with the fuel to power the mythological phoenix destined to come out of this devastation and soar!

For the good news today, esteemed colleagues, is we have all of the fuel needed to build the new world we so desperately want to create!

Our time together is limited today, so I won't go into all the details of what I am proposing. I will reveal a few of the results of my research to make my point to the world's acting leaders who might be listening. The fact is, even though they were the sites of violent military battles and an almost incalculable loss of life, the twenty three alien ships are all still relatively intact. This means we not only still have the vast quantity of waste in the alien's septic storage tanks — each the size and capacity of the Central Park Reservoir — but we have access to the billions and billions of tons of their metals in the wreckage of their ships. According to my research, this untold amounts of waste and the alien metal at those twenty three landing sites can be exposed to helium to create enough clean fuel to power us far into our new future!

*(Rousing applause from audience. Nearly ten minutes of a standing ovation.)*

Now, now, ladies and gentlemen. I am excited about all of these findings too! But please sit down and keep listening, for there is even more good news I need to report.

After the defeat of The Army of Christ, I was given access to those gigantic mass graves of the bodies of all of the dead Altoonians. It turns out their decomposition has not been normal, like most organic materials from this planet. In fact, upon dying, their bodies hardened like setting cement. The result of this is that we've been left with vast fields of statues – enough to fill literally hundreds of Louvres!

However, when these stone corpses are introduced to liquid helium, there is a changing of states of matter. In fact, I've discovered — as macabre as it is to say — we can create a "tea" from steeping the dead Altoonians in liquid helium. While this is fascinating, it is far, far more important than just a simple physics issue. This resulting "tea" can be refined into fuel as well, which means between this mixture from these dead alien bodies, the contents of the alien waste tanks, and the metals from the destroyed twenty three alien ships, we now have access to a fuel source that will last not one or two generations, but much, much further into the future!

I know what some of you are thinking. As exciting as all this is, I'm not really exposing a truly renewable resource here. Because of the finite nature of the alien supplies, you may think I'm only suggesting a mere substitute to what we had, a cleaner version of the limited petroleum-based fuels. Such a discovery would not be an upgrade from our past, especially if these new supplies could run out even quicker than the older ones. That's all absolutely true. The fuel coming from these various Altoonian sources will run out eventually because they are limited. And, once we use them up, there is no way, at this point, to make any more. Even those pockets of human population around the globe who kept a few Altoonians alive to use as a fuel source will eventually not be able to produce enough of the necessary waste products.

Does this all mean we should give up on this pursuit?

I say no. The fact is, I believe we will be able to duplicate the alien elements eventually, synthetically, if we're just given enough time and resources to research it fully. Using the clean and free fuel from the aliens would give us the power needed to accomplish this goal. I have come close enough in my own research to confidently say I think human scientists will be able to — one day very soon — be able to synthesize a version of the alien materials, and this will be the renewable source of fuel to lead us into a bright and happy future.

While most of our worldwide ecosystems were brought to the very brink of extinction by the violence of this period, and the overall populations of the planet's species, including us humans, were reduced in such a pronounced way, I cannot help but think a new world with improved societies built upon the nonpolluting alien-sourced fuels would be the very best way for us to proceed. Again, if we're not trying to avoid just recreating the flawed and toxic systems of the past, we should rush headlong into this new future, the one based on this cleaner alternative fuel.

Before I end, I want to bring up a potentially controversial topic for discussion. The Noosbits. Since they were almost completely spared from the defeat of the Altoonians, we now find ourselves living with another alien culture in our midst, but this one is going to be an integral part of our shared future together. I've met with a couple of them, and I found them to be compelling and peaceful creatures, and very similar to we humans. As we read in Vice President Hunter's chronicle, they can have an almost opioid-like effect on us, but this effect can be monitored and managed like most addictive substances.

However, the most intriguing aspect to the Noosbits might just be how their waste products create as efficient a source of energy as the Altoonian wastes. Now, while, their populations are currently too small to generate enough waste to completely fuel a global rebuilding process on their own, it is my opinion that they can certainly contribute to the powering of smaller regional and localized communities and projects. By having a thriving community of these little buggers living in a scientific research station, for example, they could power the endeavors of such a facility completely with nothing but their waste.

On a grander planetary scale, however, it may be the results from the somewhat ethically dubious sexual liaisons with the Noosbits undertaken by certain members of the United States government which might yield the most surprising repercussions. As Morty Brahmson announced to the world from the rooftops, so touchingly described in Vice President Hunter's journal, these illicit relationships did indeed produce a new Noosbit/Human hybrid species. While incredible in and of itself, the real silver lining to the story is that this pairing has resulted in the fairly equal sharing of genetic material between the two species. Because of this, I am excited to report that the waste from this new combined species is more like Altoonian/Noosbit waste, and thus is a source for clean fuel.

So, although I am not suggesting any kind of forced breeding program at this point, the fact that these alien creatures have a very short gestation period and an extremely high birth rate could mean we can, together, quickly produce a combined hybrid race between our two peoples. Even though the study of this process is only in its infancy, it is entirely possible that this assimilation between the Earthlings and Noosbits will not only continue to alter the entire genetic makeup of our species, it will also make a direct contribution to the creation of a clean energy supply for the future of the entire planet.

How soon? Mathematically, I'd say we're within four or five generations of seeing this hybrid species become the majority, population-wise, on Earth…if we encourage it to take place. If so, we're talking about a world which will have the capacity to produce its own fuel from the waste generated by the very dwellers on this planet!

Imagine, my dear esteemed colleagues, such a bright, shared future!

You see, I am excited beyond words to keep researching the untold potential of these new fuel sources to their fullest because in them lies such a wonderful possibility to go way farther than our species ever has. It fills me with such happiness to know we Earthlings will someday have a bright, new future once more. For the time being, however, we need to be patient and let things unfold.

In closing, I'd like to quote the former Vice President of the United States of America, James Fenimore Hunter. In the words of that esteemed man, who had such a role in this exciting new chapter of humanity, we should just, "sit back and watch the show."

**THE END**

# ABOUT THE AUTHOR

The facts about Sam Sumac are hazy, at best. Any details we have about his life come from his own handwritten autobiographical sketch, *Please, Don't Forget to Pay the Debt.* According to this, he was born in Buffalo, New York, exactly ten months after VJ-Day, to an unwed Polish woman by the name of Ewa. While he never knew his father's identity, Sam describes his childhood as a happy one spent with his mother in a home near the Buffalo-Kenmore border. He claims to have attended various elementary, junior high and high schools throughout his youth before enrolling in the State University College of Education at Buffalo for one year, where he majored in Physics. He dropped out to enlist in the United States Army.

Sam contends he was conscripted as a tunnel rat during the Vietnam War due to being just over five feet in height. While those early days of his military training brought him some moments of happiness, his deployment to the combat of the war only damaged him. Although unsubstantiated,

Sam alleges that he was a member of one of many of the companies of subterranean soldiers in the Củ Chi district who were given a cocktail of hallucinogenic drugs before heading into the tunnels to do battle with their North Vietnamese enemies. He believed these induced narcotic highs led him to have many out-of-body transformations, which he repeatedly calls, "his enlightenments" in his writings.

Sam attributed the combination of the violence of the war and these unauthorized military experiments for his nervous breakdown. According to him, the stress of the tunnel warfare and the impact from the unstable narcotics caused him to be briefly institutionalized in a military psych ward in Pennsylvania. Prone to fantastical hallucinations during this time – most involving alien invasions, time travel, the apocalypse, the Oil Crisis, the Middle East, and the gruesome punishments of many of the people he held as responsible for his ordeals (Especially, a Morton Hunter from Altoona, Pennsylvania – allegedly a special operative with the CIA who Sam blamed for the administering of narcotics to Sam's unit.) – he spouted a nonstop string of prophetic stories and sagas. He says his mental health gradually improved with care, until, ultimately, he was well enough to be discharged from the Army.

When he returned to Buffalo, he found out his mother had passed away some time during his hospitalization. While devastated, he decided to settle in his former hometown. He rented a house in the same neighborhood of his childhood and began working as a salesman at a local shoe store. While this job might not seem too exciting to most, Sam reported he, "had a thing for feet," so the work appealed to him deeply. During this time, while living alone and working full-time, his compulsion to write down the stories inside his head hit him. Sam spent every spare moment, including writing late every night, putting onto paper the bizarre delusions from his time in the tunnels and the military mental hospital, and, in the process, he created a series of science fiction stories.

He vividly describes not being able to contain the flow of creativity coming out of him. During these writing frenzies, he wrote without purpose or order. He merely transcribed all the imagery and characters as they came out. These manic periods never left him enough time to edit or to prepare a manuscript for publication before the next story needing to be penned demanded his attention. He aptly recounts how he felt like a faucet of stories which was unable to be shut off.

Then, one day, Sam Sumac disappeared. When his landlord went to check on him after not receiving his rent payment, there was no trace left behind whatsoever of the man. The police were called, but they quickly decided there was no evidence of foul play, so no further official investigation was needed. However, it is still unclear — even at this point in time — what actually happened to Sam. He simply vanished.

Some would like to think he changed his identity and moved to another city to resume his writing in a new locale.

Others have a darker interpretation. Regardless, whatever happened to him is just part of the mystery of Sam Sumac.

The world would have likely forgotten all about the man if it were not for several boxes belonging to him being discovered in a storage unit a year after his inexplicable disappearance. Due to the lack of an annual payment for the storage and the absence of any next of kin on his rental application paperwork, these unclaimed items were given to his ex-landlord, who, in turn, gave them to a fellow employee at the same shoe store Sam worked. When this individual opened the boxes and saw the chaotic state of their contents, he resealed them and put them in his garage, where they were undisturbed for nearly twenty five years.

Finally these boxes landed in the hands of a retired Episcopal priest who was asked to claim the possessions of a former parishioner who'd recently passed away. It was only when the boxes were re-opened that the writings of Sam Sumac were once again exposed to this world.

Sort of.

These boxes were brimming with intermixed and disarrayed heaps of handwritten pages on different types of paper and done with various writing implements. With no organization or order, the process of collating and transcribing has been a maddeningly complicated and time-consuming endeavor.

*Piss & Vinegar*, apparently written in the late 1970's or early 1980's, is the first attempt to get a Sam Sumac story into a completed format. It is hoped that, with time, more of his novels might eventually get reassembled and come out in print some time in the future, but the Herculean effort needed to accomplish this makes the task an incredibly slow process.

So, sit back and enjoy these words from an unknown genius, Sam Sumac.

P. B.
February 2014

# NOTE FROM THE AUTHOR

Word-of-mouth is crucial for any author to succeed. If you enjoyed *Piss & Vinegar*, please leave a review online—anywhere you are able. Even if it's just a sentence or two. It would make all the difference and would be very much appreciated.

Thanks!
Sam

Thank you so much for reading one of our **Sci-Fi** novels.

If you enjoyed our book, please check out our recommended for your next great read!

*People of Metal* by Robert Snyder

The well-intentioned leaders of China and the U.S. form a grand partnership to create human robots for every human vocation in every country in the world. The human robots proliferate, economic output soars, and the entire world prospers. It's a new Golden Age. But there are unintended consequences—consequences that will place biological humanity on a road to extinction. Ultimately, it will fall to the human robots themselves to rescue biological humanity and restore its civilization.

CPSIA information can be obtained
at www.ICGtesting.com
Printed in the USA
FSHW010624100120
65812FS